HIT LIST
THE BEST OF
LATINO MYSTERY

HIT LIST

THE BEST OF
LATINO MYSTERY

EDITED BY
SARAH CORTEZ
AND
LIZ MARTÍNEZ

Arte Público Press
Houston, Texas

Hit List: The Best of Latino Mystery is made possible in part from grants from the city of Houston through the Houston Arts Alliance, and by the Exemplar Program, a program of Americans for the Arts in Collaboration with the LarsonAllen Public Services Group, funded by the Ford Foundation.

Recovering the past, creating the future

Arte Público Press
University of Houston
452 Cullen Performance Hall
Houston, Texas 77204-2004

Cover design by Exact Type
Cover art by Oscar Martinez

Hit List: The Best of Latino Mystery / Edited by Sarah Cortez and Liz
  Martínez; introduction by Sarah Cortez; foreword by Ralph E.
  Rodriguez.
    p. cm.
ISBN: 978-155885-543-4 (alk. paper)
    1. Detective and mystery stories, American. 2.American fiction—
Hispanic American authors. 3. Hispanic Americans—Fiction. I.
Cortez, Sarah. II. Martínez, Liz, 1963–

PS648.D4H48 2009
813'.087208868073—dc22
                                                          2008048548
                                                              CIP

∞ The paper used in this publication meets the requirements of the American National Standard for Information Sciences—Permanence of Paper for Printed Library Materials, ANSI Z39.48-1984.

    9 0 1 2 3 4 5 6 7 8   10 9 8 7 6 5 4 3 2 1

TABLE OF CONTENTS

M y friends all have stories of their lifelong love of books. Each one is a more inveterate reader than the next. They talk, sometimes ad nauseam, about their romance with fiction. You would think they fell out of the womb with a book in their hand. In their company, I feel like a bibliofraud. As a child I was, if anything, a shameless watcher of TV. I was stunned when, in third grade, I learned my classmates didn't watch Johnny Carson. I didn't decry them to the teacher, but I made a mental note to think less of them in the future. I mean, *really*. How could they not know the *Tonight Show*?

Things change. For me, it was seventh grade and Agatha Christie. I would love to say that I was once racing around the school library with my friend Gregory, when suddenly I tripped, knocking a shelf of books down upon me. Then, in cleaning up the mess I couldn't help but open one of the Christie novels because the cover captivated me. Upon reading the first paragraph, I simply couldn't put the book down. Indeed, I got so lost in the narrative that I was accidentally locked in the library overnight. Left to my own designs, I finished not one novel, but ten. That's the sort of narrative people love to hear about reading, but alas, that's not how things played out. I didn't so much stumble upon Agatha Christie as I was forced by Mr. Martelli to read *The Orient Express* for English class. I took a moment to resent him for it. He was, after all, the very same teacher who assigned *Treasure Island*, a book that, in my twelve-year-old sense of judgment, I more than generously gave a whole paragraph to enchant me. When it didn't, I consigned it to Cleo's (the family basset hound's) box of toys.

My parents must have been on a "let's make the children more well-rounded" kick the weekend Mr. Martelli assigned *The Orient Express* because, as I remember, they made me stay in my bedroom on a Saturday afternoon until I had finished the first two chapters. Regular monsters, I tell you. But then it happened—the conversion, I mean.

I couldn't put the book down, even when Gregory stopped by to get me to play stickball. From *The Orient Express* I graduated to *And Then There Were None*, which led almost predictably to Edgar Allen Poe's mystery stories, and then to Sherlock Holmes.

Since those glorious adventures in the late seventies, I have been a fan of mystery novels. Indeed, as some readers of this foreword will know, I gave over much of the last decade to reading Latino mysteries and writing a critical study, *Brown Gumshoes*, of the Chicano detective novel. When that book came out in late 2005, I felt certain I was done with the mystery novel for a while. Having spent far too many waking hours reading novels about murder, deception and torture, my slumbers had become filled with either people chasing me or I chasing them, and we all had one goal—to kill one another. Sure, the sleep specialists will blame my insomnia on the cappuccino I like to down before bedtime, but I know it is the fear of being gunned down in my dreams that makes me dread putting head to pillow. So upon finishing *Brown Gumshoes*, I decided a respite from the detective novel was in order, and until Sarah Cortez and Liz Martínez contacted me about writing this foreword, I had been pretty successful. The mystery novels I owned sat quietly on my bookshelves, and we had come to the mutual agreement that we wouldn't disturb each other. But darn it all, Cortez and Martínez have me hooked again.

Hit List: The Best of Latino Mystery, which they have compiled, locks you in your seat and won't let you up until you finish the last page. Even then, you may very well be tempted to get in line with your ticket and ride the roller coaster all over again. It's just that good. Cortez and Martínez have assembled veterans of the genre such as Lucha Corpi, Rolando Hinojosa-Smith and Steven Torres, to name but a few, as well as newcomers to the field. Each of these authors knows the genre and knows it well. Moreover, the range of stories includes private eye tales, police procedurals, a legal thriller and even one story told from the point of view of a bullet. These authors are an ambitious and talented bunch. They craft dialogue, plot and character in such a way that you want to linger over the sentences and memorize lines to whip out at your next cocktail party. And with proper attribution, I have already started using, to great effect, Carlos Hernandez' line, "Life and limes are delicious, but sour." It's insightful and funny because it's true. That it comes couched in a story about a reality television show dealing with hit men for hire makes the line only that much more savory. Hernandez and his deliciously twisted and intriguing story are not the exception; they are the rule in this anthology.

You will find no boring Latino caricatures or stereotypes in this volume. What you will find are numerous characters (not all of whom are Latino) living their lives in all of their racial, gendered, class and sexual complexity. No predictable lives, but rather an investigation into the very multiple and protean identities people carry with them in the world, and with these mystery stories it is a world that brings us to locales as distinct as Mexico, California, Texas, Puerto Rico, Colorado and New York, to name just a few of the places we traipse through on our journey through the book.

As you sit reading this foreword, I'm guessing that you are doing so with your sole copy of the book. Run out to your local bookstore now and buy three more copies. You are going to want to give them to your friends. You'll be the person who turned them on to Latino mysteries, and they will be forever in your debt. If being haunted by nightmares of men with 9mm guns and ski masks is the price to pay for fiction as wonderful as that in *Hit List: The Best of Latino Mystery*, I'll turn my paycheck over every time and call my pharmacist for a refill on the Ambien.

Ralph E. Rodriguez, Ph.D.
Providence, Rhode Island

We came to this ground-breaking project—the creation of the first anthology of short fiction by Latino mystery writers—with many similarities in our backgrounds. As kids, we were both enthralled by reading mysteries. It didn't bypass either one of us that in our reading, most of the sleuths lived the adventurous life we craved, replete with fast cars, villains and a satisfying participation in serving justice.

Years later, we both take pride in bringing to you, our reader, this collection featuring many, if not most, of the Latino mystery writers who have functioned as pioneers in their use of the mystery genre to reveal their unique cultures, neighborhoods and realities. Reading these award-winning writers is as exciting as reading the new voices of emerging writers in the field, who are also featured in this volume.

We are eager to introduce readers to a cast of sleuths, murderers and victims of crime who reflect contemporary society's preoccupations with identity, with self and with territory—both internal and external—and its concomitant complex allegiances and surprising compromises.

Some of these stories display a wickedly inventive use of traditional mystery apparatus, e.g. the use of a Macguffin in Manuel Ramos' *The Skull of Pancho Villa*, or the dazzling modern twist on the locked-room mystery in Carlos Hernandez' *Los Simpáticos*.

We admire the way so many of these stories lead the reader to a darkly wry consideration of the ethical issue of whether or not there can be a moral murder: John Lantigua's *A Reunion with Death*, S. Ramos O'Briant's *Death, Taxes . . . and Worms*, Steven Torres' *Caring for José* and Sergio Troncoso's *A New York Chicano*.

Some of these stories unwind in the rich interior of domestic spaces in the central character's home or garden: Sarah Cortez' *In My Hands*, Arthur Muñoz' *Made in China*, R. Narvaez' *In the Kitchen with Johnny Albino* and S. Ramos O'Briant's *Death, Taxes . . . and Worms*. Others spin us through a dizzy array of urban spaces as the central character, whether PI or crook, either solves the mystery or commits the crime: Carolina García-Aguilera's *The Right Profile,* Rolando Hinojosa-Smith's *Nice Climate, Miami,* Carlos Hernandez' *Los Simpáticos,* A. E. Roman's *Under the Bridge* and Sergio Troncoso's *A New York Chicano.*

Two of the stories take us to Mexico: Alicia Gaspar de Alba's *Shortcut to the Moon,* for a noir set in contemporary times, and Bertha Jacobson's *A Broken String of Lace,* for a haunting historical tale. We are even treated to a glimpse of small-town Puerto Rico in Steven Torres's *Caring for José.*

The narrative voices in this collection range from the hardboiled in *Nice Climate, Miami* to the softboiled in *Death, Taxes . . . and Worms,* more reminiscent of the cozy. *Los Simpáticos* introduces a narrator who is the chilling epitome of the entertainment industry's greed and ruthlessness, while Lucha Corpi's *Hollow Point at the Synapses* introduces the most intriguing narrator you'll meet in the mystery genre. The tone and mood of narrative voices ranges from the frantic sense of borrowed time in L. M. Quinn's *A Not So Clear Case of Murder* to the confident sense of unquestioned superiority in Mario Acevedo's *Oh, Yeah* and Hinojosa-Smith's *Nice Climate, Miami.*

We bring these stories to you with the same sense of anticipation as we have experienced since childhood when reading mystery. Whatever your preference—traditional, historical, chick lit, PI or police procedural, revenge, dark domestic, ruthless noir or cozy—you'll find something to delight you in this collection.

We thank these authors with whom we have worked, and whose writing has helped to fill yet one more publishing void for Latinos. And, most of all, we thank our publisher, the ever-innovative Arte Público Press.

Sarah Cortez
Houston, Texas

Oh, Yeah

anela held up his Browning 9mm HP. The slide was stuck halfway.

I took the pistol from him and removed the magazine. "You got the bullets in backward. Like I told you before, the pointy end of the bullet goes to the front."

Canela hunched his beefy shoulders and squinted at the Browning. He mumbled, "Oh, yeah." He took the pistol, handling the gun like he still wasn't sure how it worked.

I didn't like or dislike Canela, it was just that he was as dumb as a Labrador. Canela got his name from the cinnamon-colored scars on his face. My *abuelita* said that Guatemalans weren't too smart, and she got that right. Canela was the king of the *pendejos*.

I hadn't known him until a couple of weeks ago, when Enrico and I were looking for a third partner, and we found Canela in the warehouse district loading stolen furniture into a truck. His intimidating bulk and eagerness for serious bread, plus the fact that no one around here knew him—not the hustlers, not the snitches—meant I could use him. Quick in-and-outs didn't require much upstairs, and that described Canela for sure.

Enrico and I had done time for armed robbery, and neither of us was going back into the slammer. Canela was my guarantee. He was slow on the uptake about everything, and if things went into the crapper, I'd leave him behind to get pinched.

I wrapped my sawed-off shotgun in a newspaper. Canela folded the laundry bags for the loot under his jacket and zipped up the front. We tucked our pistols into our pants so they were hidden beneath our jackets.

"Your disguise?" I asked Canela.

He yanked a knitted ski cap from his jacket pocket and pulled it over his watermelon head. The eye slits and mouth hole were stretched crooked, and Canela looked like an obese, spastic clown.

I remembered what had happened during our first robbery last week, a practice run at a convenience store. "And this time," I said, "when you pull your gun, it's 'Hands up,' not 'Trick-or-Treat.'"

Canela removed the cap. "Oh, yeah."

We went outside and got into the Ford Maverick, Enrico and me up front, Canela in the back. On the way to our heist, a savings and loan south of Brandt Avenue, Canela put his gorilla-paw mitts on the top of my seat. "So tell me again, the plan?"

Man, was this guy a bowl of dumb ass. I had told him seven, eight times already. A chimpanzee would have known it by heart, but not this stupid ape. I repeated the plan and added, "Nothing's changed."

Canela scratched his head like thinking made his brain itch. "Oh, yeah."

Enrico parked across the street and left the motor running. Canela followed me through the front lobby. Easy as one-two-three, we put on our masks, pulled our guns and yelled for everyone to stay cool. Canela stuffed the laundry bags while I made scary moves with my shotgun. When I turned around to leave, I looked out the front plate-glass window toward Enrico.

He was climbing out of the getaway car and raising his hands. Cops with rifles bobbed around him, using the Maverick for cover.

Panic poured through me like ice water.

Okay, I was ready for this. Now, to ditch the big stupid Guatemalan and escape. "Canela, cover me while I find a way out the back."

Canela leveled the Browning at my face. "Drop the gun and get on your knees." His mask was off. That flabby expression of his looked suddenly threatening and hard, like it belonged on the front end of a Buick about to run me over. "You're under arrest. Oh, yeah."

Hollow Point at the Synapses

She stops outside a store, glances at the garments in the window, thinks. Then she looks at her hands, her long fingers. Her right fingernails cut short, her left clipped closer to the flesh line. She walks into the boutique.

For days, the man and I have watched her from the café across the street, where the man has breakfast, the only meal he can afford. He and I have rested outside her apartment, under the stairs leading to a vacant basement. He has lost everything looking for her, and now we follow her day and night.

Next to me, the man stirs in place. What is he thinking now? Does he know her as well as he thinks he does? What does he love most about her? Her young dark beauty, perhaps. Her nose tilted a bit to the left. The roundness of her breasts or hips. The way her hand rises slightly over the frets until it finds that precise chord as she plays every morning before the open window of her studio a few blocks away. Her music. Does he love her at all?

I don't know what love is. I wasn't meant to know. In this cold place, encased by steel, I wait. The man and I wait. I feel the beating of the man's heart. Faint just a moment ago, racing now, relentless —the marching of its minutes and seconds.

She comes out of the store holding two shopping bags. The man and I follow, but not close enough to be detected by her. No one sees us. Everything goes dark for an instant. Then I see the cars. I know she has walked into a parking lot.

We're now very close to her. Unaware of our presence, she is humming as she walks. "The Concerto de Aranjuez Adagio," the man whispers next to me. She pauses. The man and I scurry behind a truck. She looks around. No one is there. We move again when she does. She picks up the melody again a few bars earlier and this time hums past the point of her hesitation.

She opens the trunk of her car, puts the bags in it and closes it. She begins to walk toward the driver's door. The man and I show ourselves, but we keep our distance. She recognizes us.

"Pablo." She sucks in breath. "Why? You said I could go." Her words are hardly a whisper. "I didn't tell them. I swear I didn't."

Her hand holding the door handle shakes. She fusses with the keys, finds the right one. Too late. The man is upon her. He holds her from behind in a tight embrace.

"Clever girl. Caroline Serrano—a new name, a new country, a new identity, a brand new destiny. Did you really think I would never find you?"

I am now very close to her temple. Through the narrow scope of vision allowed me, I see her right eye sweep the parking lot, hoping, praying for someone to be there in the hour of her need. There is no God here, no shiny guardian angel, no Good Samaritan. There is no one but she and the man and I—he, all obstinate feeling, and I, no feeling at all.

She struggles, trying to free herself from his hold. In vain. She falls to her knees. I am now looking at strands of black hair, piling on one another like slender black saffron reeds.

I feel the pull of the hammer. The pressure mounts. I am now in place. The moment is upon me. Swiftly and efficiently, I will do what I must, what I was created for. In an instant, I am off, traveling at a speed reserved only for death. I hit my target and explode into tiny, fulminating particles, each conceived to trigger a process that will end where mourning begins.

I am many now, grazed by sharp splinters of bone, cutting through mass gray and warm, tearing away the flesh from the spirit seam by seam, cutting paths to dark nights and bright mornings, the stars like swarms of fireflies, awakening with echoes of half-forgotten melodies in my head, *estrellita del lejano oriente*—a star in the eastern sky—, her voice is all mine now, her heart and mind all ours, *erre con erre cigarro*, faces I should remember and I don't, *erre con erre carril, Perla, qué lindo es tu nombre*, you're my pearl, I was seven, *rápido corren los carros, siete años*, Papá plays for me on my seventh birthday, his hand slides down frets *como los carros del ferrocarril*, Mamá's pleasure in nights of fitful sleep, footfalls in the dark, "Wake up, we must go, move to another safe house, *Sendero Luminoso, sendero de luces, somos las luces que alumbramos*, we are The Shining Path to a new life, we are the path and the path-makers," Morning and Evening Star, make a wish, *un deseo*, desire, "*Te deseo*—I want you," say it, "I'll always want you, Pablo," "I want you to suck me hard," "I can't, *no debo hacer esas cosas*," but Pablo says, "Perlita, *no eres nenita*," thirteen, you're not too young, *mírate esos volcancitos*, pointed nipples, *ya eres mujer y yo sé que te gusta*, you love it when I lick them with my tongue, *déjame comerte ese pollito entre las piernas*, NO! A+B=C, C-A=B, positive plus negative where negative is positive plus, *"Mamá, los soldados mataron a mi papá*, they killed him, the soldiers, no, no, no, *entre cielo y tierra, cielo y tierra* heaven and earth, *qué vamos a hacer*, what can we do, no, Mamá, don't die, please don't die," Mamá swallows gasoline, "Perla, leave this place," dying, Mamá's gone, I am alone and I feel nothing, nothing, nothing, I want my father's guitar, all I want is his guitar, play, play, forget, "Perla can go," Pablo says, no one questions his authority, "You can go," he tells me, "but you can never tell anyone who and where we are, they don't understand what Sendero Luminoso is, what we are about, they'll kill us all," and I promise, "I won't tell, *nunca les diré*," the moon is full, I walk alone, down the mountain, to the American school, my school for two years, Dominican Sisters, Sister Teresa, "Help me, I'll play for you my father's songs, let me stay, I'll play and sing at the market and pay you," Sister Teresa weeps, "Oh, my dear child, for God's sake no, but play for Father Juan, he'll teach you, you'll always have a home with us," the priest looks at me and I'm frightened but I go into his room, "Yes, good, that's right, raise your fingers slightly, just so over the frets, we don't want to mar the purity of sound and feeling, that's what made your father's style superb, yes, Perla, I will teach you, come to my room every afternoon," I'm wrong about him, I'm happy, "Perla, Perlita, *vente conmigo, mi amor*, why are you calling me now, Mamá, it isn't time yet, two stars, two faces, Mamá *y* Papá, *y todo lo demás no importa, pero sí importa*, no, I don't want to remember anymore, "Perla, open your legs," NO, please, Father Juan, NO, "I've taught you, loved you, I know you want us to be together, you owe me," Sister Teresa, she knows, "Padre Juan . . . , *por Dios Santo*, Padre, *es una inocente*, she's so young," Sister Teresa takes my hand, "*Hijita*, don't say anything, Padre Juan will never again hurt you my child, no one will, you must come with me, play, I told them you've joined the convent in the States, the Sisters, we'll take care of you," I want to go home, I have no home, music is my home, I play and play over and over, this is my life, Papá, music the biography and geography of your sorrow and mine, play, forget, forget the storms raging day and night, *tempestad que hace temblar las campanas de la iglesia*, church bells clanging wildly, then quiet, moonlit nights, nights so dark, desire, *noches tan obscuras como el hueco negro del deseo y la desesperación del que nacen las estrellas*, but the stars are so far away, Father Juan and Pablo one and the same, just wearing different clothes, play, play the darkness away, raise your fingers slightly over frets and strings, no unpleasant screeching of the strings, sound clear and simple, pure feeling, sustain those melancholic notes just enough, pause, imagine a hummingbird hovering in mid-air in search of the purplest sweetest sage blossom, Oh, Papá, why have you forsaken me, you'd be so proud of me, how did that reporter find out, "The talented guitarist, Caroline Serrano . . . at the Met with the Cleveland Orchestra . . . is in fact Perla Sandoval . . . daughter of Rafael Sandoval . . . Peru's foremost classical and Spanish guitar soloist . . . 1971, Maestro Sandoval and his wife . . . members of the urban guerrilla . . . *Sendero Luminoso* . . . killed by the Peruvian Army . . . daughter

Perla . . . raised by the Dominican nuns in San Francisco, California . . . " No, please . . . Pablo will kill me . . . I'm going back . . . home . . . I'll tell Pablo . . . I said nothing . . . I don't know how . . . they found out, where's home, Mamá forgive me, why can't I . . . remember . . . your face, my father's face . . . wait for me . . . I'm coming, I couldn't bear the loneliness again, Our Father who art in heaven, forgive me Father for I have sinned . . . Have I . . . sinned, God, How . . . could you let them . . . No, I haven't sinned, forgive Father Juan . . . Pablo . . . they have sinned . . . YOU all powerful God YOU let them, Pablo and Juan, one and the same . . . now You have . . . to forgive them . . . forgive . . . Yourself . . . I . . . forgive . . . You . . . Lord . . .

We feel the light tremors of the dying heart we share. Our spirit rises as our body readies for the long sleep. Our last sigh is the thinnest blade ripping the ultimate seam at the flesh line, at every synapse, at every point of the thin blue line where death ends and irremediable sorrow begins.

But now, who will tell our story?

In My Hands

Winston and Elizabeth were a beautiful couple. It's easy to remember seeing them that first time at the firm's annual spring golf tournament. His roguish darkness a contrast to her cool elegance. He had come in as a full partner recruited from an East Coast powerhouse; I was there pretending to be the date of a one-year associate who didn't want them to know he was gay.

No one would have predicted that Elizabeth and I would start hanging out together. Everyone says married women only like to be around other married women. But my looks didn't compete with her tall, nonchalant gold-blonde beauty. She was gorgeous; I was capable. Besides we were both passionate about golf. Winston didn't like golf—he kept his excellent physique by God knows what means since all those partners do is sit behind impossibly large, impossibly expensive, hand-carved desks. So, she and I would meet at least twice, maybe three times, a week for eighteen holes. With my crazy schedule selling real estate, I could always fit it in. Besides, being at the Sweetwater Country Club had its advantages for my business.

She liked telling the other pampered wives of rich husbands about my brains and savvy in real estate—she even bragged about me as her "one smart friend." I was practiced at turning a casual conversation into an appointment to show houses. Women like her had their husbands buy houses for them to decorate as a hobby—as soon as they finished with one, they would get bored and look for another. The real estate equivalent of serial monogamy.

The first inkling of trouble I had was at the club sipping on our perennial Diet Cokes in the casual dining area after a round of golf. We never ate—we always said we were like orchids—getting nutrition from Houston's humid air. That, and heart-shaped Charm Pop suckers.

She leaned to one side and said in her usual blunt way, "Winston is unhappy, Calais."

"Did he lose that big case?"

"No, I mean personally unhappy."

"Elizabeth, unhappy about what?"

"He's sleeping on the sofa."

"You never told me he snored."

"Take me seriously. Last week he started sleeping on the couch in the media room. I have no idea why."

"Ask him."

She lowered her chin and delivered one of her drop-dead stares. "Are you kidding? I just want to find out who the bitch is and kill her." She gave me a look that could have kindled thunder. I thought she might cry, but her golden cheeks didn't show any tears—right then anyway. I was careful not to mention that good-looking husbands with the testosterone to be successful trial lawyers rarely possessed an "off" switch when it came to sex. My gay friend was still an associate at Winston's firm, and the rumor mill had been going full blast about Winston and a Barbie-look-alike paralegal. I had hoped there was no factual basis.

It went downhill fast from there. He moved out and filed for divorce. He negotiated paying a huge alimony (probably because he felt guilty—which he should've), and moved in with the cheap tart who had somehow wormed her way into his heart, his bed and his wallet—not necessarily in that order.

We had to stop playing golf because he only kept up the membership at Sweetwater for the rest of that year. Instead, we went for manicures together, or for Thai food on Wednesdays with her friends—the other affluent wives. I could tell Elizabeth felt lost without him—everyone else in Sugar Land is married (to a doctor, lawyer, dentist or engineer), except for me. But I'm an anomaly. Elizabeth is not: she's a beauty, and accustomed to being protected by a mantle of endless funds earned by a charming, powerful man wearing a matching wedding band. After seventeen years of marriage, he had left her and all of Sugar Land knew it, or it must've felt that way to her.

At first, at those Wednesday lunches we all joked about Winston's new wife's chain-smoking, and her hideously long acrylic fingernails with applied decals of bluebonnets. We heard that one of her large breasts had plopped out of the skin-tight shimmy of a dress she wore to a partner's dinner while she was leaning over the green felt of the pool table—apparently, an unsafe maneuver after silicone augmentation for both under-muscle and over-muscle. She took the shot and aced it, before tucking her breast back in. But then the weekly lunches moved onto other topics and no one mentioned seeing that hand-some Winston at the Club or buying his aged Scotch at Spec's. I hadn't seen him since before the divorce, but I could visualize his hard pecs stretching the fabric of a polo shirt tight across his chest as he ran a few errands on the weekends.

Late one night, I got an uncharacteristic call from Elizabeth. Her voice sounded one octave lower than it normally is. Rather than sultry, it was downright dangerous.

"Calais, I saw Winston today at the grocery."

Since when did Winston shop for groceries? I didn't want to say it out loud but implicit in my question was the fact that I knew Elizabeth had shopped and cooked for him all those years of marriage. I doubted he knew the difference between a tomato and a lime anymore. The waiters he always tipped extravagantly would discreetly tell him the name of anything on his plate if he wanted to know.

"I'm drunk, I'm afraid."

"Where are you?"

"Sitting at my kitchen table polishing off a fifth of Johnny Walker Black."

"Elizabeth, you can't drink a fifth of Scotch in one sitting."

"Don't worry. There wasn't that much in the bottle. He looked happy. Ridiculously, exuberantly, youthfully happy."

"Maybe he won one of his big cases."

"I don't know. But he was with her, positively gliding down the imported vegetable aisle. I hate him. I hate her. I will never go to that goddamned store again."

I began to worry; Elizabeth doesn't curse. I could hear the tears that she must be holding down because her voice kept dropping lower and lower. I'm not sure why but I pressed the button on my voice mail to record the conversation.

"Promise me one thing, Calais. You've got to promise."

"Sure."

"If I ever get killed, find a PI or go to the police because Winston will have done it."

"Are you crazy? Why would he?"

"Because he will want the money he is paying me in alimony. He only agreed to it because he felt guilty. But I can tell he doesn't feel guilty anymore. He's enjoying that damn doll-woman, and I'm worried. He's a devious man. How the hell do you think he made partner so early?"

The next Wednesday the girls met for lunch, and I waited for Elizabeth to confide more details of her uncharacteristic drunk the previous Sunday. But her friend from college, Kathy, was in from Chicago, so I couldn't get Elizabeth alone. Frankly, I was barely listening to the conversation bouncing along topics like preparing for hurricane season and the new little shop selling fabulous turquoise jewelry. I was trying to formulate the most logical plan to deal with a recent string of unexpected financial crises that had forced me into a cash crunch. Six months previously I had made a down payment on an exciting commercial property that would house my own real estate firm. I had passed the testing for my broker's license, and after ten years of working as a sales associate in someone else's firm, I was ready to be my own boss. To have my own cadre of productive sales associates. But the capital infusion required to build-out the space and acquire fixtures, furniture and equipment was more than I could afford right now—almost $70,000. I would have been able to make the smaller payment my banker had initially arranged, but the recent interest rate fluctuation had made him up the ante. Now I needed more than twice the amount to get the loan. I was close to losing the initial money I'd put up, and I was close to losing the chance to finally be professionally independent. The worry had been keeping me up nights and ruining all my days. I had even lost my last three closings—bad timing, pushing the clients too hard. Typical mistakes for a newcomer; mistakes a seasoned veteran like me should never make. And I couldn't talk to Elizabeth or any of her friends about it—none of them worked, none of them wanted to work. They wouldn't understand an economic downturn—they didn't have any. Besides they all saw me as the epitome of success and independence—a woman who didn't need a man to earn her money for her. And I didn't need a man for money; I just needed the money desperately.

I wasn't prepared for the call from Kathy that next morning. I was dressing to go into the office to make sure the title company was on track for my next attempt at a closing.

"Calais, this is Kathy, Elizabeth's friend."

"Of course."

"This is really strange, but Elizabeth was supposed to pick me up this morning so we could go to an early yoga class. She didn't show up and I can't reach her cell or landline. Did she call you? Do you know where she is?"

"No."

"Well, I thought you might know because I heard we're meeting you for lunch . . . ." Her voice trailed off.

"Look, I'm sure it's nothing. She might have gone for a long walk and forgotten to check the time or something."

"Maybe. But she's always so punctual. You know how she is about time."

"I'll be glad to swing by her house on the way to the office."

"I'd feel better if you checked up on her." She sighed. "I know that you're the one friend she has that she says always takes care of everything. I'd just feel better putting this in your hands." She sighed again.

I had only offered to go by Elizabeth's house to make Kathy feel better. After all, she was on a mini-vacation here in our lovely metropolis. Besides, Elizabeth's subdivision was only a couple blocks off the route to work. As I cruised into it, I counted off the houses I'd sold along the tree-lined blocks. I could recite to the penny the amount of commission I'd made on each one. The good thing about supporting yourself is that you don't need a husband to do it for you. I'd never be in the position Elizabeth was. I would never have to wait for a man to give my life meaning.

Elizabeth's SUV was in the driveway, so I rang the bell about a million times, giving her adequate time to get out of the shower wet, grab up her reading glasses, get into her Greek isle cotton robe from her last married vacation and peer through the front door's beveled lead glass-panes and see me. I tried to raise her on her cell. No luck.

I walked up the driveway to the back door and tried that doorbell. Still no luck. I unlatched the gate and went inside her lush landscaped back yard. The back porch door was often unlocked. Elizabeth had taken to long walks on the manicured pathways that ran behind the houses. When she finished these "philosophical journeys," as she jokingly termed them, she would go into the house through the screened-in back porch. I had noticed that whatever she thought about on these journeys was not conducive to locking doors afterwards.

Sure enough, the screen door was unlocked. I knocked loudly on the door, looking into the kitchen. Still no response. I could see her purse sitting inside on the kitchen countertop, so I knew she was still here. I knocked louder. No answer.

I poked my head inside the door and yelled. This nicely contradicted my mother's adage that I was "such a quiet girl," always followed by "still waters run deep."

Entering her spotless kitchen, I saw one coffee cup in the sink —odd because Elizabeth doesn't drink coffee. I continued calling her name walking toward her bedroom half expecting her to appear slightly breathless from the shower, hair twirled up in a towel. But no, I made it all the way into the bedroom without finding anyone.

She had moved into a different downstairs bedroom when Winston had left; she had redecorated it "sans husband"—ecru and black toile everywhere, sheets, curtains, notepads. I had only seen it impeccable. Today, it looked like a tornado had hit. Bedcovers were on the floor; one lamp lay on its side on the carpet. I felt goosebumps go up my back. Where *was* Elizabeth?

Then I saw what I knew was their wedding photo. I'd seen it in her dressing room—when there was still a "master" for the master bedroom—in an outdated pewter frame. It was face down in the middle of the bed. Mostly out of nervousness, I picked it up. When I turned it over, the glass covering the photo was hopelessly shattered and the broken shards radiated out from her hopeful radiance and his devil-may-care *GQ* grin.

The door to the bathroom was open and a quick glance confirmed that no one was in there.

My mind raced along a million possibilities. What had happened to Elizabeth? It looked like there had been a wild scuffle in the bedroom. And why had the sentimental wedding photo been smashed and left in the middle of the bed? Hadn't Elizabeth told me at the time of the divorce that she was wildly superstitious about the karma of photos and given every single one of them back to Winston? Besides, who else had a key to the house? Had she changed locks after the divorce? Who had been there to drink coffee? And, most importantly of all, where was Elizabeth without her purse (unthinkable) and without her big, gold-toned Escalade now sitting with a cold engine in the driveway?

I went back into the kitchen to look at the coffee cup. It was sitting in the pristine sink, a faint smell rising from the dark coffee still in its bottom. I frowned, trying to remember if this was something Winston had taken with him when he left or something that had stayed. It had his firm's name in gold. The gold script meant that it was a partner's cup; the associates' had gray lettering.

Things were beginning to shape up in my head. Winston must've come over and gotten in through the unlatched screen door (as I had done), or with his own key. Maybe she had made him a cup of coffee —he was a fiend for just-brewed strong coffee. Somehow he had gotten her into the bedroom and overpowered her. I guessed that he couldn't resist waving around that wedding photo. It would be just like a trial lawyer to glory in waving around one last Exhibit A, even if the only onlooker was an ex-wife, that is, a bound-and-gagged ex-wife. He must've spirited her off in the dark. She had tried to warn me that he might want to kill her to save the hundred grand a year. I couldn't believe he'd pulled it off. The closest place to dump a body near this subdivision was the acres of nearby rice fields. It would be easy—no one goes out there except teenagers late at night in 4X4's and pickups to go "mudding." In the dark, in those huge vehicles, a body could get run over and squashed in the mud a million times. No one would be the wiser. But Winston's plan had a flaw. That flaw was the fact that he had left the coffee cup and wedding photo.

I walked back into her bedroom. The photo was laying face up near one side of the bed. I perched on the bed and studied it. They both were just out of college. I remember her telling me once that it had been a fairy-tale courtship. Yes, Winston's brown eyes showed a liveliness and warmth that any girl would've gotten lost in. I was not, and never had been, the kind of woman that Winston would look at with any kind of focused attention or genuine desire. Yet, here I was —the only person who knew he had killed his ex-wife to save a hundred grand a year. Maybe, just maybe, he would be willing to donate half of the money he had just saved himself to me and my new real estate business, if I removed the coffee cup and smashed photo before I called the police? Maybe he would be willing to give me about seventy grand if I offered to "forget" Elizabeth's recorded remark about his wanting to kill her to reduce his out-of-pocket expenses? Certainly, it was worth a try. Being a partner in a law firm, he would be a logical thinker. Logic would tell him to cut a deal with me. All I needed to do was appropriate the coffee cup and the wedding photo without destroying any fingerprints and keep them, together with the tape, somewhere very secret and very safe. I'd persuade Winston by threatening to turn them over to the police if he didn't do as I wished.

I looked under the sink for the Playtex gloves that I'd seen Elizabeth use countless times for washing dishes to preserve her manicure. As I was reaching for the coffee cup with a gloved right hand I heard the back porch door swing open. Oh, my God, was it Winston? Right there and then? Would he kill me before I explained my tidy little plan?

I swung around to see the back door open, and Elizabeth strode in as big as Dallas. She gave a little smirk when she saw my hands and the cup, and said, "Hey, it's nice of you to come over to wash my dishes . . . but?"

I let the question hang in the air for a second or two, so I could get my breathing back to inhale-exhale.

"Kathy called to say she was worried about you and asked me to come by and check. Are you okay?" I had noticed the dark circles under her eyes. She looked like she'd been up all night.

"Oh, yeah. I forgot I told her I'd be by early today for that yoga class."

"Are you okay? We've been really worried."

She plopped down at the kitchen table and waved me into the other chair. She put her face into her hands, sighed deeply, then uncovered her eyes.

"I've a night from hell."

"What happened?"

"Well, I was feeling unusually depressed. I couldn't take sitting here alone anymore. So, I went up to the Starbucks and sat at one of the outside tables, reading. Then, one of my contacts fell out. I must've made quite a picture crawling around trying to find it in those fake cobblestones. Anyway, this very nice man helped me. We started talking, and he was an engineer or something. I guess because I was so depressed, I did something I absolutely don't condone—I asked him home with me. I didn't really have sex in mind. But I guess he did because in the middle of some very nice snuggling, he got way too friendly and I had to hit him over the head with the nearest handy object, which happened to be the wedding portrait I had out from my drunk last Sunday." She gave a wry grimace in my direction when she said "drunk."

"Needless to say, it dampened his ardor, but my bedroom's a mess. I had to revive him with coffee before sending him packing. And I was so completely and totally depressed—even more so than at the beginning of the evening—that I decided to go talk to a counselor, thera-pist, whatever, at the Women's Shelter across the freeway because I really do think if I hadn't had that big portrait to hit him with, I would've gotten raped last night. By a goddamned engineer, of all things. But you know what? I couldn't even tell the counselor about it. All I did was talk about Winston leaving me after seventeen years for that sleazy, little nymphette half his age, and how he would like nothing better than seeing me disappear out of his life forever."

"But your car? Why didn't you take your car and your purse?" I managed to stammer out.

"Everyone in Sugar Land knows my Escalade. I couldn't take it. I didn't want people to know that I was there. I took a taxi."

"Are you alright now?"

"I think so." She shook her head ruefully. "I just need to not do that again."

"I'm so sorry that happened to you, Elizabeth. You're sure you're okay, right?"

She grimaced and nodded her head up and down. "Just a lapse in judgment. Don't worry. It won't happen again."

I marched myself over to the sink and took out the Palmolive dish soap and washed that goddamned coffee cup. That little activity gave me some time to think with my back to Elizabeth still at the kitchen table.

Then I turned around and peeled off the Playtex gloves.

"Listen, darling. I'm so dreadfully sorry about the horny engineer, but thank God, you're safe now. Take a warm shower and a Valium before we meet Kathy for lunch. I've got to continue to the office and make sure the title company doesn't muck up my closing for tomor-row. Call Kathy and tell her you're okay."

She smiled and straightened her shoulders. "Let's not tell her about it, okay? I'd be terribly embarrassed. I'll just tell her I slept late and couldn't hear the phone."

"Sure," I smiled. "Your secret's safe with me."

Outside, the late August heat was stifling and the cicadas had already started their late summer song of dying. I eased my car through the pristine neighborhood and past the high school with its two-acre lot of student parking where Lexus, Mercedes and custom trucks waited for 3:00 p.m. I cranked the AC to maximum power. All the excitement was making me sweat.

After lunch I'd go to Wal-Mart and buy one of those prepaid, non-traceable cell phones. Late afternoon I'd call Winston. We'd meet. I'd do a little bargaining. I'd sell him a foolproof plan for saving his alimony. He'd understand my logic, and donate plenty of cash my way for a quick capital infusion. In fact, I'd always wanted to see him up close, naked and in my own bed. His custom-made, hand-stitched and monogrammed Norton Ditto shirt draped at the foot of my bed. I didn't want him for a husband—he was too handsome and would be far too much trouble. But I'd make sure he'd visit regularly because soon his balls would be in my hands—literally, figuratively and completely. Right in my capable hands.

The Right Profile

The third of the back-to-back episodes of *Law and Order* I'd been watching that night had just ended when my cell phone rang. I looked over at the clock on the bedside table and saw it was two o'clock in the morning. Only a few individuals would dare call me at that time, and just then I didn't particularly want to speak to any of them. So I ignored the ringing. I figured that if my curiosity got the better of me, I could always listen to the voicemail during the commercial break. The fourth episode of *L and O* was about to start, and I didn't want to miss the beginning teaser, when the crime was committed. Less than a minute later, though, instead of hearing the familiar beeping sound letting me know the caller had left a voicemail, the phone rang again.

I moved Sweetie, my dog (no easy task, as she tips the scale at two hundred pounds), so I could reach for the phone to see who the fuck was calling me at that time. Bobby O'Meara—I should have known.

"Fuck you, Bobby, this better be a fucking emergency. I'm missing *Law and Order*. It's an episode I haven't seen."

"Now, Maggie, what kind of way to greet me is that?" Bobby protested. "Especially as I'm calling you to do you a favor."

I didn't have to ask Bobby where he was calling from. In the background I could easily hear the familiar sounds of the Alibi, a seedy bar on the Miami River, located just north of downtown. I'd been working as Bobby's private eye for the past ten years, so I was well acquainted with most, if not all, of his habits (of which there were many), all risky and growing. It didn't take all of my crack investigative skills to know that the fact that Bobby was still at the Alibi at two o'clock in the morning on a Tuesday was not a good sign.

"Favor? What favor? You're trying to weasel your way out of paying me for the last two cases I worked for you? You still owe me five large for those," I pointed out.

"Maggie, Maggie, darling, don't you go all postal on me." Bobby's voice was thick with the cocktails he'd drunk. "I'm not holding out on you. I haven't been paid myself, darling. You know I'll break yours off when I get paid. I promise."

Robert O'Meara was a fine criminal defense attorney. He could have been an outstanding one, except for his bad habits, worse work ethic and nonexistent morals. Even so, in spite of all those negative character traits, he was still quite successful. But then, that had to be taken with a grain of salt, as in Miami, the bar was set pretty low for lawyers. Bobby's law office was located in the northwest section of Miami, in a dingy building, on an even dingier street, in a neighborhood so seedy that I was always pleasantly surprised when I walked out to the parking lot after work and saw that my car was still there, hub caps and all.

As his private eye, I knew how Bobby worked his cases and advised his clients—not exactly according to the ethical standards set up by the Florida Bar. Lately, I'd become increasingly convinced that Bobby was one case away from being disbarred (for all I knew, he could be under sealed indictment right now), which was why I insisted on being paid up front for my work, and in cash. For now, though, I was annoyed with him, and with myself, of course, that I had allowed the money he owed me to add up. Still, Bobby had that Irish charm that, in spite of my best efforts, I couldn't resist. So, occasionally he was able to get away with not paying me. I have to admit, every so often I'd been tempted to walk away, but he always managed to pull in some really interesting cases—and the sex wasn't bad, either.

I pressed the mute button on the television. "So, what's the favor?" I had to admit I was curious.

"I'm going to get you to Heaven, Maggie. Thanks to me, St. Peter is going to open the Pearly Gates to Heaven for you and let you in," Bobby announced in a disturbingly cheerful tone of voice.

"Oh, Heaven, is it? I can't believe you're bringing up the Catholic stuff, Bobby!" I could hear the tinkling of ice cubes hitting his glass as he spoke. Bobby may have been drunk, but he still remembered my vulnerabilities. In spite of five divorces, I still aspired to be a member in good standing of the Catholic Church. My dearest wish was to take Communion, but, based on my dismal marital history, so far the Church, unsurprisingly, had denied that to me. I'd even written to the pope himself, to see if he would grant me five annulments. But to date, His Holiness hadn't responded. Even though the prospects for my being granted a papal dispensation were kind of grim, I had not given up hope. I may have been cynical—most Cubans are—but I did believe in miracles.

"Well, Maggie, if you help me out on this, I'll write the Vatican on your behalf to let them know what you did, darling girl." Bobby would not let it go.

"Cut out the crap, Bobby. As if you had any influence with the pope!" I replied. "And fuck you for talking about the Church that way. And, while you're at it, fuck the blarney, save it for your Latina chicks. They buy your bullshit." I was annoyed, and I was going to let him know it. "I'm missing my show. I put it on mute, and I can't read lips. So just come out and tell me what the fuck you want from me."

"Okay, Maggie, you're right." Bobby had this uncanny ability to sober up at a moment's notice, a skill that had gotten him out of numerous DUIs. "Time's a-passing. Listen, I've got this client—she's a waitress at the Honey Bee. Anyway, I've known her for years. I represented her in the divorce from her scumbag husband. They have three kids, and he owes her twenty grand in child support payments. The bastard paid the first coupla times, then *nada*. The husband comes into court looking beat-up, walking with a cane, blood on his clothes, pretending to be senile. He actually dribbles spit and drools as he talks, tells the judge he'd love to make payments, but he can't work, he's too fucked up. Judge Simmonds—he's the family law judge assigned to the case—falls for the husband's sob story every fucking time. Gives the guy a pass. Fucking bleeding heart." Bobby spat out the words. "Wife knows he's working. He's a photographer, has his own business. He just doesn't want to pay what he owes her."

"So, Bobby, all this is very tragic, really unfair, but I'm still missing the show." I was in no mood to listen to Bobby tell me his sad story. "Get to the point. Where do I come in?"

"Well, Maggie, my love, this is where you earn your entrance to Heaven." Bobby said. "Well, at least, your annulments."

Bobby was fucking unbelievable. "I get it, you want me to prove the husband is working, and, not just that, but there's no investigative fees. I'd be doing it for free, out of the kindness of my heart. That's why St. Peter's going to let me into Heaven—and, of course, the pope will grant me my annulments." At that point, I'd missed so much of the show that there was no point in watching, so I turned off the television.

"I always knew you were smart," Bobby replied. "But wait, Maggie, darling, there's more." I could hear him take a sip of his drink. "Good news. Judge Simmonds is going away on vacation. There's a new judge assigned to the case while he's away. We have a hearing day after tomorrow. The new judge, Judge Shapiro—I have a good relationship with her—says if I can prove the ex-husband is working, she'll throw his ass in jail. It's our one chance to get justice for the client—our lucky break. We have to do something, and do it now."

I thought about what Bobby had just said. "Bobby, I hate to burst your bubble, but if the ex-husband is in jail, he won't be able to pay your client what he owes her." I pointed out the obvious. Bobby must have been drunker than I had thought. "So, she's back to square one, except she gets revenge and the satisfaction of knowing the bastard is in jail. That's worth a lot—it would be for me—but it won't pay her bills."

"Right. But now that we have a new judge, I can go after him for what he owes and actually have a chance of getting it for her. I know from having represented other clients in similar situations that usually the threat of jail is enough to make them cough up the money," Bobby said. "Listen, I'll have Adrienne e-mail you the information you need in the morning: ex-husband's name, address, contact numbers, etc. You'll come up with something tomorrow to prove he's working. I know I can count on you, Maggie. This is our one chance. We can't blow it. Our client, she's a nice lady, a good woman." Bobby had been about to hang up when he added. "And the hearing's set for nine o'clock Thursday morning—bright and early—so you only have tomorrow to work your magic." I could hear the clinking of ice cubes. "And Maggie, she's a compatriot of yours—a Cuban!" Bobby knew how to twist the knife. He had saved the best for last. "Love ya, Margarita. You're the best!"

"Fuck you, Bobby!" I yelled into the receiver, but Bobby had already hung up.

All the talking had woken Sweetie up, and she got out of bed with a hopeful look in her eyes. I looked at her, now all excited at the possibility of going for a walk, and began putting on my jeans and T-shirt.

Although I'd had Sweetie for ten years, I was still occasionally startled by her totally strange appearance. Sweetie was massive, with a head that sprung directly from her shoulders, so she was virtually neckless; she was missing an ear, and the other stood six inches straight up in the air. One of her ancestors must have been a Dalmatian, for she had splotches all over her body; she had one blue eye, the other, brown. My vet said that in the twenty years he'd been practicing, he'd never seen a dog that even remotely looked like her.

Sweetie had been a rescue dog. She'd had one hour left before she was going to get the needle. I hadn't planned to adopt a dog. I'd gone to the pound that day with my friend Violet, a pet detective, who was hot on the trail of a stolen pug. I'd walked around the pound while Violet interviewed one of the clerks, a woman Violet had heard trafficked in stolen pedigree dogs. I'd stumbled on Sweetie, who was on her way to the death room. One look at her, and I knew I'd take her home. No wonder I'd been married five times.

"Well, kiddo, you're in luck that Bobby called. You're getting an extra walk tonight. I have some thinking to do." I leaned over and kissed her. I never carried my Glock when I walked Sweetie. No rapist would dare touch me when I was accompanied by such a strange creature. By the time we returned to the house, the sun was coming up, and I had a plan.

Early the next morning, when I turned on my computer, I saw that, just as Bobby had promised, his secretary Adrienne had e-mailed me the information about the ex-husband. Bobby had said the scumbag was a photographer, so I decided that instead of following him around for days, documenting his actions as he went about from job to job, I would, instead, pose as a customer. We didn't have the luxury of being able to carry out any kind of long-term surveillance on him.

I waited until I'd had my third cup of coffee before making the call. I used one of the disposable cells I kept around for just this kind of occasion. The ex-husband answered on the third ring.

"Mr. Santiago?"

"Sí. Thees ees heem speeeking," a smarmy, heavily accented voice replied. "Who ees thees?"

I hated the guy already, making what I was planning way easier. "My name is Lillian O'Connell. I'd like to make an appointment with you to have my photograph taken."

"Ay, sí, of course. Weeth my pleasure," the ex-husband replied. "But, pleese, how do you get my number to call?"

The guy may have been a bastard, chiseling asshole, but he was no idiot. He wasn't about to set up an appointment with a stranger over the phone, as he had a court date pending in the next twenty-four hours. I was prepared for him, though. "I met a lady at Macy's the other day, at the perfume counter. She was with some friends. She was showing some photos to them. I looked over and saw them, and we got to talking. She said you had taken them last Christmas. The photo was beautiful, just beautiful. I asked her for your name. You're a true artist."

I hoped the flattery would be enough to convince Santiago that this was not a set-up and I was a real customer, but the guy wasn't buying. Not yet, anyway. "What was thees lady, her name?"

I stayed quiet for a bit, as if I were trying to remember. "I think it was Maria. Yes, I'm pretty sure that was it. Long, black hair, about thirty years old, very pretty, dark eyes." Hell, I figured it was safe enough, as that description could fit just about half the female population of Miami.

Now it was Santiago's turn to be quiet. I had the sense he was still suspicious he was being set up, so I decided to help him make up his mind. "Oh, please, Mr. Santiago. My husband is in the army. He's shipping out to Iraq at the end of the week. That's why we're here, to have a little vacation before he goes. I'd really like to give him a good photograph of me before he leaves. He said that's the only thing he wants before going." I pleaded with the scumbag.

"Okay. You want to meet in my studio?" Santiago asked.

Thank God. Greed had won out. I'd passed his test. "No, I don't want the photo to be inside. My husband, he's an outdoor kind of guy—we're from North Carolina. We love the outdoors." Even though Bobby hadn't said anything about Santiago being violent, I wasn't about to go inside with the guy in case anything went wrong. "Is there a nice park someplace we can go? One you've used before to take photographs outside?"

"Sí, I've taken clients to Kennedy Park in Coconut Grove. The ladies—they like it there. Pretty. *Muchos* trees, near the bay," Santiago said.

"That sounds perfect. I'll be there at two o'clock this afternoon." I said. "Is there anything special I should wear?"

"No, Señora O'Connell, just your pretty face," Santiago replied.

I was so repulsed by the guy that I could feel the coffee I'd drunk come up in my throat. "Oh, you're so nice," I managed to say, then added brightly, "See you in a few hours!"

Promptly at two o'clock that afternoon, the taxi I was riding in dropped me off in the parking lot across from the park. I could see two men standing at the entrance to the park, and from the way they kept looking around, they were apparently waiting for someone. The older one was Santiago. I recognized him from the photo that Adrienne had e-mailed to me that morning. The younger man must be his assistant. Still inside the taxi, I snapped a couple of pictures of them with my digital camera, then paid the driver, got out and walked toward them.

"Señor Santiago! Hi!" I called out to the older one. "It's me, Lillian O'Connell!"

Santiago walked toward me, the younger man staying a few feet behind. Santiago was immaculately dressed, completely the opposite of how Bobby said he had turned up in court. He was wearing a crisp, blindingly white dress shirt, neatly pressed dark brown gabardine trousers and black leather shoes. His hair was cut stylishly, and he was close shaven. The assistant, although informally attired in blue jeans and a cotton shirt, was still well dressed.

"Señora Lillian." Santiago reached for my right hand and brought it up to waist level. For a moment, I almost panicked, thinking he was going to kiss it, but, instead, he did some kind of stroking thing with it. The minute I got home, I told myself, I would wash it with Clorox. "It is a pleasure of mine to be here, to take a beautiful lady picture."

Santiago took my hand and led me into the park. I'd told Santiago I was from North Carolina and that my husband and I were outdoor people, so I knew I had to dress the part. After speaking with him that morning, I'd gone to an Outdoor World kind of shop in Little Havana and purchased the most outdoorsy outfit I could come up with. To have my picture taken that afternoon, I was wearing khaki pants, a camouflage shirt, hip waders and a pith helmet on my head. I smelled like mosquito repellent. For jewelry, I had hung a compass on a string around my neck. I looked totally demented, like a cross between a fly fisherman, an explorer from deepest Africa and a bloodthirsty hunter. So much so that I was surprised the taxi driver let me into his cab. But then, the driver had been Haitian, which also explained why he had driven me there.

"Here, Señora. I theenk I like you in a tree." Santiago posed me against one of the royal palm trees by the bay.

I watched as Santiago opened the bag his assistant had been carrying and looked at the contents. I couldn't believe my eyes! The motherfucker had a Hasselblad camera, the Rolls Royce of photography equipment. That thing must have cost thousands of dollars—at least thirty grand—and that wouldn't even include the lenses. I'd worked a couple of undercovers on South Beach, cases that had involved the fashion industry, so I knew a bit about the kind of cameras photographers used for their shoots. The Hasselblad digital camera was the one that the top fashion photographers used—vanity cameras—to prove how successful they were.

I leaned my body against the palm tree just as Santiago told me to do, all the time keeping an eye on what he and his assistant were doing. I knew it was highly likely I would be testifying in court against him the next morning, so I had to get the details right.

"Señora, you speek Spanish?" Santiago asked me.

"No, sorry, not a word," I replied, although I did speak it quite fluently. Not only was I Cuban, but husbands two and four had been Hispanic—number two had been Cuban; four, Venezuelan. I wanted to be able to listen to Santiago speak to his assistant without worrying that I could understand what they were saying. "I'd like to learn, though," I added cheerfully.

The minute I told Santiago I couldn't understand Spanish, he began talking about me to his assistant in that language. He freely criticized my hair, my skin, my outfit, but, mostly, he had it in for my profile, especially my right side. He sure hated my profile, but still, he kept taking pictures of it in a condescending manner, making me move this way and that, in a way that I knew emphasized my flaws. He pointed out to the assistant that my eyes bugged out; my nose looked like a volcano about to erupt; my neck sagged. It took almost all my self-control to stop myself from lunging at him and showing him how I felt about his own profile.

After taking several dozen shots of me in different poses that mostly consisted of me leaning against the palm tree, Santiago suggested we change venues and showed me the way to a eucalyptus tree by the water. As we walked, he kept talking to his assistant in Spanish, mocking me and criticizing my right profile. He was fixated on it. Every so often, Santiago would address me, speaking with such a thick accent that I had trouble understanding him.

Finally, a couple of hours later, the shoot was over, and it was time to leave. As much as I hated to admit it, Santiago knew what he was doing. The guy was a pro. Santiago and I watched as the assistant packed the two bags—the second contained both a Canon *and* a Leica camera and a lot of other expensive equipment. We walked back to the parking with Santiago telling his assistant how it was going to take him hours to fix the shots of me taken in profile so that I would look decent.

"Señor Santiago, thank you very much. I know my husband will be very happy." I addressed the photographer. "We discussed a little how much you were going to charge for the photos. You said you would charge for the shoot—two hundred per hour—then the rest according to how many pictures I ordered, so I'd like to pay you that now, in cash." I dug into my backpack for the plain white envelope into which I'd placed the four hundred dollars I'd taken out of the ATM earlier and gave it to him. "Here's four hundred dollars in cash." I smiled at him. "I'll give you the rest tomorrow, when I come to your studio to pick out the photos."

Santiago took the envelope and slipped it into his pocket. "Gracias, Señora Lillian. I have your number. I call you tomorrow, after the noon, so you can come and pick the pictures."

I watched as he began to walk toward his car. "Oh, please, Mr. Santiago, one minute. Can I have a receipt for the cash, please? For the four hundred dollars?" I put my hand on his arm. "I'm trying to keep records for myself to know where I spend my money while we're on vacation."

Santiago looked toward the assistant, then shrugged as if to indicate how stupid I was. He reached into the pocket of his shirt, and took out a business card and wrote "$400. For photo shoot."

I watched him write, then asked, "Could you put the date, please, so I'll know when we were here?"

Santiago shrugged again, but wrote the date under the amount. We shook hands, and, after safely placing the card in my wallet, I got on my cell phone to call a taxi. Santiago actually offered to drive me back to my hotel, but I declined, saying I wanted to go shopping in Dadeland.

As he and the assistant walked toward his car, I heard Santiago say to the younger man in Spanish, "With the profile that woman has, it's a miracle she found a husband. It's going to take me hours to Photoshop her, to fix that right profile so she looks human."

I smiled and waved at them as I dialed Bobby's office phone number. "Got it. We're going to nail the bastard. It'll be fun tomorrow." I proceeded to give him an account of what had taken place in Kennedy Park that afternoon.

The next morning, I was at the courthouse at eight-thirty. The hearing wasn't until nine o'clock, but Bobby wanted me to stay out of sight until I had to testify, so I hung out in the court reporters' room. I looked very professional, dressed in a dark blue suit, stockings and heels. My long blond hair was pulled back in a ponytail. For jewelry, I had on only a simple wristwatch and a pair of pearl earrings. There was no trace whatsoever of the nutcase outdoorsy woman of the previous day. Still, though, Santiago's comments must have gotten to me because on the way home, I had stopped at a drugstore and picked up a couple of jars of neck-firming cream.

It was close to ten o'clock when Ernie, the bailiff, came in to get me. I stood up, smoothed my skirt, and followed him into the courtroom. Without looking around, I walked straight to the witness chair and was sworn in.

Bobby had been standing in front of me, so I'd not been able to look over at the defense table, which was a good thing. I would have passed out if I'd seen Santiago earlier. Gone was the neat, smartly dressed, perfectly groomed man from the day before. In his place, I saw an old man dressed in a torn polo shirt with some kind of brown stain on the collar, ripped black pants and flip-flops. And it hadn't been only the outfit that had thrown me off: Santiago's face looked as if it had been bashed in. There was dried blood on his forehead, his hair was all matted and filthy and his right leg was in a cast.

Santiago just kept staring at me as if he knew me but couldn't quite place me. He whispered something to his lawyer and sat back in his chair.

Bobby walked toward me, put his arm on the railing of the witness box and addressed me, speaking in a loud voice: "Please state your name and occupation."

"My name is Maria Magdalena Morales. I am a private investigator here in Miami, license number C 8802651," I replied.

"Thank you," Bobby said. "Please tell the Court how you came to be involved in this case."

"I received a call from you two days ago telling me that there was to be a hearing today here and what the hearing was about—that it concerned child support payments that Mr. Santiago owed his former wife. You asked me to come up with a plan proving that Mr. Santiago was indeed working, earning money and that he was capable of paying his former wife the money that he owes her."

Bobby nodded. "And, Ms. Morales, were you able to do that? To prove that Mr. Santiago was working?"

"Yes, sir," I replied.

It was at that exact moment that Santiago realized who I was. He sprung out of his chair, pointed at me and screamed, "She's lying! The bitch is lying! She's a hooker. She tried to pick me up, and I turned her down. She got violent on me when I refused her! That's why she's telling those lies about me." I noticed his English was pretty fluent when he was upset.

Judge Shapiro looked at Santiago's lawyer and said, "Mr. Ramirez, you will either calm your client down *right now*, or I'll have the bailiff remove him from the courtroom."

Mr. Ramirez put his hand on Santiago's arm—hard—and pushed him back into his seat. "Sorry, Judge."

Bobby just watched without saying anything. He waited until Santiago calmed down, then turned to me and said. "Now, Ms. Morales, you just heard Mr. Santiago there call you a liar." He smiled at Judge Shapiro. "Can you prove to the Court that you are telling the truth, and that it is Mr. Santiago who is the liar?"

I reached into my purse and brought out an envelope, then slowly pulled out the photographs I had taken of Santiago and the assistant yesterday, date—and time—stamped. Then I pulled out the business card on which Santiago had written "$400. For photo shoot," and the date, and handed the items over to Bobby, who, in turn, passed them to the judge. Next, I began telling the events of yesterday, not leaving out any details. I finished nailing Santiago by telling the Court that I had conducted some research into the price of the photographic equipment that Santiago had used. Hell, the Hasselblad camera alone, without lenses, cost over thirty-one grand.

When I finished, Judge Shapiro looked at Santiago in disgust. She pointed at him and declared, "Mr. Santiago, right now, this very minute, I'm throwing you in jail for fraud, for perjury and for as many other charges as I can think of."

She looked over at her bailiff. "Ernie, take him to Booking, please."

Bobby and I smiled at each other. I stepped down from the witness stand and slowly walked past the defense table. I stopped, looked at Santiago, and addressed him in perfect Spanish. "At the jail, they're going to take two mug shots of you: one face-front with you looking out, and one of your right profile. Make sure the one of your profile comes out nice. There's no Photoshopping in jail. No Hasselblad cameras."

Santiago lunged at me, the rage in him causing his face to turn crimson. "You lied to me, you bitch! Your husband is not going to any Iraq. I bet you don't even have any husband. No one would marry a bitch like you!"

"Oh, but you're wrong about that, too, Mr. Santiago, as you've been about so many other things." I gave Santiago my sweetest smile. "I've had five!"

I kept on walking up the aisle. At the door of the courtroom, I turned and called back to him. "Don't forget what I said about the profile shot. Remember, there's no Photoshopping at the Dade County Jail!"

Santiago lunged at me. I blew him a kiss and walked out.

Shortcut to the Moon

On good days, I think of Iowa City. Those are the days I find coins in the street, someone gives me a smoke or treats me to their leftovers. When I've eaten and appeased the god of bile in my gut, or when the nicotine hits the bull's-eye in my blood, I allow myself to remember that year in Iowa City. That's all it was, for me: one year of college. But for lots of reasons, the place is etched into my mind like it was a foreign country, or maybe another planet.

When you're from El Paso, you get used to the rough grain of the wind. The leaves turn piss yellow or brittle brown in the fall, not every shade of red and gold and purple, and the winter wind doesn't frostbite your thighs or turn your tears to icicles. In Iowa City, you learn the meaning of seasons. At the Black Angel Cemetery, where I spent untold hours practicing Iowa Writing Workshop techniques that felt like they were making me change from being left-handed to right-handed, the colored leaves of oaks and maples stood out among the headstones like fiery panes of stained glass. What I loved most about that year in Iowa, other than the cornfields and the blizzards and the daffodils blooming under the snow and the juicy double cheeseburgers at George's Bar, was getting blitzed on Cuervo and Colombian with my cousin Ivon in all-night, heart-to-heart sessions that we called "shortcuts to the moon."

That's what I like to think about on good days, but I haven't had a good day in a long time. Till today, when that *gringa* tourist felt sorry for me, I guess, and handed me a five-dollar bill. I wasn't even asking for it. Just sitting there, huddled at the foot of the Cristo Rey statue that's perched at the top of the lookout over the little lumber town of Creel in the Copper Canyon. The days are longer than the nights, so it wasn't cold, but I was shivering, and I guess the *gringa* could tell that I needed something to ease the pain, so without a word, she just walked over to me and handed me a bill. Two Abe Lincolns stared up at me, and I realized my eyes had crossed. I was shocked

29

and forgot to thank her. Just opened my mouth and watched her walk away.

Took awhile for it to sink in that this was not another fantasy of mine, and finally I dragged my ass up from the nest of newspapers I'd made and went to the mission store to buy some essentials: a couple cans of tuna, a pack of Faros, a bar of soap and a roll of paper towels that I can use for drying, washing and wiping. I could barely fit it all into my grungy backpack. Who knows what happened to my suitcase, but I got three bikini *chones*, three baby T's and a pair of khaki shorts rolled up in the pack, along with my journal and my battered copy of *Siddhartha*. The pack is heavy to lug around all day, but makes a nice pillow at night. The lady who runs the mission store just shakes her head every time I go in there, but she always throws in some tamarindo candy or a little pack of Chiclets and tells me to go with God. I want to say I'm trying, but she won't get it.

So today is a good day. A double good day, 'cause I'm not passed out yet. After I've washed up at the public toilet in the train station, and changed into a clean pair of *chones* and an almost clean T-shirt that says "Don't Worry, Be Happy," I wander down to the little plaza in town and allow myself to be around people. Sometimes watching the people breaks my heart. I remember my dad and my grandma and my stupid cousin Ricki—I never, ever allow myself to remember my mom, even though the smell of roasting *chiles* from a restaurant brings her front and center, whether I like it or not—and it hurts so bad I have to fuck somebody so's I can get the money for a bottle.

The train station is the best place to pick up men. The Germans and the Spaniards are the easiest. The Germans, to a man, have these burly pink bodies and perfect dicks. I haven't seen a crooked dick yet on a German. They have a strong smell, though, and their armpits are rank. Even their elbows smell. The Spaniards don't smell as bad (though they've got more body odor than a Mexican any day), and they're funny as hell, but their dicks aren't as nice to look at. A lot of them aren't circumcised and they get this crazy tilt to their erections that makes me laugh sometimes. Except I don't laugh often. Only on good days.

These days, most of my clients have been from the States. I go for the young ones traveling in packs because all the beer they drink on the long, slow train ride from Chihuahua City makes them horny when they get to Creel. "Hey, stud," I call out, and the first one to turn around is my prey. They don't have a choice but to prove their studliness to their buddies. Me and Araceli, the local whore, have worked out a deal. I get the Americans, she gets everyone else. Works out fine with her. Americanos are cheap, she says. Besides, I got me some regulars that won't touch Araceli with a ten-foot condom.

And since today is a double-good day and I'm cleaned up and I don't have to fuck nobody for money or food, and since even the families strolling in the plaza aren't putting a bug up my ass, I think I'll send another postcard to my dad. I bought three postcards when Ricki and I first got here, for our spring break, and sent one right away, a picture of polka-dotted Tarahumara men in headdresses and loincloths dancing their traditional *Pascua Florida* Easter dance. The other two I saved for later in the trip, all stamped and everything, a picture of the quaint little kiosk in Creel and another of a spectacular sunset over the copper and crimson formations of the canyon. But that was before Ricki went on that Holy Week excursion to the waterfall and didn't come back. Before I read in the paper that the decomposed body of a young man had been discovered by some hikers about two weeks after he disappeared. Nothing left to identify him but his teeth and his tattoos. I didn't need to know the results of the dental plate match. Ricki had a juvie record in El Paso, so I knew the police would eventually find out who he was. It was the tattoos that told me everything. "Rita" on one arm; "Cunning" on the other. Not his mother or his girlfriend's name, as they surmised in the local rag, but her own name, or rather the name of the woman he was becoming. From Richard Cunningham to Rita Cunning.

"Rita, as in Hayworth," he would say, all husky-voiced and dreamy-eyed, naming off all the Ritas that he knew, in person or by reputation. "As in Moreno, as in González, Magdaleno and Mae Brown, as in Santa Rita. Don't you see, Mary? It's sexy and dark and down-to-earth at the same time. It can be the name of a tía or a saint, of a sister-in-law or a dyke." Though, of course, he wasn't interested in the least in having sex with women. The Cunning part, short for Cunningham, he was especially pleased with until I pointed out it sounded a lot like cunnilingus to me. I have a way of bursting people's bubbles.

When I found out about the tattoos, I went to the little police station in town and said I was Ricki's cousin and wanted to see the body, see the tattoos with my own eyes. Health hazard, the police chief told me. Against the law to expose a body in that advanced stage of decomposition. The man asked me Ricki's full name and his age and where he was from, and what we were doing in Creel. What else would we be doing in Creel but visiting the Copper Canyon, I said, brave as usual on tequila. I watched him clench down on the cigarette he was smoking, getting pissed off at the way I was talking to him, so I knew I was pushing it. Why did he go into the sierra? To bare his asshole to a Tarahumara, I wanted to say, but I just shrugged and mumbled something about a Holy Week excursion.

He looked at me all shifty-eyed and asked for my passport, said he was going to have to hang on to it for a few days. When he asked me if I knew where Ricki's passport was, I lied and said he didn't have one, just a tourist visa. I gave him the name and address of his parents, Uncle Michael and Tía Fatima, and wrote them a stupid note saying I was sorry and didn't know what had happened to Ricki.

To prove I was really his cousin traveling with him on vacation, he made me pay the fee to transport his remains to Chihuahua City and from there to El Paso. "Five hundred dollars," he said. "Are you crazy," I said, digging into my jeans and pulling out the rest of my cash: fifteen hundred thirty-one pesos in one pocket, a hundred-dollar bill my dad had given me for emergencies in the other. That's all I got, I said. He scooped it all into his fat palm and gestured with his head for me to go. Fact is, as I learned from the jail keeper a few days later, they'd had no way of lifting the body out of the canyon and had set it on fire, instead. They sent his parents a box of bones and ashes. DHL Ground Delivery. I'm sure as hell it didn't cost them two-hundred-fifty bucks. That motherfucker took all the money I had left.

I toyed with the idea of putting in a collect call to my cousin Ximena, Ricki's older sister, and sort of the captain of all the cousins. If anyone could handle bad news it was Ximena. I got as far as dialing the number, and then. . . . I don't know. I snapped, I guess. Next thing I knew I was waking up in some seedy room crawling with cockroaches next to some naked Asian guy, empty bottle of Hornitos between us. I took a couple of twenties from his wallet and slipped out of there fast. Weird thing was I had all my clothes on, even my shoes, but when I went to the bathroom I found my *chones* drying on the sink and my backpack stashed behind the toilet.

Next time, it was a white guy in Iowa Hawkeye boxer shorts I woke up next to. Talk about serendipity. Then the custodian of the jail, who didn't pay me but at least he knew how to break in to the police chief's desk and got me my passport back. Then a black guy, a safe-sex freak that wouldn't let me even jerk him off without a rubber, followed by a couple of Germans. I didn't care who it was or what he wanted, as long as he didn't try to stop me from drinking myself to death. And before I knew it, the sad little marching band playing the Mexican national anthem told me it was *cinco de mayo*, long past Easter, and I hadn't called anybody to let them know about Ricki. By then, I figured they already knew, so what was the use of calling. Somewhere in the small, sane part of my brain, it occurred to me that maybe my dad would be worried about me and that I should call him to let him know I was okay, so to speak. But like I said, it was a small thought, easily overrun by a couple shots of tequila.

If you really wanted to be generous you could say that I stayed in Creel to figure out what happened to my cousin. And I did, for a while. Five days in a row, I went to that motel with the cute cabins we had stayed at when we first arrived and waited for the tour guide who'd sold the Basaseachic Falls Canyoneering Adventure to Ricki. He'd taken the two of us on a tour of the Tarahumara dwellings and the so-called Valley of the Monks that looked more like a forest of giant petrified penises, and the guy kept disappearing into the woods to fuck his girlfriend. I didn't trust him, but he'd talked Ricki into the Basaseachic tour by saying it was a special tour for men only, led by a real Tarahumara guide, that took them to an area of the falls used only by the native men for some kind of spring ritual of renewal. Smelled real fishy to me, and I begged Ricki not to go, even threatened to get on the next bus back to Juárez if he did.

"Come on, Mary, you know me better than that. What's my favorite movie?"

"Wizard of Fucking Oz," I said, knowing what he was getting at.

"Exactly. 'Somewhere over the rainbow, dreams come true,'" he sang the whole stupid song as he packed his gear and his second-hand Polaroid camera into his Old Navy duffel bag. He didn't even care that I held on to his passport.

Horny little idiot. That tour guide must have seen the queer in him to tell him the excursion was for men only. Fact is, my cousin had this fantasy of getting laid by a Tarahumara, and figured this could be his one and only chance. When the tour guide finally showed up at the motel, swaggering under his cowboy hat, he acted like he had no idea who I was or what I was talking about. I told him I was going to report him to the police chief, but he laughed, said the police chief was his brother-in-law.

"I'll report you to the tourist bureau, *hijo de la chingada!*" I shouted at him, but all he did was spit in my face and saunter away. So much for detective work.

I took to showing Ricki's passport picture to folks in the train station and the post office and the plaza, but every time I'd see a pretty guy in a ponytail, or a guy who walked with his elbows close to his body, like Ricki, I'd black out and wake up in some bed with some stranger. Most of the time I'd be fully dressed and they'd be naked, so I figured I'd worked them over pretty good with hand or mouth, and that was worth at least forty U.S. dollars a pop. So I had a fee. A steady clientele. And a broom closet of my own at the rinky-dink Hotel Tarahumara.

Things turned to shit after they put me in jail, though. Tiny, stinking icebox of a jail behind the police station with an old drunk who kept farting "*pedos de la muerte*," as the jail keeper called them, because they stunk of death. Stayed there for a week, I think, because I refused to blow the police chief, and that spoiled my reputation. I got kicked out of my room. I didn't look so hot, and I smelled even worse with the stench of *pedos de la muerte* in my hair and clothes. No more easy clients at the train station. And Araceli gave me a major tongue-lashing and a good *desgreñada*, pulling-my-hair pissed at me when she found out about my regulars, said I'd been crossing the line into her territory and poaching on "her" men.

"*Pocha sin vergüenza*," she called me. "Go fuck the dogs in the plaza. This is my station from now on."

I had no money except the few pesos I could make in boxcars and the Cristo Rey lookout after dark, and no place to sleep but the great outdoors. Once, I gave a blow job to one of the ticket takers behind the station and got a free ride to Divisadero. Figured I could ply my trade in dollars again up there where my reputation wasn't anything anybody cared about, where they didn't know I was the cousin of a young man found dead in Tarahumara country.

As far as customers were concerned, I had a pretty good stretch of luck for a few days doing the ticket takers while the train waited for the tourists to pose for pictures and buy some extra trinket or greasy quesadilla from one of the Divisadero stalls. I'd walk up to them after all the tourists had stepped down from the train, sidling up close enough to touch their belts, letting my hand wander down just far enough so they understood what I was offering for two hundred pesos.

Things changed when someone reported a homeless drunk woman loitering in the lobby of the five-star hotel that hangs off the ledge of the Copper Canyon. Before long, I was burnt up in Divisadero. So I got another free ride back to Creel, and been here ever since. My address now is Cristo Rey. Reminds me of home, except our Cristo Rey in El Paso is bigger and presides over desert and freeway. If I squint real hard at the limestone Christ statue, it transforms into my mom, arms outstretched, going, "don't be afraid, Xochitl." She's the only one who ever called me by my first name, Xochitl, the one the Catholic nuns took away as soon as I started first grade, making me go by my middle name, Maria or Mary, the rest of my life. I tuck in to a nest of newspapers each night, just me and the bottle or me and *delirium tremens*.

Sometimes I dream that I'm on the phone to my dad. "It's nobody's fault, *mi'jita*, your mamá was sick," I hear him saying, but his voice sounds like it's coming from a walkie-talkie underwater. Maybe it's me. Maybe I'm just swimming in tequila until I find my way back to the womb. It's funny what you can get used to. But I guess I'm getting tired of the party I've been on since before Easter, tired of blacking out and sleeping on concrete. I've been trying to clean myself up, dry out enough so that I can bring myself to write that postcard to my dad. Maybe it's time to go home.

There's a kid sitting next to me on the bench now, watching me stare at Ricki's passport picture. A little snotty-nosed boy in a red jacket, about four or five years old. Looks like a Tarahumara kid, except they don't usually travel alone, not this young. I crane my neck over the plaza and spot a Tarahumara woman with a baby slung over her chest, sitting in front of the gazebo surrounded by palm-leaf baskets of all sizes. Must be the boy's mom, I think. For some reason, the kid is bugging me. Just sitting here staring at me, trying to figure out if I'm somebody he should beg from. My clothes are dirtier than his, but my face and hands are clean, and I've got a full pack of cigarettes and two empty tuna cans next to me on the bench. I could be sending some mixed signals to this kid. I sure as shit ain't gonna be sharing what's left of my five bucks with him.

I'm praying nothing happens between now and dinnertime so I can take that eighteen pesos I have left and buy me a bowl of soup at Lupita's Restaurant. They're the only ones who won't kick me out, if I come in with money and can pay for my food. They got the best *coci-do de res* I ever tasted, other than my grandma's. A beef broth thick with carrots and *calabazas*, potatoes and cabbage, the meat practically dissolving in your mouth, bones rich with marrow and a big order of soft homemade corn tortillas. That's what I want more than anything. If nothing happens, I mean. I go back to staring at Ricki's picture. Little showoff with his slicked-back hair and bleachy smile.

Goddammit, Ricki! I pound my fist into the bench.

If this kid doesn't stop bugging me, staring me at me with those crybaby eyes, waiting for me to fork over a peso or two, I'm going to take my money into that liquor store over there and get me a quart of Los Mochis Tequila.

Two Tarahumara girls, about eight and ten years old, in bright flowered skirts and scarves run up to the boy and one of them whispers in his ear, all three of them staring at me like I'm some circus freak.

"*Váyanse*," I tell them, gesturing with my arm for them to get away from me, but the girls hold up a flat basket filled with magnets, little woodcarvings in paisley skirts and bandanas, torsos wrapped in white rebozos, tucked inside a tiny palm leaf basket.

"*¿No quiere?*" says the older girl.

As long as I've been here, I've never seen a Tarahumara girl or woman begging. Only the little boys beg. Older boys and men don't usually come into town. Only the women deal with the tourists. More stoic than Apaches, they don't talk much. They'll tell you the price of whatever they're selling, and that's it. No "good morning" or "*buenas tardes*" or even "*gracias*" from them. And don't even think of haggling with a Tarahumara. They don't give a shit if you walk away. Money is just a daily means to an end for them, and they don't believe in possessions, either. Their measure of a good life is not "he who has the most toys wins." It's the one with the least toys that gets a ticket to Tarahumara heaven. You could say I've been trying to live by the Tarahumara code, you know, learning how to make do with as little as possible, for the last . . . what? . . . six weeks, give or take?

"*¿Cuánto?*" I say, picking up one of the magnets, the figure is carved of canyon piñon, and the face and legs are striated with brown and gray. I lift the skirt and see that it's wearing tiny paisley panties.

"*Diez pesos*," the girls say in unison.

Maybe I could send this magnet to my dad, ask him to telegraph me some money for the fare back to civilization. I could still get a small cup of *cocido* with eight pesos. But there's this fucking hopeful look in the boy's eyes that does me in, makes me think of Ricki when we were kids playing *muñecas* in Grandma Maggie's backyard.

"One day I'm gonna be a mommy," he'd say, diapering his doll.

"Not me," I'd say. "I'm gonna be an astronaut so I can go to the moon."

Fucking memory dries out my mouth, makes me feel like I swallowed the saltshaker. I need something to wash it down.

"*No, gracias*," I choke out the words, returning the magnet to the girls.

Before I know it, I'm making a beeline for the liquor store. What can I say? The only place I want to be right now is on the moon. When I come back to the plaza with my paper-bagged bottle, the girls are still there, like they're warming the bench for me. I roll my eyes at them and start to walk in the opposite direction, toward the church.

"*¡Foto!*" One of them calls out.

"Leave me alone," I say, unscrewing the bottle. "I don't have a camera." I take a nice long burning swig of probably the cheapest tequila ever made. Feels like a live flame touching my gizzards.

The older girl comes up to me, points to Ricki's passport still in my hand. "*Foto*" she says again, furrowing her little eyebrows.

What is this kid trying to tell me? "This is a passport," I tell her. "My cousin's passport. He's dead."

The girls shake their heads.

"*Allá arriba*," the older girl says, pointing to the hills. "*Foto.*"

I watch her reach into the paisley pocket of her skirt and pull out a picture. She shows it to me, holding on tight to the corner. And there he is, the son of a bitch, posing shirtless in his own Polaroid moment with the two girls and the little boy. They're standing next to a wash line strung on timber and hung with dozens of colored Tarahumara skirts drying in the sierra sun, the tattoos on his arms clear as day.

I grab the girl's arm. "Is he alive? *¿Está vivo?*"

Eyes round like pennies, the girl nods. "*Allá arriba*," she says again.

I'm so startled I drop my bottle and it shatters on the flagstones of the plaza, all that good tequila soaking into the scuffed blue leather of my cowboy boots.

I try to take the picture from her but the girl slips it back into her pocket.

"*Diez pesos*," she says, then wrenches her arm from my grasp and she and the other girl and the boy scurry out of the plaza.

Fuck me running, I think, except I can't stand, much less run. My knees are giving out and I feel like I'm going to black out again. The bench. I have to reach the . . . fuck! My head hits the edge of the arm-rest.

When I come to, there's a familiar face—two of them—leaning over me. My eyes feel crossed and I have a hangover headache even though I haven't had but one sip of my daily deadly dose today.

"Don't move," she says, "Are you okay?" Her two faces dissolve back into one. It's her. The *gringa* who gave me the five-dollar bill earlier.

"What's your name?"

"He's alive," I tell her. "My cousin's alive. Those girls took a picture with him."

"How many fingers am I holding up?"

I try to focus on the fingers she's wiggling in front of my eyes, and for a moment, I think I'm going to vomit. I feel like I got kicked in the head.

"I'm okay," I say.

"Can you sit up? Let's get you some water."

She helps me sit up against the bench and holds a bottle of water to my mouth, but I turn my head. The thought of drinking anything makes me want to puke.

"My cousin. They said he died in the canyon. Found him decomposed," I tell her, and I can't figure out how I could've gotten drunk on one sip of tequila. My words are slurred and I sound like I'm deranged. "Those girls took a picture with him."

"Just be still, okay? You may have given yourself a concussion. I think you need to go to a hospital. You need help."

I turn to face her and try to fix my gaze on something other than her blue eyes. "What I need is to make a phone call," I say, staring at the spray of freckles on her nose. "I have to call my family. See if they know . . . if they know about Ricki. Can you help me get to a phone? I'll do anything you want." I put my hand on her thigh to help her get my meaning. "Anything," I repeat.

"Brigit! Where've you been?" calls someone behind us. My head hurts too much to turn around, but soon enough, I have the misfortune of recognizing who it is.

"Jesus *pinche* Christ. Espinosa, is that you?"

"Now I know I've lost my mind," I say. "You couldn't be for real."

It's my cousin Ivon Villa, partner in crime from my Iowa City days, standing there gaping at me with this horrified, pitiful look that makes me want to punch her.

"There but for the grace of the goddess go I," she says.

"She's the one, Ivon," says the *gringa*. "The one I saw up at the lookout, the one I told you about. I didn't even recognize her. She's lost so much weight."

And that must be Brigit what's-her-name, the woman Ivon married in Iowa City.

"When you said you said you'd seen a drunk woman up there sleeping in newspapers," Ivon says to her girlfriend, "I was afraid it might be my cousin, but I didn't want to believe it. Boy, am I glad Uncle Joe's not here to see this."

"You know, sweetheart, maybe you should open a business for finding missing relatives," says the *gringa*, helping me get to my feet and sit down on the bench. "Careful, now," she says to me, all maternal and shit. "Don't move too fast, or you'll lose your balance again."

Lose my balance? That's a good one.

"At least this one isn't mauled by dogs," says Ivon. She's squatting down peering into my face now like she's extra nearsighted or something. "Unlike what happened to my little sister, this is all self-inflicted damage. Huh, *prima*?"

"What in the holy hell are you doing in Creel, Pancho *Pinche Puchi* Villa?" I ask, using her childhood nickname and sounding like a total drunk. I know it doesn't seem that way but I am alert enough now to be aware of my embarrassment. "Don't tell me my dad sent out the troops."

"Girl, your dad is a mess. Ever since your phone call, his ulcers have been killing him. The whole family's practically in mourning."

"My phone call?"

"I don't know. He said you sounded sick. That you were ranting and raving about Ricki's tattoos. Sick, my ass. You were drunk, weren't you?"

"They know about Ricki, huh?"

"It's *you* everyone's been worried about, *pendeja*. Your dad was getting ready to come look for you himself. It would've killed him to have found you like this."

"So what? Did they get Ricki's remains or not? The fucking police—"

"Ricki's remains? Girl, what the fuck are you talking about? Ricki went home weeks ago. Said he looked for you all over town when he returned from some side trip he took."

"Are you shitting me?"

"The police told him you'd gotten on a train after having caused a disruption at the motel you guys were staying at. They made him pay a fine, too. He figured you'd gone back home, so he went back, too."

"The son of a bitch has been home all this time?"

"Pigging out on Tía Fatima's pancakes the last I heard."

"His parents never got any notice of his death?" I'm beginning to put it together in my tequila-logged brain.

"Notice of his death? Girl, you must have been really tripping. All they got was a charge on their credit card that Ricki was using, to pay for the damage you caused at the motel. Seems you set the room on fire, or something."

"A charge on their credit card?" I hear the *Twilight Zone* theme in my head and start to laugh. "Doo-doo-doo-doo Doo-doo-doo-doo," I say, still laughing.

"I think she's hysterical," says Brigit.

The police had played the both of us, and taken us for whatever they could: two fifty on my end, who knows how much on Ricki's. There I'd been wandering around like the town lush, mourning my decomposed dead cousin in jerk-off sessions and blackouts, entertaining the locals with my theatrics. And there he was eating his mom's pancakes at home, no doubt showing off his Polaroid pictures of the Copper Canyon. I'm laughing so hard I can feel the piss soaking up my jeans. Not that it's the first time.

"You're a total nightmare," Ivon says to me. When did she get so holier-than-thou, I wonder?

"Be kind, honey. You don't know what she's gone through."

"Let's go," says Ivon, pulling me to my feet.

"Look at that bruise on her forehead, Ivon. She should really see a doctor," says Brigit. "There's that little hospital by the train station."

"I don't want to go to no hospital," I say.

"Let's take her to the hotel," Ivon says to her girlfriend. "We're getting on the first train back to Chihuahua tomorrow."

"You need a nice hot shower," says Brigit, unzipping my backpack. "Do you have any clean clothes?" She looks inside and gags like there's a dead animal in there.

"Fuck that," Ivon sneers. "We're dumping all this stinky shit. She can wear some of my clothes."

Each of them puts an arm around my waist, and I feel like I'm five years old again, walking between my mom and my dad.

"What is it with this family?" Ivon is grumbling. "Do we all have a self-destructive gene or something?"

"Remember Iowa City?" I ask Ivon, tears bubbling down my face, not so much because I want to remind her that she'd had her own pant-pissing days in college, but because I want her to say something nice about that year we shared in Iowa. I'm the one who talked her into going there, and she's the one who ended up staying. Got her Ph.D. and everything, the first doctor of the family. "Remember our shortcuts to the moon?"

"Shortcut to hell is more like it," she says.

We pass Lupita's Restaurant, and suddenly my mouth is salivating and the god of bile sends up a wave of nausea that makes me puke a bitter yellow liquid in the street.

"Get it all out," says Ivon.

Brigit hands me the water bottle and I rinse out my mouth.

"Hey, do y'all want some good soup? They got the best *cocido* in the known universe here at Lupita's."

"Not until you do one thing," says Ivon, getting in my face.

"What?"

"Admit that you're an alcoholic, Mary. Admit that you're killing yourself and that you need to stop drinking to save your life. Admit that you need help and that you have to start going to AA meetings as soon as you get home."

"What the fuck!" I can't believe what I'm hearing. This was a woman who could drink *me* under the proverbial table. We'd been getting loaded together since junior high. From the Smeltertown graveyard in El Paso to the Black Angel Cemetery in Iowa City—Ivon was my drinking buddy, my Dark Shadows blood sister in the Almighty Order of the Agave. And now, here she is doing the Twelve Step Shuffle on me? "No fucking way!" I am in serious regret mode here.

Ivon knuckles my head and kisses me square on the mouth. There's tears in her eyes the size of Texas. "Admit it, *esa*!"

"Fuck you," I say. I glance up at the lookout and see my mom again in the outstretched arms of Cristo Rey. I can almost hear her going, *No tengas miedo*, Xochitl. Don't be afraid while I shoot myself up with insulin and trip out to talk to the Virgin. Trouble is, she died. My mom died on my watch. So what if I was only thirteen years old and just doing what I was told, counting nine hundred minutes before I woke her up from her self-induced insulin overdose with a cup of sweet tea? That's enough to terrify anyone for the rest of their motherless life.

"Look, *cabrona*," I say, "the only thing I'm gonna admit to is that I'm happy to see you guys, okay? And if I weren't so messed up, I swear I'd kick your high and mighty ass all the way back to El Paso."

Ivon threatens me with her fist. I thrust my chin at her, like daring her to go ahead and hit her cousin when she's down and out. She punches me in the arm, just the same.

"*Cabrona*," I say, and she hugs me hard enough to split a rib.

Los Simpáticos

Y ou don't know my name, but if you are Latino, live next to a Latino, or have watched television within the last year, you know my work. My name is Desideria Belén Ayute, and I am the sixty-one-year-old executive producer for *¿A Quién Quieres Matar?*, the reality-TV show where we find *fulanos* who want to hire a hit man and get them to admit on hidden camera all the filthy details as to why. Oh, it's a good show. Three years on the air in every Spanish-speaking country on the planet, and still on top—even today, even after all this ugliness. Wait, who am I kidding? Even more now. The show's reruns are doing better than this season's crop of *telenovelas* and variety shows. Advertisers have never been so eager to catapult money at us. I'm in talks right now with a half-dozen networks about creating an English version. If only, somehow, Xavier could enjoy all this success with us, life would be perfect. But that's not life, *mi vida*. Life and limes are delicious, but sour.

Theoretically, *¿A Quién Quieres Matar?* could run forever. You wouldn't believe how many Latinos out there are willing to pay tens of thousands of dollars to kill a friend or family member. I'm an old woman, so I can remember a time when, if you wanted to kill someone, you'd go grab your machete and do the job yourself. But this new generation, with their American ways and their American dollars, they don't want to get their machetes dirty. They'd much rather hire some poor *guajiro*, fresh off the boat and hungry for money, to do it for them. And there's never any shortage of hungry *guajiros*.

Xavier Morales was the actor who played the hit man on our show. We pixilated his face and slowed his voice in post-production, made it low and robotic so people wouldn't recognize him on the street. We thought the series would be ruined if they did, but we were fools to think we could keep it a secret. Before the first season was over, some Internet idiots with too much time on their hands uncovered his identity.

We thought the show was over. But it wasn't—because even though millions watch our show, billions do not: they watch something else, or don't watch TV, or whatever. In fact, once his cover was blown, ratings went up, especially with women viewers ages eighteen to thirty. You know why? Because Xavier was gorgeous. *Ay*, what a *guapetón* that man was! Beautiful and manly and gentle and powerful and funny and, my God, what a dancer! Just watching him walk was enough to make modest women press their thighs together and less modest women open them a little. And though he was Cuban through and through, he was born in the States, which meant that most of the nasty parts of machismo (for instance, the part that will backhand a sassy woman) had been shrunk to almost nothing, like successfully treated tumors, while the good parts of machismo—the valor, the tenacity, that almost savage cheeriness that is impervious to neurosis —remained perfectly intact. I had sexual fantasies about that man six days a week. At least.

So you can imagine how upset I was when the police called me that morning to tell me he'd committed suicide.

Earlier the previous evening, we had wrapped up shooting our special New York City edition of *¿A Quién Quieres Matar?* It was the weirdest shoot we'd ever had. We were all set up in our rented third-floor apartment in the Bronx to receive our mark of the week, a lanky Dominican named Tito Angelobronca. Seventeen years old, going on twelve, he slumped in his chair and only spoke to adults when spoken to, and even then only with the sullen one-word replies of someone who wants to get out of there and go run around with his friends. He wanted Xavier to kill another high school boy named Miguel Fernández for, as far as I could tell, no good reason: he gave half reasons like girls and neighborhood slights and "that *puto*'s a punk-ass bitch! He's got to go, yo!"

So Tito was coming to the apartment to finalize all the details with Xavier, to give him all the information a real hit man might need for the job. And Tito had a special request: he wanted Xavier to make it look like a suicide, and wanted Xavier to leave a note behind that read "*Soy simpático*," which means "I'm likable" and/or "I'm sympathetic." It was a damned weird thing to write on a forged suicide note. Xavier was going to ask him what that meant when he showed up.

Besides Xavier and the hidden cameras and my crew, in the apartment were a half dozen of New York's finest who, once they had all the evidence they needed, would burst from their hiding places and wrestle Tito's chicken-bone frame into a chair. Then, if he waived his rights—and they almost always did—Xavier would interview him and try, in an avuncular if sanctimonious way, to show him the error of his ways. And then the police would haul him off, and we'd start breaking down the equipment and heading to our next location: Miami, our bread-and-butter city. There's never been a hit man in Little Havana who's been unemployed for more than twenty minutes.

So there we were, waiting, ready to get the whole dirty business on camera. Only it wasn't Tito we saw, courtesy of our hidden cameras, walk into the apartment building. It was an old woman, dressed in the humiliating motleys of some chain restaurant: Hawaiian bowling shirt, red slacks, black visor, disintegrating sneakers. Her eyes looked as big and black as a horse's. She was stooped but sure-footed; she climbed the stairs like someone who had ascended Machu Picchu every day of her life. In one hand she carried a brown bag that said "Large Brown Bag" on the side.

We weren't ready for her, but in the reality-TV biz you learn to adjust fast. While the rest of us hid, Xavier slipped into character: a laconic, efficient sociopath. He dragged a chair in front of the apartment door and sat facing it, waiting for her to knock.

She didn't. She turned the knob and walked in and didn't close the door. Her huge eyes were shut into slits, her mouth was pursed, her hands were fists. She looked at Xavier with the combination of derision and fear that we Latinos usually reserve for the Antichrist.

Xavier, smiling like the Antichrist, said, "I think you have the wrong apartment, Abuelita."

She replied in Spanish, but I'll translate: "This is the right place. One look at you, and I know this is the right place. You're the assassin. You're the man Tito wants to hire to kill Miguelito. Well, you won't be killing anyone today. Tito is not going to hire you. I found out about his plan. I know everything. That's how I knew to come here. And I have put a stop to it." She dropped the bag on the floor. "Ten thousand dollars. Consider yourself paid. All I ask is that you leave Tito alone. He will never say anything to anyone about this, and neither will I, may God split me in two with a lightning bolt."

All of us were stunned. But Xavier could handle anything. After a short pause, he stood and went over to the bag, took out a rubber-banded brick of bills, rifled through them appreciatively. Then he smiled and in Spanish said to the old woman, "Okay, Abuela. Paid in full. So it's over."

The old woman squinted her horse-eyes. "Don't try to find Tito. Don't try to hurt him. You'll never find him."

"I kill for money, woman, not for pleasure. I have been paid, and I didn't have to lift a finger. Why would I want to kill him?"

"Because he has seen your face. He can report you to the police."

"But you won't let him. You told him he could never say anything to anyone, because if he did, I would kill him."

"Yes. Just as you say."

"But, Abuela, now you have seen my face, too. Maybe you think I am going to kill you?"

"Yes," she said. Sudden tears fell like ballasts from her eyes. "I do."

I saw Xavier's character waiver—the hit man persona shimmered, almost dissipated. But he collected himself. "I understand. I see it all clearly now. You think I won't let either of you live. You have done everything you can, but you think I will kill you both anyway. But listen, Abuela. Killing clients is bad for business. I have a reputation to maintain. So long as you and Tito keep quiet, it's better for me to take the money and be on my way. We can all win."

She was still crying, but she didn't let that get in the way of scrutinizing Xavier. "Don't lie to me. God is watching you. You are going to let Tito live?"

"Yes, Abuelita. And you too."

"I am an old woman. If you don't kill me, soon enough something else will. But Tito is just a boy. Swear to God you will not kill him."

"I swear in the name of God that I will not kill Tito Angelobronca."

She narrowed her horse-eyes. "How can I trust an assassin?"

Xavier laughed and replied, "I don't know, Abuela. All I can offer is my word."

She studied him for a moment. Then she said, "You are going to hell. Unless you change your ways, God will punish you for your terrible sins. You should pray every night to Jesus Christ, and confess your sins, and change your evil ways."

"I know, Abuela. I know."

"If you keep your word, I will pray for you. One rosary every day." She turned to leave. "Perhaps the Virgin Mary will hear me and intercede on your behalf. Perhaps your heart will open up to God's love. You can still be saved from eternal damnation. Pray every night, and in the end you may spend eternity in God's loving presence." She pulled the door shut and was gone.

We watched the monitors, jumping from one to the next as she left the range of one staircase camera and entered that of another. It wasn't until she left the building that we started breathing again.

The crew and cops erupted in an astonished disputation: "What the hell was that?" we asked each other, laughing and scratching our heads. Could we still make an episode out of this weird twist of an ending? And then there was the money, all that money: We had to return it to the Abuela. It was her money, not Tito's, we were sure—scrimped and scoured from who knows where to save the life of her unworthy grandson. Well, that could be our ending right there! We could have Xavier return the money to her, tell her it was all pretend, all just for TV and that she didn't have to live in fear. We'd just have to make sure she was ready, so that she wouldn't do anything rash—like have a heart attack—when she saw Xavier again.

Xavier. He sat with his elbows on his thighs, hands covering his face. I went over to him, put a hand on his shoulder. He knew it was me by touch. "Oh man, Mami," he said. He always called me Mami, which I kind of hated and kind of adored. "That was hard. I shouldn't have done it that way. I should've told her it was all an act."

"Are you kidding?" I said, and moved around to the front to give him a hug. The first rule of being a good producer is hug first, talk money later. "You were perfect. Thanks to you, we'll still be able to salvage a show out of this. And she'll get her money back. Everyone's going to benefit from this, thanks to you."

He groaned. "I tortured her, Mami. I made her suffer. I could've been so much kinder. Why didn't I just tell her the truth? Why did I stay in character?"

"Because you're a good actor, and you had a job to do. We're going to fix everything. We're going to make everything right."

Into his hands he said, "I have to make it right, Mami. I have to."

"You will," I said. "Don't worry. We'll fix everything. First thing tomorrow."

As I entered Xavier's hotel room the next morning, tears dragging clots of mascara down my face, I thought to myself, *I told you we were going to fix everything, Xavier. Why didn't you believe me?*

This part is a little sick. I know it is. I am ashamed, but not so ashamed as I should be, and that makes me even more ashamed. I brought a camera crew with me to Xavier's hotel room.

Look, I'm a TV producer. This was a legitimate international news story. I had a responsibility to the public. Plus I didn't want to go there alone. So I brought Eugenio, the oldest cameraman in the industry, and Constancia, the show's viper-tongued director, to whom I would trust my eternal soul.

The only reason I got into that hotel room in the first place was because, after many shoots in New York of ¿A Quién Quieres Matar?, I'd made friends with a lot of NYPD detectives and, in a small but real way, helped them arrest some dangerous people before they could do any real harm. And everyone wants to be on TV. Even NYPD detectives.

Enter Detective Dan Burdock. I always think of him when Billy Joel sings the line: "He's quick with a joke / or a light of your smoke, / but there's someplace that he'd rather be." Yes, poor Danny always dreamed of being a star, but since he had a complexion like a post-poisoned Viktor Yushchenko, he was better off as a detective, where he could use his looks to intimidate lowlifes.

He was the one who had called me, who was now leading me and my crew through the room. The detectives, crime scene investigators, and the coroner had all done everything they needed to do. At Dan's request they had left a few key items in place so that I could film them. But not Xavier. They had, of course, removed his body. They had even remade the bed. He had utterly disappeared from the room.

Once my crew was parked, plugged in and rolling, Dan, with a kind of dilettante expertise, looked into the camera and set the scene for us. "Here is where the apparent suicide took place. I say apparent, because the official report won't have been filed yet, but it's pretty cut and dry. The victim, Xavier Enamorado, was found this morning at 7:30 a.m. by Alonzo Gutierrez, his personal assistant. Xavier was on that bed, seemingly asleep, but Alonzo couldn't wake him, checked his pulse and found none, and immediately called the front desk for an ambulance. There were no signs of struggle, forced entry or robbery in the room."

He smiled at the camera like an idiot. Didn't he realize how much more he had to explain? In a voice that displayed not a hint of irritation, I asked, "Detective Burdock, how did Xavier do it?"

"Oh, right," said Dan. His face grew appropriately grave, and he said, "Cyanide."

I could literally hear Constancia making a face. "Cyanide?"

"And how do you know it was cyanide?" I followed up.

Detective Dan looked into the air philosophically. "You see, as a New York City detective, you become an expert in identifying poisons just by using this," he said, tapping his nose. "Cyanide has a unique smell. A little like almonds, but bitter. Furthermore, the victim often changes color, because what cyanide does is it causes cells to suffocate. Mr. Enamorado was pretty blue when we found him." I could see him trying to formulate a bad pun, but luckily he restrained himself and continued. "We're waiting for a toxicology report to verify this hypothesis, of course, but really, that's only a formality. I'd bet my shield it was cyanide."

Before I could follow up, Constancia asked, "Potassium cyanide?"

"Toxicology will tell us for sure. But yes, probably."

"So where'd he get it? Where's the container? How'd he get it into his system?"

Dan didn't like Constancia's tone—she had a way of making everybody sound incompetent—but he didn't break character. "We believe we've successfully reconstructed Xavier's last hours. Basically, the answers to all those questions can be found right there," he said, pointing to the nightstand. Besides all the other typical nightstand-y stuff, there stood a large milkshake cup with the word "GruuvyJuuce" written in a groovy, juicy font on the side.

"The way we figure it," Dan continued, "Xavier was feeling depressed about the shoot yesterday. Yes, we know he was upset; Alonzo told us. So he goes out, picks up some cyanide on the street, then stops at a GruuvyJuuce, takes the cyanide on the way home, washing it down with the shake, gets back to his hotel room and goes to sleep. Forever," he said grimly, looking straight at the camera. You can always pick out the reality shows on TV; they're the ones with all the bad actors.

"Picked up cyanide on the street?!" screamed Constancia. "That is the absolute stupidest theory—"

I covered her mouth. She mumbled for a second in my palm, but then finally shut up. I removed my hand, but gave her an admonishing look. "What's GruuvyJuuce?" I asked Dan.

"It's one of those new powershake places that're popping up all over the place. Can't see the appeal myself. They're really expensive, and they have all these weird fruit flavors I've never heard of. Like this one: it's got this neon-peach-orange color, and it smells like nothing I've ever seen before."

"You see smells?" asked Constancia.

I shot her a look, then went over to the nightstand, leaned over the cup and took a long whiff. "It's mamey," I said.

"What?" asked Dan.

"Mamey," said Constancia. "Also called *sapote*. It's a tropical fruit that's popular in the Caribbean and South America. Cubans love it."

Something was bugging me. I turned to our cameraman and asked him in Spanish (since that's the only language he knows), "Eugenio, mamey. Don't people use them for home remedies?"

Like any good cameraman, Eugenio was loathe to talk while we were still rolling. But he was also too polite not to respond, so after a moment's hesitation he said, "Of course. They use it to cure everything: good for headaches, stomach problems, VD, warts, malaria, everything. They make a hair tonic with it in El Salvador to keep you from going bald. I should get me some, eh?" he said, patting his bald head.

We all laughed, even Dan, whose Spanish was so bad he can't even order at Taco Bell. But I could tell Eugenio wasn't done. It took a minute of staring at him expectantly, but finally he continued: "And you can use the seed to make a drink that will induce an abortion. I had a cousin from Pilar del Río. You know the type: one of those *bobas de la yuca* who can't keep her legs shut. Well, she got herself into trouble, and there was only one way to fix trouble like that. That mamey potion almost killed her, but she lived, and it worked. It got rid of the baby all right." Eugenio's mouth clapped shut. He hid behind his camera so I wouldn't see him getting choked up. "Poor little baby. Never got to be born. My poor little nephew."

"What'd he say, Desi?" Detective Dan asked.

I was about to answer Dan when Constancia's cell phone/computer/surrogate brain went off. "It's Alonzo," she said, handing that overcomplicated gizmo to me.

I took it, struggled to figure out how to work the stupid thing, let Constancia press the right button for me and then, finally, said "*Ay,* Alonzo. How are you doing, *niño*?"

"I'm okay," he said. "You know, rough day." A beat. Then, "I shouldn't have left him alone."

"*Ay, niño, no sea estúpido*. What were you going to do, crawl into bed with him? There was nothing you could do. This isn't your fault."

He wasn't convinced. But like a *niño bueno*, he said, "Okay."

"Hey, you're not alone, right? You keeping busy?"

"Yes, Mami," he sighed, just like Xavier would've. He imitated Xavier in everything.

"Don't lie to me. What are you doing right now?"

"*Ay*, my job, Mami, okay? In fact, I have good news. I found the Abuelita. We can return the money to her."

"That was fast. Good work."

"She works at this place called GruuvyJuuce. Mami, it's perfect. I was thinking we could give her back the money right there, right at the store while she's working. Man, what a great moment that's going to be." And then he added sadly, "Xavier would've loved it."

I pulled the phone away from my ear. For a few seconds I thought I could hear the roar of the ocean. But it was the sound of my own blood surging into my head.

"What is it?" asked Detective Dan.

"It's a homicide," I said to him. "Xavier was murdered. And I know exactly where to find your prime suspect."

Latinos don't like mysteries. The Brits, they're a mystery-crazy people. Americans too, if to a lesser degree. But us? All that confusion and ambiguity at the beginning, all those subtle clues to make you feel stupid when you see the solution at the end, all those red herrings purposefully put there to trip you up. No, what the New World mind likes is *intrigue*. Just lay it all out: this person wants this, that person wants that and here's everyone's sordid past, and here are all the evil things everyone is planning to do. Now sit back and watch it all play out. And judge them. Oh, that woman, she's the biggest *puta* I've ever seen in my life. Oh, that man, he's a *salvaje*; he'd eat his own father down to the skeleton if he thought it would help him get ahead. That's the reason why the *telenovela* has become the art form of choice for us. Look, just let us know everything up front, so that, for once in our lives, we can make a full and fair judgment about something. To hell with mystery. Real life is all too full of them.

Like the one I had on my hands now, concerning our seemingly courageous, self-sacrificing Abuelita. More and more, she was looking like a monster. Or, to use the technical term, a killer. Maybe even a serial killer.

Detective Dan had discovered through a little research that there had been a strange upswing in cyanide poisonings in New York. The victims were almost exclusively boys and young men, African Americans, Latinos, Asians—no Caucasians—ages fifteen to twenty-five. Almost all the victims had some gang affiliation, so the first thought was some kind of gang rivalry. But how would a gang get hold of enough cyanide to carry out more than a dozen poisonings? So that's when the focus switched. Investigators started looking for a chemist, exterminator, someone who worked at a job, probably at a large corporation, where he might have special access to deadly poisons.

Yes, he. They were looking for a serial killer now, one with a score to settle with young men of color, and serial killers were almost always male. *Almost* always.

You with me? Here's what they had been looking for: a male, middleaged, science nerd of color—probably African American or Latino—who was picked on all through school and who now wanted to punish his former, or current, persecutors. The police didn't once imagine that an old woman, who was probably illegal and probably had next to no education, would know how to extract cyanide from the seed of a mamey. Almost any Abuela of a certain age remembers the old ways so well, they can never learn the new ways of this country. I'm sure our Abuelita never learned to work the computer cash register at GruuvyJuuce. But drawing the poison out of a mamey seed? What could be simpler?

So now a new profile was forming: Abuelita was worried about her little Tito. She was willing to do anything for him. But he was reckless, dangerous. Getting involved with gangs. She had to remove the bad influences from his life. Keep him safe, no matter the cost, the risk to herself. So she takes a job at a GruuvyJuuce so she will have a ready supply of free mamey seeds, and she uses her campesino knowledge to kill the men she thinks are corrupting her Tito.

But why kill Xavier? Sure, she thought he was a hit man, but she had paid him off, had collected that huge amount of money to do so. Why go to all that trouble just to kill Xavier a few hours later?

Dan's theory was that she had "buyer's remorse" and wanted her money back. Constancia thought that her plan all along was to find out where the hit man lived, used the money as an excuse to get through the door and then poison him when he wasn't looking. Eugenio thought she was "*arrebatada*," and that you can't figure out crazy people's motivations. That's what "crazy" means, right?

All three of them were wrong. The money was found in the hotel room; if that's why she did it, why didn't she take it back before the police confiscated it? And unless she was an idiot, she wouldn't have poisoned him using a cup that came from the place where she worked—and one look into her horse-eyes told you that woman was no idiot. And as for Eugenio: sorry, *viejo*, but even crazy people have motivations. They may be crazy motivations—they may think they are being chased by wolves or are covered in ants or were José Martí in a past life—but they're still motivations. We just hadn't figured out what motivated our Mamey Murderess to poison poor Xavier.

But we didn't need to figure it out. We just needed her to tell us. There were several ways you could do that. You could haul her ass into the station, stick her in a room with Bad Cop and Worse Cop and let them throttle it out of her. Or . . .

"Or," suggested Detective Dan, in a low, conspiratorial voice. We were going over the evidence in the police station, and he didn't want anyone else overhearing us. "Or, we can go to her apartment, set up a few cameras, get some nice incriminating footage, *then* bust her. That way, we get our killer, and you get your ending. Everybody wins."

"What's in it for you?" asked Constancia. That girl has all the finesse of a blind rhino, but I was wondering that too.

"I've been a detective a long time," said Dan. "I'm actually overdue for retirement. Maybe it's time I tried a new career."

Uh-oh. I knew this day would come: the day Dan Burdock would ask me for a job. How do you tell someone whose help you desperately need that he's too ugly—way, way, way, *way* too ugly—for television? Well, if you're Constancia, you blurt it out, consequences be damned, and then you don't get what you want. If you're Eugenio, you're embarrassed, you don't say anything and you fill your network with ugly people and you go bankrupt, and all those ugly people have to go out and find new jobs anyway.

Me? I am a producer. Managing talent is what I do best. I hugged him. "Oh, Dan, I can't believe how lucky I am! We've been wanting to hire a police consultant forever for *¿A Quién Quieres Matar?*, but we just haven't found the right fit. But who could be better than you? Oh, I'm so happy!"

I kept on hugging him; it was the best way to monitor his reaction. I could feel his whole body processing what I had said. "Consultant?" he asked, bewildered.

"Oh, you'll love it!" I said, hugging him even harder. "Easy work, great pay and you're there on the set of the hottest show in Central and South America."

"And the Caribbean," Constancia added.

"Consultant," Dan repeated. But this time it wasn't a question; it was an answer. "Well, I guess that does sound pretty good."

He hugged me back to seal the deal. Constancia came around so I could see her. She mouthed, "You're my hero." I smiled at her and, making sure my chin didn't touch Dan's shoulder, I mouthed back, "Watch and learn."

There are two kinds of justice: fairness and revenge. Fairness is infinitely better, but most of the time it's impossible. For instance, absolutely nothing about Xavier's murder was fair. So what can we do? The only thing left is to get revenge.

But you have to be strong. You have to have the stomach for it. Take Alonzo, for instance. He was so shook up, he might not do anything, or worse, he might even harm himself, stupidly feeling guilty for something that wasn't his fault, while the person who's actually guilty suffers no consequences. Me? No way was I going to let that *hija de la gran puta* get away with killing Xavier. I was going to get justice. Let the state stick her in jail for the rest of her life. Better yet, strap her to a chair and fill her veins with poison. That'd be nice. I'd be in the front row to watch her die.

Yes, I believe in the death penalty, and no, I don't give *tres pepinos* if those *comemierda* criminals suffer like hell on the way out. You and I can fight about that after I finish my story.

I set Alonzo to tail the Mamey Murderess (code name: MM). He sat in that GruuvyJuuce all day, sucking on tropical shakes infused with *Hoodia gordonii* and ginseng and all sorts of expensive, worthless crap. He was suffering so much about Xavier, the worst thing I could've done was give him time off; instead, I gave him a job that he had to do in public. That would keep him safe, and it would help us nab his murderer.

So Alonzo was watching the MM while we set up hidden cameras in her apartment. It was a dingy little place in the Bronx, almost as big as a Rubik's Cube, but without all the happy colors. Dan was the only person from the NYPD with us, both because we weren't exactly going by the book on this one and because the place was so small, we wouldn't have had any place to put more cops. As it was, I had to give most of my crew the day off. It was me and Constancia and Eugenio and our two skinniest audio/video interns. We paid off the landlord, set up our control room in his apartment (which was two floors down from MM's) and armed every stairway and every room of her apartment with all-seeing cameras no bigger than the eye of a rat. Dan dragged himself under her futon frame. It was even money whether he would be able to pack his beer gut under there, but somehow he managed. Everything was in place. We were ready. All we could do now was wait.

So we waited. And waited. Apparently Abuela was working a double shift. Great.

We were half drunk with boredom—Dan had fallen asleep under the futon—when the front door opened. There in the control room, with the landlord peering over our shoulders, we scrambled to our battle stations, scanning the monitors. Into the apartment walked two teenagers. One I didn't know, but he wore the GruuvyJuuce work uniform: it was just like Abuela's, save he wore a yellow button that read "Employee of the Month." The other teen was Tito.

As they walked through the door, Tito said, "She's not going to be home until late tonight. You know, you work there. Jesus, stop being such a pussy."

"I'm not a pussy," said the employee of the month. "Didn't I prove I'm not a pussy?"

Tito turned to him and, with a tenderness I didn't think he was capable of, hugged him. "Yeah, you proved it," Tito said into his ear. "You're a Simpático now. No one's going to fuck with you ever again."

Employee of the month hugged Tito back. And started to cry. "Tito, I'm scared. I guess I am a pussy. I'm sorry. I don't want to be. But I am. I'm scared."

Tito broke the hug, but held his shoulders and shook him encouragingly. "It's okay. This was your first time. The first time is always the hardest. You hear me? It gets easier from now on. You know why? Because now you're a stone-cold killer. You proved you got it in you. You proved you're worthy of being a Simpático. And nobody messes with the Simpáticos, Miguel."

"Miguel?" the entire control room asked in one voice.

That name was all Detective Dan needed to hear. While they had their little moment, Dan scurried out of his hiding place and, with a viciousness you'd expect from a man twenty years younger, proceeded to beat the will to live out of them. It was the most savage attack I've ever witnessed. All of us in the control room were wincing and oohing like a professional-wrestling audience as Dan landed blow after merciless blow. It made me a little afraid of Dan, knowing he had that kind of sociopathy available to him. I mean, he really beat the shit out of them. They were crying and begging for mercy, and they got none. I felt bad for them.

I mean, I would've felt bad for them, if they hadn't killed Xavier.

Little Tito, eight years old, has a toothache. Bad. Mom and Dad can't afford a dentist, so Abuela whips up a home remedy, a poultice made mostly of mamey seeds. It's worked for generations. He'll be better in no time.

Instead Tito gets cyanide poisoning. The emergency room doctors save his life, but always after that he has a little trouble breathing. Before his life has barely begun, his *abuela* had ruined it.

That's what Abuela thinks, anyway. She blames herself for all the misfortunes that have befallen the family. Her son died, then her daughter-in-law died and then it was just her and Tito. And she had poisoned Tito.

When you're a chicken-boned asthmatic going to high school in the Bronx, you've got to compensate for your body if you're going to make it out alive. The good news is that anyone can fire a gun. As long as you're crazy enough to bring one to school, you get the kind of rep that will keep you alive.

And the kind of rep that will draw people to you. Tito finds himself surrounded by friends even more desperate for protection than he is. So long as he'd shove his piece in the face of anyone who messed with them, they would do anything he told them to. Almost accidentally, Tito starts a gang.

Tito calls it "Los Simpáticos." Like *Goodfellas*, Tito's favorite movie. The gang grows fast. He names some lieutenants, whips up a completely clichéd and plagiarized loyalty oath. As for initiations, well, there are plenty of *putos* he wants dead. But when the Simpáticos kill some *puto*, he wants all the other gangs to know who did it. And he's been fascinated by cyanide since he was eight years old. He knows an old family recipe that will give him all he needs.

One day, some Simpáticos and initiates are sitting around Tito's *abuela*'s place—she lets him do whatever he wants, her unassuageable guilt silencing her objections—watching *¿A Quién Quieres Matar?* Everyone loves the show, except Tito. "Xavier Enamorado is bullshit," he says. "He's a poser. *We're* the real deal. We kill people. That *puto* is bullshit."

Miguel makes the mistake of saying, "He's got money and women, and he's on TV. That ain't bad."

By the time the show's over, the only way Miguel's ever going to be a Simpático is if he kills Xavier.

But Tito likes Miguel, so he's going to help him. "I'll pretend like I want to hire him to kill you. I'll get him to come see you at work. You get him to buy some GruuvyJuuce. And that's when you poison him."

It takes over a year to arrange everything. The hardest part was getting our attention, making us think Tito wanted to kill Miguel. Tito trolls the same chat rooms we troll when we're looking for marks. He starts posting comments, making it clear he wants to hire a hit man. We saw his posts and thought we had an easy mark. We were so used to being right, we hardly even checked out his story. We were so proud and stupid, a high school kid fooled us.

Once we make the first contact with him, Tito assumes we're going to tail him so we can get film footage on him before the hit. So he and Miguel have to start playing their parts. He fakes a big fight with Miguel at his *abuela*'s apartment in front of his friends and Abuela, whom he sometimes forgets is in the room. She, however, sees everything with her big horse-eyes and doesn't know the fight is fake. Later that month, she hears Tito on the phone, talking to Xavier, arranging the hit on Miguel. Though her English is rocky, she catches the drift of the conversation. She is terrified.

For the first time since she poisoned him with her toothache remedy, she comes alive. She confronts him. And since he thinks we've bugged the place, he confirms her worst fears—he is paying someone ten thousand dollars to kill Miguel. She pleads with him. Threatens him with eternal damnation. He laughs and says, "Look around, old woman! You're already damned!" He thinks that's a good line for television and hopes we will use it.

Tito and Xavier arrange a meeting. He leaves the address on the kitchen table for his *abuela* to see—that is how impotent he thinks she is. But she has resolved to save Tito from himself. She steals ten thousand dollars from the GruuvyJuuce safe, where she is a shift manager, and, on her lunch break, takes it to Xavier before Tito's meeting is to occur.

Remember Xavier after his meeting with Abuela? *Demasiado simpático*, you might say. He can't wait until morning to try and make everything right. He has to find her, set everything straight. But he doesn't know where to find Tito or his *abuela*. The only person he has any information on is Miguel. So he goes to see Miguel at his job. GruuvyJuuce.

Miguel had trouble telling us about the conversation he had with Xavier at GruuvyJuuce. He kept saying, "He was a good man. He just wanted to fix everything."

But in spite of all the new wrinkles, Miguel, who'd been carrying cyanide with him since Tito's first conversation with Xavier, stuck to the plan. He told Xavier that he would call Tito's *abuela* and have her come to his hotel to collect the money. Xavier was frazzled, febrile with guilt. He wouldn't have been hard to convince.

Miguel even gave him a mamey shake. On the house.

I am not heartless. I am *demasiado simpática*. But I believe in justice. And this time, that meant revenge.

But you have to know how to work it. Otherwise you make too many sacrifices. I wasn't going to shoot those two little *comemierdas* myself, and I wasn't, in some made-for-television act of supreme stupidity, going to hire a hit man to kill them either. Why would I have to, when the government is more than happy to take care of the details for me? I have plenty of money. All I do is hire a pack of bloodthirsty lawyers to go to court and prove that Tito and Miguel should be tried as adults, and poof!, they're tried as adults.

I hear you saying: "Okay, but there's no death penalty in New York." That's true, but that just means the government won't go through the hassle of killing them itself. Instead, they're going to be incarcerated with hundreds of hardened criminals who know what those two skinny little *putos* have done. You know how many fan letters a week we get from American jails? If I were Tito or Miguel, right now I would be praying to God for a heart attack before I set foot in prison.

But here's how you know I'm not heartless. I've hired lawyers for Abuelita. Right now, they're negotiating with GruuvyJuuce, trying to convince them of what a PR coup it would be for them to drop the charges, especially since we returned the money she stole. I think it's going to work. My lawyers are good.

So everything's about as good as I can make it. But it's not great— poor Xavier is forever dead. But you work with the money, talent and time you have to make everything the best it can be. That's all you can do.

Well, and develop a taste for limes.

Nice Climate, Miami

The next day, a cloudless Monday after three days of thunderstorms, a bluer-than-blue sky and a white sun shimmered on a hamburger joint not far from Grant's tomb, when O'Hara hailed a cab: "Take the tunnel. We're going to LaGuardia."

He bought a one-way fare to San Francisco for the following week. From there, he took a different cab, this one to Kennedy, where he bought two more one-way e-tickets: one to Montreal, the other to Miami.

Two days later, he went to Barney's at midmorning and paid cash for two lightweight summer suits, a pair of Chucks, a pair of Ray-Bans and some Oxford cloth shirts. He then bought a cashmere pullover.

"Here," he said to the clerk. "Mail this to my sister, Kathi Luckman. Here's her address. A hundred ought to do it. You can keep what's left."

"Thank you, sir."

On Thursday, a carry-on in hand, he took another cab, this one to Grand Central Station. Once there, he looked around for a moment, then headed for a rental unit nearest the east entrance.

Back in his Village apartment, he oiled and cleaned his Totter caliber 2.72—a keepsake once used by a woman, a Russian Mafia hitter out of Brighton Beach. Earlier that morning, O'Hara had spent three hours shredding his identity as John Rienzi, beginning with his driver's license, the credit and debit cards and on to his Social Security card. He then used his disposable cell to call the movers and remind them of the following morning's appointment. The next day they pulled up to his apartment on time.

"That's it? The desk, the chair and six boxes?"

O'Hara nodded and gave the movers an address in Astoria. The apartment was not much different and just as bare.

"Here's a key to the new place. When you're through, leave it with the man at the corner bodega. Tell 'em it's from Rienzi. Got that?"

61

The driver nodded, took the money and looked at the tall man, who then handed him a fifty-dollar tip.

"Live it up. It's Friday."

At eight-thirty that evening, the humidity hovered in the thirties, with the temperature a couple notches past seventy degrees. O'Hara left the Astoria apartment and, taking an unhurried look at his few belongings, he locked the door and took the subway coming in from Twenty-Third Street/Ely Avenue. Crossing the river into Manhattan, he took the subway to Eighty-Sixth Street in Yorktown—the old German section. He then took a cab south to Midtown and stopped by a flower shop on Lexington.

Sure he wasn't being followed, a quick swipe to his upper lip removed the fake mustache. He then put on a pair of horn-rims.

Flowers, he thought, that's the ticket. A dozen gladiolas and another cab, this one to Sutton Place. He glanced at the bridge as three young, smartly dressed girls laughed when they saw the flowers. O'Hara smiled sheepishly. "You're right, they're for my wife. I've been a bad boy."

One of them pointed a slender index finger as if to say, "That's what you get. You ought to know better, a man your age." And she laughed gaily as O'Hara smiled and shrugged, as any middle-aged husband resigned to take whatever awaited him at home might do. They waved at him, and the three said, "Good luuuuck."

He smiled again and looked at his watch—five till nine. He hurried toward the river, and within seven minutes he stood on the corner of Fifty-Ninth Street. He'd written the apartment's address on the palm of his left hand: 362 E. 59th, Apt. 2-B.

He looked up. The light was faint in the apartment. He went back mentally to the layout of the place, and he crossed the street to wait. The woman appeared, fifty if a day, he thought, in a tailor-made coat. Ha! As usual, pulling on that overweight hairless dachshund. He made as if fumbling for his keys and, looking up, the woman smiled and opened the door for him.

"Thank you."

"Oh, it's no bother. Billy and I are going out for our walk. Come on, Bill."

O'Hara looked at the flowers: the best passport. He immediately pressed the elevator button to the second floor. Refurbished, the apartment building no longer had a firebox in the basement. O'Hara left the flowers in the elevator. He pocketed the horn-rims, turned right and stood in front of 2-B. He pressed his ear against the door. Not a sound. He frowned and checked his watch again: nine-fifteen; the woman had taken the dog for a walk; he's supposed to be in there.

O'Hara reached into his left-hand pocket, drew out a credit card and jiggled it. The door opened noiselessly. With his back to the wall, he crossed his arms and waited for his eyes to become accustomed to the faint darkness. The sofa, by the piano; to the left, the window with an impressive view of Midtown. The TV was at the furthest reach of the bedroom, and the john was . . . he heard a slight noise coming from the direction of the toilet. A faucet was turned off. Then he heard some steps, a sneeze followed by a cough and a clearing of the throat.

"It's him," he said to himself.

The man coughed again and blew his nose as he entered the room.

"Mr. Rusconi."

The man looked up. "Who are you? How'd you get in? And what do you want?"

"I'm a bit slow, Mr. Rusconi. I came to see you about a debt."

Rusconi blew into the wet handkerchief again, hesitated a bit and said, "Yeah. I suppose it's about the vig, right?"

O'Hara looked at him and shrugged.

"Hold it, hold it. Look, I can pay, yeah, really. Right now."

"A bit late. I've got my orders." With this, he showed him the Totter 2.72.

"Hey, what are you doing? If you kill me, I can't pay up, right?"

O'Hara shook his head slowly. "They don't want the money. The debt's been placed on the debit side. They'll eat it. It's a lesson to the others, that's all. A lesson."

"But, ah, we, ah, we, we can make an arrangement, you and me, right? I mean, well, really, you see . . . Can I sit down?"

"Sure. It's better that way. An arrangement? Sounds like a bribe. No, I can, but I won't. Besides, it's not to my advantage, if I can put it that way. I either kill you, or they'll come after me. Is that simple enough?"

"Oh, you're not a member of the Family, is that it? And you don't look Italian. A contract?" Rusconi rubbed his face. Money, he thought. That's the only thing these people understand. They've all got a price.

O'Hara smiled, as if he'd read Rusconi's mind. "What? You're going to offer me five thousand, is that it? Look, I'm getting twenty-five hundred, a freebie. You understand?"

"Sure, of course."

O'Hara interrupted him and laughed. "No, you don't. The silencer's a great friend, by the way. You won't hear a thing. C'mon, close your eyes."

Rusconi raised his hands and shook his head. "No. Twenty-five, what do you say? Twenty-five." Breathing hard now, Rusconi sneezed again. "Listen, no, no, listen to me. Fifty, how's that? Fifty thousand for you. Alone. Think on it. Fifty thousand. Right now."

O'Hara turned and said, "To the bedroom. Move it. Now, take your pajamas off."

"What was that?"

"Take 'em off and throw 'em on the floor. Do it."

He aimed the Totter at Rusconi. "Unmake the bed, throw everything on the floor." His voice became colder: "To the john."

O'Hara pushed him and said, "In the shower. Turn it on."

Rusconi began to whimper.

A minute or so later, O'Hara said, "Okay, that's enough. Turn the water off. Forget the towel. The bedroom, let's go. No, don't dry off. Move it."

The phone.

"Let it ring. You've got an answering machine."

Rusconi hesitated as O'Hara raised the handgun.

A woman's voice. An apology for not having called sooner. "At Chapin's, tomorrow morning. Ten o'clock, don't forget. I'll wait, but don't make me wait too long, John."

After the click, Rusconi looked at O'Hara. "My wife."

"You're a bachelor, Rusconi. That machine mark the hour?"

Rusconi nodded and kept wringing his hands.

"Okay. The money. Where is it?"

Rusconi sneezed and signaled to an end table by the bed.

"That?"

"It doesn't look like it, but it's a safe. I had it made like that."

Rusconi looked at O'Hara as if trying to read his mind. "You really gonna let me go?"

"If it's fifty. Otherwise . . . "

"Hey, it's all I got on hand right now, but it's fifty, all right. Maybe even a little bit more."

"Stand by the wall there. Face it. Get your hands up."

Rusconi sneezed again. "I'm soaked. What'd you make me take a shower for?"

"Look at it this way: I walked in, you were in the shower, I held you up and I wounded you."

"What?"

"Look, this is a Totter 2.72, nine-millimeter with a special charge. If I hit the meat part, shoulder, leg, it doesn't matter, the bullet goes right through you. Got that? There'll be blood, but it won't be a serious wound. Now, turn around."

"No, I can't stand pain. No."

"Listen to me, Rusconi. I take the money and leave you to call a doctor, or I'll take the money and do the deed. Nothing to it."

"Not many big bills there, how're you gonna carry 'em?"

"Get one of your bags and stuff it in there. Hurry. Now, here's the story. The cops will come when you call them . . . you got anything else? This has to look like a robbery."

Rusconi crammed the money in and stopped. "My friend's earrings, a pearl necklace—nice—and some rings. Oh, and two pair of cufflinks she bought me. Cartier's, I think. They're in here."

"Good enough. Go on, fill it. You tell the cops that they . . . that they took a good amount of cash. You got that?"

Rusconi relaxed a bit and nodded. "There, I'll zip it."

"Good job."

"What do we do now?"

"Don't move, and listen carefully. Stand by the bed, leave the safe wide open. Good. Now, what will it be, an arm or a leg?"

"The arm, the left one. Be careful, please."

With a bored look on his face, O'Hara said, "Closer to the bed, I said. Stick your arm out. Good. You're not going to die, Rusconi. Look at me."

"Careful, okay?"

O'Hara took a deep breath, aimed and shot him in the heart. Rusconi fell on the bed, then slid off the silk sheets and onto the floor. O'Hara waited a few seconds, then used Rusconi's phone.

He looked at Rusconi again and said, "It's Rienzi."

"Just a moment, sir, I'll get my dad."

As he waited, he hefted the bag.

"Everything all right?"

"Yes, sir. And with a bonus. He offered me money. Something like eleven or twelve thousand. I've not counted it yet."

"Ha! Little chiseling Italian Jew. Look, take another two for you. You want someone to come by and pick you up?"

"No, sir, I think I'll take the route you gave me. Go down to Midtown, come back up again and down to Mulberry. How's that?"

"Forty-five minutes, you think?"

"Or less, yes, sir."

He walked casually to the phone plug and kicked it. Another casual look around as he headed for the door. Once outside, he stood in the shadows. Clear sailing, he said to himself. A man with a suitcase.

He walked the three blocks south and went downstairs, making his way to the subway platform. He waited there five minutes, walked up to Fifty-Seventh and stopped when he got to Madison.

He turned the corner, bag in hand and hailed a cab. "Grand Central. Go by Riverside."

"Riverside? That's kind of a long way."

"There's no hurry."

Fifteen minutes later and a few blocks from the station, he asked the cabbie to parallel park.

"You pronounce your name Achmed, do you?"

The exact pronunciation of his name made the cabbie smile. "It sure is, but the fares usually call me Atchmed."

"Well, Achmed, I'll walk from here. It's a nice, cool night. By the way, do you know if the trains run this late to Westchester County?"

"Oh, yeah. I think they go all the time."

A glance at the watch: ten on the dot. "A couple of twenties, Achmed."

"I'll help you with the bag." As the driver walked to the trunk, O'Hara drew the Trotter. He kept his eyes on the Arab and set it at the ready.

"Look, I found this on the seat. Is it yours?"

"Oh, no. We can't carry."

"I'll keep it, then."

He strolled by the newsstand and picked up a copy of that morning's *Times*. From there to the locker to pick up his clothes. A glance at his watch: ten-fifteen. He waited until ten-thirty, then stepped outside to hail a cab.

"JFK."

"Catching the red-eye, are you?"

"Business. Delta departure. Look, there's an extra fifty if you can make it in twenty minutes."

"From here, at this hour? Piece of cake."

O'Hara casually shoved the Totter under the seat and leaned back. He nodded and said to himself, "Nice climate, Miami."

A Broken String of Lace

Analú Soto opened the window from her tiny room. The fresh air hit her flushed face. Young men from the city had come to celebrate Flavio Ríos' engagement. Because of her reputation, they wanted her there. She knew that under normal circumstances, there was no chance that Flavio would even notice her, but tonight was different. She would have to act fast. Still feverish from restless nights of illness, her body ached. She didn't feel like attending, but if she were to succeed with her plan, she'd have go.

Analú dressed as simply as she could and applied only a dab of makeup and lipstick. At five minutes till midnight, feeling a little nauseous from her sickness, she entered the large room and wandered among the drunken guests with indifference.

Flavio had waited for her all night. New to Guerrero, a small agricultural town in the northern state of Chihuahua, he was eager to meet the girl all the men talked about. Analú's beauty and elegance was legendary in the surrounding area, and he wondered whether she would be there. Slouching at the opposite end of the large room, his eyes lit up as soon as she entered. No one was as attractive as Analú, and he knew the moment she walked in that she was the girl everyone had spoken about. He smiled and started toward her. Two less fortunate girls, who had tried to get his attention all evening, sighed with resignation. Analú, a master in the art of subtle communication, moved her head slightly and indicated that he should meet her outside.

The sounds of laughter and music flowed out the windows, into the open field. Flavio smoked a cigarette and waited for her, wondering whether he had misunderstood her meaning.

It was a cold night, and he pulled up the collar of his wool sweater. He went to the back of the building. He crossed the terracotta tiled patio and followed a flowered path. In the background, the apple grove cast sharp shadows under a full moon. The girl sat by an old stone wall. She seemed like an apparition. Her long hair fell around the contour of her back, and her beautiful profile was illuminated by the moonlight.

"I wish for time to stand still, so I could bathe in your beauty," Flavio said.

He went to her side and placed a hand on her dark hair. The cold smoothness of it made him shiver with delight.

"The goddess of love has come to earth," he murmured.

Analú barely moved. She tucked her hand into the pocket of her jacket and gripped a sheathed dagger. She didn't know how she was going to do it, but she knew tonight would be her only opportunity.

"I didn't think you'd come," he said, his strong hand still resting on her hair.

"I came because I heard you'd be here," she said and lifted her gaze to meet his. The handsome young man was looking at her with sincere admiration. Since she had begun conceiving her plan a week ago, she had expected him to be different.

She stood up, and his hand moved down from her shoulder to her hand, which she hastily removed from her pocket. Holding her hand in his, he lifted it to his lips to place a tender kiss on her long fingers. The sensation made her skin tingle.

Analú looked back toward the house.

"Not here," she whispered. Her hand barely touched Flavio's cheek. "I want this night to be unforgettable for you. Let's go elsewhere. I know the perfect place. Do you have a vehicle?"

"We brought horses." Flavio smiled mischievously.

Of course they did. None of them would have taken the risk of having anyone see their cars at the whorehouse, Analú thought.

"That will do," she said.

Holding hands, they walked to the barn. Analú kept turning her head nervously toward the house, hoping that Lola, the *doña*, wouldn't see her.

Flavio helped Analú mount his horse and placed her sideways in front of him while he held the reins on both sides of her slender body. It was comfortable for both of them, and Analú placed her head on his shoulder. Lola had drummed into her for so many years how to use her charm: "Make them feel you need their protection. Show yourself vulnerable. Men love that."

Leaning against Flavio, though, was not part of her show. His strong shoulders felt comfortable, and his aroma was different from that of other men. His aftershave spoke of elegance, good upbringing and money, of a city boy playing Don Juan in the country. It was a pleasant change from her normal clientele. The drunken farmers certainly didn't smell this good, and they didn't talk to her as Flavio did.

Avoiding the main road, Analú directed Flavio through the brush in the direction of a ravine. She knew it would take days to locate anybody in that abrupt area of the countryside. The moon lit the way while Flavio whispered love songs in Analú's ear.

On the ride, Analú caught a glimpse of the hacienda where she had spent her childhood, and her heart jolted. The whitewashed mansion that had been there long before she was born, before her mother was born and even before her grandmother, was a magnificent mirage under the cold moonlight. No one lived there now. It was being remodeled for Anaí, the youngest of the Castillo children. Anaí was about to return to the estate as a new bride.

A myriad of forgotten childhood memories flooded into her mind and invaded her restless spirit. She had not been back in seven years, ever since that fateful night when her destiny changed forever. Flavio felt her body trembling.

"Are you okay?" His hand rested on her shoulder.

"I lived in that house when I was a little girl," she whispered.

"You lived there?" His eyes opened wide. "Are you the girl who disappeared?"

"I didn't disappear. The Castillos knew where I was. It was easier to say that to cover their guilt." There was bitterness in her tone, but then, pulling her chin up, she added, "Let's go in."

"No!" Flavio's eyes shone with fear. He couldn't be seen in her company.

He hadn't told her yet who he was.

"Don't you feel adventurous?" Her slender fingers ran down his face, teasing him.

He gave in to her wishes.

They tied the horse by a tree and walked in silence. Analú led Flavio to the back entrance. He dug inside his pocket for matches to light the way, but she stopped him.

"That is not necessary. I know this house like the palm of my hand."

The door was not locked. They entered the house that had once held Analú's dearest dreams. For her, it was an emotional journey.

They stood in the middle of the great moonlit kitchen. Analú put her hands on the wood stove and sighed.

"Mamá was the cook. She made the most delicious meals."

Memories of the long hours spent kneading dough, cutting vegetables and baking desserts filled her mind. She could almost smell the sweet aroma of *pan dulce* and cornbread, and the fresh coffee prepared with cloves and a cinnamon stick. The kitchen had been the place where the women of the household gathered. Many conversations took place inside these walls. With her eyes closed, she took a moment to savor memories that filled her senses and took her back to happier times. She allowed herself to forget the knife in the depths of her pocket.

Flavio observed her with a new interest.

"Mamá and I lived here. The Castillos raised me as one of their own. Rita Castillo was the best godmother I could have hoped for. I was born a few months after Ana Inés. Everybody called her Anaí. I was named Ana Luisa, after her. Everybody called me Analú."

Then she hurried out of the kitchen as if an uninvited ghost had appeared in front of her, and Flavio followed. The shutters in the house were closed tightly. She made her way along a pitch-black corridor with steady steps. Flavio struggled to keep up with her by holding his hand to the wall to maintain his balance. He couldn't see anything, and Analú moved as though she walked in light. She entered one of the rooms.

"Analú?" he called into the dense obscurity.

"I am here," she said. The sound came from the end of the room. "This used to be my bedroom."

Flavio followed the voice and stumbled into the low bed where she sat. She reached out a hand to help him find her. His hand was large, his grip strong and reassuring.

"Anaí and I slept here. We had little twin beds with a white headboard painted with blue flowers. Our bedspreads were baby blue with tiny yellow lines. I always thought it was the most beautiful room in the world. Herminia, the nanny, brought in fresh flowers everyday. We would wake up to the smell of gardenias, roses, carnations, lilies, whatever she picked from the garden.

"Anaí and I were best friends. There was no difference between us back then. My godmother insisted that I call her Tía, and she bought as many beautiful dresses for me as she did for Anaí. We attended pri-

vate lessons together, and we did our homework at the same table. I used to think I could have it all, just as she would."

Flavio caressed her hair to encourage her.

"Anaí sleepwalked." She giggled. "That's how I came to sleep here, next to her, and not in the back, in the maid quarters where Mamá slept. Herminia tied a string of lace from her sewing basket to both of our wrists so that I would wake up whenever Anaí drifted into those dreams that made her walk around the house, and sometimes even beyond. My job was to follow her and keep her from harm. I walked this house a thousand times in complete darkness. I used to know where every turn was, where the tile was uneven, which step would squeak. At first, I was afraid of the nocturnal noises. I feared the crickets' sad song, the hushed steps of mice, the wind blowing —even the cracking logs in the fireplace. I used to think this house was haunted and almost fainted every time I had to follow Anaí on her nocturnal wanderings. With time, I learned to control my fears, and I got used to it. I even enjoyed the uncertainty of not knowing where her dreams would take us. It became a game."

The dim light of a match glowed when Flavio lit a cigarette. His eyes shone, entranced by her story. He offered her a cigarette, and she moved her head to decline. She took his hand again and led him to another room, to another memory.

The library bookcases were covered with tarps, and the sofas were sheltered with old sheets. Analú could tell the workmen were painting, for there was an acrid smell of turpentine. They opened the large window to ventilate the room. The moonlight allowed them to see each other much better. Analú's profile against the window was so delicate. Flavio couldn't refrain from touching her with his finger —barely—tracing her silhouette against the scrubby brush outside.

"I used to love this room, with all those leather-bound books. All that knowledge stored on page after page. We would spend hours going through them. I was a better reader than Anaí. I used to think I would go on to become a teacher." Her hand touched the black telephone on the desk. "Then they installed this wicked thing in the house. Anaí and I were mesmerized the day they brought it. It had taken months of preparations: Workmen dug a long ditch from the main road, engineers with hard hats came in and out of the house, and Mamá cooked for all of them from sunrise to sunset."

"We no longer needed a horse boy to go to town and fetch the doctor when somebody got sick. We could just lift this thing and summon him, by magic. Anaí liked to make prank calls. I didn't see the point, but I humored her. I had to. She soon got bored calling the pharmacist to ask whether his refrigerator was running and the church to mock the old maid who took care of the priest. I was almost thirteen when we found a matchbox in the barn with a number scribbled on it. It said 'cabaret.' Those letters stuck to Anaí's mind like glue, and she couldn't stop talking about it. 'That's the place where bad girls work,' she said. We knew her father and all the men from the household would go there once in a while. They would come back pregnant with the nauseous aroma of cheap perfume, alcohol and lost souls.

"Anaí started calling relentlessly. She would ask to speak to the girls, or to the manager, or to the bartender. She pretended to be interested in a job there. She asked how old she needed to be. Were there requirements, like height, weight and bra size? How much did they tip? She couldn't stop thinking about that evil place. Every day, she formulated new questions to ask them. Eventually, that was not enough. She wanted to go and see for herself." Analú's voice cracked with emotion. She paused for air, and Flavio, guessing what was coming, held her tight in his arms. For the first time in many years, Analú let her emotions flow.

"I could have stopped her, but I didn't." She continued between sobs, her voice barely audible. "That horrible night, in the summer of 1968, just weeks before we were to move to the city and attend school, before going to bed, Anaí smiled at me and tied the lace around our wrists. It had been months since she had walked in her sleep. In the middle of the night, I felt a tug on my wrist. Anaí was up. I got up as fast as I could. In her feigned sleep, she covered herself with a wool blanket, and I did the same. We left the house. We walked through the grove and up the hill under the stars. We crossed the valley. I knew she was faking it all, but I was as intrigued as she to discover the mysteries of the cabaret, so I didn't stop her. And then . . ." Analú trembled with emotion.

"We were there. We could hear the laughter and the music from the outside. We could smell the alcohol and the cheap tobacco. We couldn't believe our eyes as we spied through the window. We finally knew about the cabaret. I didn't hear anyone approach, but a strong hand grabbed me by the neck, and I screamed.

"'Interested in coming in?' A man with foul breath spoke into my neck. Anaí tore the lace from her wrist and ran away. I was pulled inside. That's the last time I saw her. Life has been nothing but a hell for me ever since."

Flavio held her tight and let her cry for a long time. The sobs subsided, and, with a delicate movement, he lifted her chin. The moonlight reflected in her eyes. He reached down and kissed her on the lips. Analú responded with unexpected urgency. Analú let Flavio lift her in his arms, and they left the library. Feeling his way around the house, he took her to the master bedroom. Amidst cans of paint and scaffolding under the cathedral ceiling, he reached the bed. Carefully, he set her down. The moon shone directly into a skylight, and her face was illuminated with a pale halo.

The tender kissing gave way to passion and then to lovemaking. Analú was shaken, for Flavio touched her in a way that no other man ever had. Flavio seemed to care about her satisfaction. No man at the cabaret had ever cared about her feelings, much less whether or not she reached the pinnacle during those brief encounters that always left her so empty, so bored. She was the object of their desires, not a human being with feelings. Flavio seemed sincerely moved by her story and didn't seem to care who she was or where she had come from. He even ignored the rules of prevention for this type of encounter.

Flavio, with his gentle yet passionate ways, made her experience the dignity of being loved, not the degradation of being used. Somehow, the sincerity of his actions allowed him to touch a part of her soul that had been locked up long ago in order for her to survive.

Wrapped in the old washed-out sheets, Analú awoke with her heart in her throat. A tiny line of burnt orange on the horizon announced the new day. The night had certainly not gone the way she had expected. She had mixed emotions toward the man who slept by her side. This man, who should die at her hand, was also the only one ever to treat her with respect and consideration. Should she go on with her plans?

She reached for her crumpled jacket at the end of the bed. From the pocket, she extracted a newspaper clipping and the sheathed knife.

The newspaper announced the engagement of Anaí Castillo Mora and Flavio Ríos Terán. It had a picture of the young couple smiling, followed by an article detailing their courtship and the upcoming wedding in the city. It spoke of their plans to move to the hacienda in the Sierra Madres, where Flavio, a veterinarian, would take care of the Castillos' forgotten property. He was to come before the wedding to start overseeing the business of restoration while the bride-to-be stayed behind, making preparations for the most talked-about event of the year.

The day she had read the article, Analú started forging her long-awaited plan of revenge. Every man who came to town, young or old, was destined to come see her. Some came once, out of curiosity for her reputation. Others returned time and again. She had waited that week for Flavio, but she had fallen ill and almost missed the opportunity. But now, here she was. She had come with the intention of taking revenge on the Castillos. They had ruined her life, her dreams, her dignity. She blamed Anaí for taking her to the cabaret that night, running away and not sending someone to rescue her. She blamed Quentín Castillo, Anaí's father, for coming to the cabaret and using her under the excuse that she was already a prostitute. When she cried for help, he spat in her face. "Who would want you now? You are better off here. Your mother would die of shame." Two weeks later, the Castillo family returned to the city, taking with them her grieving mother, who later died.

Analú wanted revenge for all the pain inflicted in those early days of her abduction, for the horror she had to face when those men walked into the room burning with lust, for the beatings she had to endure, for the fact that she would never be able to bear children. In her mind, the Castillos were responsible, and they had to pay.

She remembered bitterly that a few months into her prostitution, she had discovered that she was pregnant. She had tried to get rid of the baby using the archaic methods she had only half overheard in hushed conversations at the Castillos'. Injured and bleeding to the point of death, Analú was taken to the *curandera*, who botched a hysterectomy on the young girl. Her anticipated revenge had been for Flavio to die and ruin Anaí's future. She knew that she could count only on that first night when a newcomer might be lured to her. After that, she didn't know whether he'd come back. And if Flavio didn't come back, it would be too late. That's why she had come tonight, even though she was ill; she had to finish her plan.

The knife's blade was long and narrow. A sharp and direct slash to the jugular would end it all for him. He wouldn't even know what happened. Then she would cut her veins and bleed to death before the workers arrived. It hadn't been her original plan to come to this house; she had envisioned them dying in the ravine and being found days later, half devoured by vultures. But, she thought with a tinge of pleasure, it would be more theatrical to be found in the Castillos' own estate, in the master bedroom and nude with Anaí's future husband. She couldn't have envisioned a more dramatic ending.

The man who peacefully slept next to her sighed and turned over. She gazed at his pleasant face. It really wasn't his fault to be in the middle of this mess. Flavio had been unlike anybody else she had ever known. Her heart sank as she faced the mixed emotions that boiled inside her. She had lived so long on automatic pilot, going through the motions, just waiting for the opportunity to avenge herself, never quite knowing exactly what she wanted to do. The previous week, she had seen the answer she wished for upon reading the newspaper announcement. Yet she was hesitant today; she didn't want to go on.

Flavio opened his eyes, and she hid the knife under her pillow.

"Good morning, gorgeous," he smiled.

"Do you love Anaí?" Analú said without a trace of emotion in her voice. She tucked her body under his. She needed to feel his strong arms and the warmth of the living body she had originally thought she would destroy.

"How did you know it will be Anaí I will marry?" he said.

"This is a very small village," she answered. "Do you love her?"

"Yes," he said, looking straight at her. "I love her."

"But you were unfaithful."

He sat up on the bed, lit a cigarette and took a long time to answer. He stroked her bare back.

"I could probably say a lot of things to get out of this one," he said. He took a deep breath and ran a hand through his messed-up hair. "The truth is, Analú, that the attraction I felt for you was too powerful to keep me faithful." He looked up at her, his eyes moist with emotion. "When I heard your story, I wanted to give you my heart. And you know I did."

She knew it well, and that was exactly the problem. The hatred for the Castillos had driven her life for so many years. There had been nothing for her but beatings and the sweating men who used her.

She was shocked to feel her wish for revenge had been trumped by recovering her dignity, minimized by Flavio's attention and empathy as she told her story for the first time. It had been nullified when he made love to her, putting his whole heart into it.

The satisfaction she anticipated when planning her theatrical revenge seemed utterly stupid now. She decided not to be responsible for any bloodshed. She would let life be the executor, and at the end, justice would be served without the need for knives or blood-stained sheets. She kissed him, and they made love a second time.

Flavio and Analú walked back to the farmhouse. It was early enough that the morning dew still shimmered on the brush. Analú began to feel sick again. The effect of the medication had passed, and her fever had returned. Small drops of sweat beaded on her forehead. She shivered even with her jacket, but she concealed her discomfort.

"I had a wonderful night, just as you promised," Flavio said, and gave her a thick envelope.

"I shouldn't take this from you," she replied. "You did a lot more for me than I did for you."

"A pleasure," Flavio said, not knowing what else to say. "Can I see you again?" Hope in his question.

"I don't think so," she replied. "I'll be leaving town shortly. I don't want to be here when Anaí comes back."

"Where will you go?" He reached into his pocket and pulled out more money. "I want to help you."

"Don't worry about it. You have done your part," she said, kissing his cheek. She went inside the house.

She was counting the money on the kitchen table when Lola, the cabaret owner, walked in.

"How dare you go out with a client? Analú, the doctor said you are very contagious. You were put on quarantine."

"It's worse than that." Analú didn't even look up. "You know I'll die soon." With a bitter smile, she looked out the window and saw Flavio walking away, his hands in his pockets. "And he will too."

A Reunion with Death

It was Monday of the long Labor Day weekend, and Detective Sergeant Roberto Rivas of the Miami Beach Police Department was on duty.

"It's Labor Day, so I labor," he told his wife, who would have preferred that they visit Cuban relatives in West Palm Beach. Instead, she packed him a lunch of *picadillo*, rice and plantains.

The shift was quiet until 4:00 p.m., when a call came from Carla in Dispatch.

"We just got a report from the Normandy Shores neighborhood. A man shot dead at a private residence. Loud music in the background and lots of people screaming. Sounds like a party that got out of hand. Be careful, Rivas."

Sergeant Rivas hung up and winced. The last thing he needed this day, or any day, was to work a case amid a house full of drunks. He called down to Sergeant Bellows in Patrol, requested four uniformed officers to meet him there and headed for the scene.

The house was a one-story pink job, with a red tile roof, a majestic royal palm rising in the front yard and under it a pink plaster flamingo balanced on one spindly leg. From the street he could hear a salsa CD playing an old Tito Puente medley that Rivas remembered fondly. Unfortunately, he was not there to dance.

Two uniformed officers were waiting for him on the sidewalk. He was told that another two were already inside protecting the crime scene.

"Okay, let's do it," Sergeant Rivas said.

They passed through a gate in the chain-link fence and, following the sound of the music, traversed a walkway along the side of the house. It led them into a large backyard dominated by a tall, spreading flamboyant tree. Suspended from two branches of the tree was a banner that read "*Bienvenido* Pedro." On the far side of the lot stood a smaller house, what in Miami was often called a "grandmother cottage."

Around the yard stood about ten aluminum tables with metal chairs and several trestle tables covered with food. Rivas saw large platters piled with chicken, pork, rice, beans and also yuca smothered in onions. The air was thick with the savory smell of those onions. In the near corner of the yard, Sergeant Rivas saw the traditional pit, covered in banana leaves and palm fronds, where Cubans cooked their suckling pigs.

Amid all the food and furniture stood about twenty adults and several children, all of whom were now staring at Sergeant Rivas and his retinue. From the looks of things, they had been partying pretty hard, possibly all weekend. Cases of empty beer bottles were stacked at the back of the yard and next to them stood several drained bottles of rum.

Some of the gentlemen swayed slightly, as if they were seaborne, but there was none of the rowdiness that Rivas had feared. They looked like perfectly normal, hard-working Cubans who had decided to celebrate the holiday and the arrival of this person, Pedro, and there was nothing illegal in that. Murder was another matter.

Sergeant Rivas nodded in their direction and asked that the music be turned off.

"*Buenas tardes*," he said once he could be heard, and he introduced himself. "I'll ask all of you to please remain on the premises, at least for the time being. No one has permission to leave." He repeated that request in Spanish to cover all his bases.

He then assigned the uniformed officers to monitor the backyard and to find out anything they could.

"Now, where is the body?"

The people pointed toward the house. Rivas thanked them and ducked inside through the sliding glass doors. That brought him into the living room, which was arranged with wicker furniture, brightly flowered cushions and curtains and, on a sideboard in the corner, a large black porcelain panther with sharp white fangs and a bloodthirsty look that suggested it was about to pounce on its prey.

Sergeant Rivas followed the sound of voices, which led him down a tiled hallway into a small bedroom. It featured a Cuban flag tacked to the wall and also an old, black-and-white photograph of Morro Castle, the Spanish Colonial fortress that overlooks the Bay of Havana. A similar flag and photo could be found in the homes of countless Cuban exile families. In Miami, it was a decorating style.

Two uniformed police officers, a male and a female, accompanied by a heavyset middle-aged man, stood gazing down at the floor just at the door to a bathroom. Splayed there was the body of a man, about forty, slim, with a narrow, handsome face, jet black hair combed in a pompadour, gray-brown eyes that were already dry and a large red bloodstain, like a blooming hibiscus, that almost completely covered the chest of his white, pleated *guayabera*.

He had been shot right in the heart and was definitely dead. A handgun lay several feet away, an unusual weapon. Rivas recognized the Makarov 9mm. Russian in origin, it had been used for many years by the Cuban military. Occasionally one showed up in Miami.

Sergeant Rivas greeted the officers, who in turn introduced the man with them. His name was Pablo Lacasa, and he was the owner of the house. Rivas studied the corpse.

"Who is this gentleman?"

"His name was Victor Bueno," Lacasa said. "He was my oldest friend. We grew up together in Cuba, in Matanzas."

Sergeant Rivas nodded. He had been in Matanzas long ago, before he himself had become an exile in Florida.

"And how did this happen?"

Lacasa shook his head. "Nobody knows. One of the children came in here to use the bathroom and found him. She ran out screaming, and I ran in. The blood was still flowing from his chest. He had been shot only a short time before, but he was already dead."

"And nobody heard the shot?"

"Nobody. The music was loud and the children have been setting off fireworks for hours. After a while, you stop paying attention. No one heard it."

Rivas shrugged. "Except the person who fired it." He pointed at the handgun. "Do you recognize that weapon?"

"No, I've never seen it before. I don't own a gun."

"Did the deceased possibly own it?"

"No, he never owned one either."

"When was the last time you saw him?"

Lacasa pointed in the direction of the backyard. "Just a few minutes before he was shot. He was dancing mambo. He was a very good dancer. All the women loved to dance with him. He was having a wonderful time."

Rivas looked down at the departed man. Yes, he appeared to be a man who had enjoyed himself. God had given him good looks, and, despite the loss of blood, his face still appeared flushed, probably from a propensity for rum. Even his death mask betrayed a glint of mischief.

"Did he argue with anyone before this happened? Was there any evidence of tension between him and anyone else here?"

"No, nothing."

Rivas frowned. "Well, do you have any idea why anyone would want to do this?"

Lacasa shook his head. "I have no idea. Victor was the happiest person in the world. He had no enemies."

That last statement was obviously not a true observation. What had been done to Victor Bueno was not an act of friendship.

The crime scene technicians arrived just then, and Sergeant Rivas left them to their work. He escorted Lacasa, the homeowner, into the living room. From there they could see all the other guests gathered in the backyard. They were standing in groups, speaking worriedly, excitedly. The two uniformed officers were questioning some of them about what they had seen and heard. Above them hung the banner, "*Bienvenido* Pedro." Sergeant Rivas pointed at it.

"Who is Pedro?"

"Pedro's is my nephew. That's him."

Lacasa pointed at a good-looking, slim young man in his early twenties who sat at the dining room table by himself, looking crest-fallen.

"Where is Pedro coming from?" Rivas inquired.

"From Cuba. I haven't seen him in more than twenty years, since he was a baby. I left Cuba in 1980. My sister, his mother, died soon afterward on the island."

He went to the sideboard and brought back a photo album full of old snapshots of Cuba. He turned a page and pointed to a shot of a young woman with light skin, dark hair, recessed dark eyes and a serious expression, holding a child, a little boy, who looked to be about one year old.

"She was very beautiful," Rivas said.

"Yes, she was," said Lacasa. "But she died young, and after that, the boy went to live with the family of his father in another town. I lost touch with him for more than twenty years. Then, just weeks ago,

I heard from him. He had qualified for a visa to leave Cuba, tracked me down and told me he was coming. He got here just three days ago, and we haven't stopped celebrating . . . until now."

Rivas listened attentively to Lacasa's account. It resembled the stories of many Cuban exile families: relatives on either side of the Florida Straits, apart for a long, long time, finally reunited years later—sometimes decades later. The size of the celebration didn't surprise Sergeant Rivas, either. The arrival of the long-lost family member was a major event, a biblical occurrence among the Cubans.

On the other hand, a murder in the midst of such an otherwise joyous occasion was unheard of. That anyone invited to such an important event would sully the proceedings by an act of violence was a travesty. Then again, when people had been drinking for a couple of days, old conflicts tended to float to the surface on the tide of rum.

The two officers who Rivas had assigned to question the crowd outside came in to deliver their report.

"No one saw or heard anything unusual," said the female officer. "They all say the victim had been in a good mood at the beginning of the afternoon's festivities, had a few rums, got in an even better mood and danced. After a while, he stopped dancing, spent a few minutes welcoming the young man who had just come from Cuba, went inside to use the bathroom and never came out."

"Did they notice anyone else who went to use the bathroom about that time?"

She shook her head. "Nobody can remember."

Sergeant Rivas asked the two officers to continue to oversee the people outside, and he turned back to Lacasa.

"Tell me more about your friend, Victor Bueno. When did he come here?"

"I came during *Mariel*," Lacasa said, speaking of the 1980 boatlift that had brought tens of thousands of exiles from the island. "Victor followed a couple of years later. He came on a raft and was rescued at sea."

"What did he do for a living here?"

"He worked as a bartender on and off." Lacasa pointed at the cottage in his backyard. "He didn't always have work, so a few years back he came here to live with us in the cottage. If he couldn't make the rent one month, he would make it up the next."

"He lived by himself?"

"Yes."

"So he didn't marry once he was here."

Lacasa shook his head. "No. Victor had his heart broken by a woman in Cuba in those two years after I left and before he came. He didn't want to leave Cuba without her, which is why he didn't come with me, and then she left him for another man. After that, he never wanted to marry. He was what they call a 'good-time guy.' He was always ready for a party."

Sergeant Rivas shrugged. "Sometimes 'good-time guys' irritate people, especially women." Rivas gazed out at the people grouped in the backyard. "Did he ever have anything to do with any of the women here? Did he give them or their husbands any aggravation, any reason to kill him?"

Lacasa looked out over the crowd and finally shook his head. "He never had trouble with any of these people. I would know. I'm acquainted with all of them."

"Maybe you're not as well acquainted with them as you think."

Sergeant Rivas turned to look at Lacasa and his eyes fell on the nephew, Pedro, who was still sitting stoically at the dining room table. Rivas drifted over, sat next to him and introduced himself.

"I'm very sorry this happened," Rivas said in Spanish. "Your first days here with your family and you have to witness something like this."

Pedro nodded but said nothing. He had the nervousness of all new arrivals when confronted by a cop.

"I understand that Victor Bueno spoke to you just a few minutes before he went towards the bathroom," said Sergeant Rivas, "and just before he died."

"Yes, he brought me a rum, we drank and he wished me well."

"Did he say anything to you that made you think he was afraid? Did he make you think anything worrisome was on his mind?"

Pedro shook his head. "No. He was happy, maybe a little drunk. He was pointing out which women were the best dancers." The boy suddenly looked sheepish. "He told me to pick out a girl I liked and he would arrange it for me to get to know her better."

Rivas cocked his head. "One who might make your welcome even sweeter."

"I guess."

"And what did you say?"

"I didn't say anything, but he said he would take care of it."

Sergeant Rivas looked up at Lacasa who was standing next them and listening. He shrugged.

"That was just Victor talking," Lacasa said. "He wasn't some kind of pimp."

Rivas shrugged. "I believe you, but maybe Victor Bueno, with a few rums in him, said something to somebody that got him shot by an outraged father, brother or husband who also had a few rums in him."

Pedro stared at Sergeant Rivas with eyes full of fear, the kind of fear that came from feeling you might have caused a murder. Rivas patted his leg.

"Don't worry, you didn't do anything, son."

He stood up, hoisted his slacks and readjusted his Panama. "Okay, now we really have to talk to these people."

Sergeant Rivas sat at one of the tables outside and over the next hour questioned the assembled adults, one by one. He asked exactly how long each person had been acquainted with Victor Bueno, even back in Cuba. But in particular, he was interested in any interactions they'd had with him in recent years. He questioned men and women and learned quite a bit about the life of the deceased, from his childhood to his untimely death.

Sergeant Rivas asked specifically about any love affairs in which Bueno may have been involved, and he also inquired about propositions a slightly drunken Bueno might have made in his attempts to supply Pedro with female companionship. Sergeant Rivas carefully studied the replies and the faces looking for signs of dissimulation, or out-and-out lies.

But just like the patrol officers who had interrogated those same people initially, he found no reason to suspect any of them. Victor Bueno had been a bit of a rogue, they all agreed, but he always had avoided any serious unpleasantness with his old acquaintances.

As for his promises to Pedro, they were typical of Victor Bueno's boasting, especially when he was bit inebriated. But he apparently hadn't approached any of the girls. He would probably have done nothing more than point out Pedro's good looks, and apparently Victor Bueno had been murdered before he could do even that.

After questioning the last of the guests, Sergeant Rivas drifted across the yard and entered the small cottage. It contained what amounted to an efficiency apartment: one large room with a pullout bed, bathroom, kitchenette and dining nook. The bed was unmade, dishes sat unwashed in the sink and the décor, apart from the small Cuban flag tacked above the bed, consisted of empty beer cans standing here and there.

Rivas searched closets and drawers, found a manila folder containing immigration documents and an envelope stuffed with various letters addressed to Victor Bueno over the years. Rivas read them carefully and then slipped them into the inside pocket of his sport jacket.

He left the cottage, reentered the house. and fell into a chair at the dining room table, next to Lacasa and his nephew.

"Did you learn anything, Sergeant?" Lacasa asked.

Sergeant Rivas shook his head slowly, his face full of frustration.

"I've been in this business a long time, and I'll tell you something: In situations such as this, it usually doesn't take long to solve the crime. People have been drinking for two or three days and you get bad blood boiling, tempers taking over, some screaming and, finally, the fatal shot or the stabbing.

"These types of murders usually come after a considerable amount of noise between the victim and the perpetrator. You can count on witnesses who watched or heard it all. You walk in, and the guilty party is pretty much served up on a silver platter. Here, all there is on a platter is the *arroz con pollo* and the pork. Nobody saw or heard anything."

Sergeant Rivas removed his Panama hat, passed his hand over his bald pate as if trying to stimulate his brain, and replaced the hat.

"The other matter that makes this case difficult is the character of the victim, Victor Bueno. Apparently no one had anything against him. Yes, they say he was a bit of a scoundrel, but a good-natured scoundrel, and he never allowed his appetites to affect his friendships. Many of the guests here grew up with him, have known him all his life, first in Cuba and then after they left the island and came here. He seemed to have no secrets from anyone and lived a normal life."

Sergeant Rivas opened the photo album that lay on the table and turned the pages, stopping now and again at a photo that illustrated his words. "He grew up in Matanzas, in a neighborhood with cobblestone streets near the sea. He went to its schools, played baseball in its park and went bathing at its beaches, just like everyone else."

Sergeant Rivas tapped an old photo of several young women wearing swimsuits. "The girls in Matanzas are very beautiful, and before long, he gave up baseball for following girls, just like most of us. But he was more handsome than most and more successful with the ladies." He glanced at Lacasa. "That's right, no?"

Lacasa nodded. "That's true."

"He liked to dance and to drink and was playful by nature," Sergeant Rivas continued. "His good humor made him hard to dislike. He made no enemies."

Lacasa nodded. "None. Everybody loved Victor."

Rivas turned another page in the album. "He graduated from secondary school and then found work as a bartender at a government-owned beach resort in Varadero because Victor Bueno wasn't the type to go on to the university.

"He prospered in the job, largely because of his winning personality, earned a living and also enjoyed the social life. But then came the great exodus of 1980—the *Mariel* boatlift—and almost all his friends decided to leave Cuba, including you, Lacasa. You tried to convince him to come along."

"Of course. Me and many others."

"But he didn't. Why not?"

"He had that girl in a town nearby, a girl who didn't want to come to Miami. I never met her, but she must have been quite something. He had just met her and didn't want to leave her."

"That's right. He refused to go without her; he remained loyal. She apparently was the one and only serious love of his life. And what did it get him?" Rivas glanced at Pedro and shook his head. "Nothing. He begged the woman to marry him, but she said no. Within a short time, that same lady left him for another man, a man with a bit better position and a bit more money.

"She had taken advantage of his sweet nature, and now Victor Bueno was left by himself, all his good friends far away. He was driven to despair and decided to set out on a raft. The acquaintances he still had in Matanzas begged him not to risk it. The woman did too, pleading with him not to lose his life at sea. But he told her it was too late. Nobody could stop him."

Sergeant Rivas was about to continue, to depict the heroic journey at sea, when suddenly Pedro leapt to his feet, swung his arm and swept the album off the table, dispatching it across the dining room, photos flying in all directions. Rivas had felt the tension building in the boy, and now it had exploded.

"None of what you're saying is true," he screamed. "Victor Bueno was a beast. He didn't beg that woman to marry him, and she didn't leave him for another man. He got her pregnant, and once she told him, he made plans to escape Cuba. When she found out, she pleaded with him to take her, and he agreed. He told her to meet him at night on the beach with her bag, and then he left her there. He didn't leave on a raft but on boat that he stole from some poor person, and he never stopped to pick her up. He came here by himself. When she wrote him, he didn't answer. Even after the child was born, he didn't answer. And finally she died from hardship and grief. He was no hero. He was a womanizer, a coward and a tramp."

Pedro was out of breath, his face flushed red. Outside, the other guests were frozen in astonishment. Lacasa's mouth had fallen open in disbelief.

Sergeant Rivas gazed up at Pedro. "And the child wrote to him as well, but didn't receive an answer. Isn't that true?"

Pedro just stared at him desolately, his chest heaving.

Sergeant Rivas reached into the inside pocket of his sport jacket and removed the packet of letters he had uncovered in the cottage, letting it drop on the table.

"These are from you. You are Victor Bueno's son, and your name is Sergio. Somehow you met Mr. Lacasa's nephew, Pedro, in Cuba. Both of you had lost your mothers very early in life and you formed a friendship.

"From Pedro you learned that Victor Bueno and Lacasa were childhood friends and that Victor Bueno was here. You obtained a visa in your own name, but when you arrived here, you took Pedro's identity, announced your arrival and insinuated yourself into this house. No one here had seen Pedro in twenty years, so how could they know who you really were? The whole idea was to find your father and to avenge your mother."

The young man's eyes had filled with tears and his voice was choked with them as well. He stared at photos that had fallen out of the album and lay scattered on the floor.

"After he spoke to me, I saw him go toward the bathroom, and I followed him. In the bedroom I stopped him and I said, 'I am your son.' He looked me in the face for several moments and I could tell that he knew I was speaking the truth. He knew who I was. But then I saw the lie rise up in him and glaze his eyes. 'I have no son,' he said to me, and he turned away.

"I hadn't planned to kill him if he had acknowledged me, but he wouldn't do it. He would not say I was his flesh and blood. I pulled the gun from my pocket and told him to stop. When he turned, I told him it was for my mother who was left waiting broken-hearted on the beach, with me inside her. Then I shot him." His teary gaze fell on Sergeant Rivas. "It was the only way."

Sergeant Rivas nodded solemnly. "I understand, son."

The patrol officers had placed themselves around the boy as he spoke. Sergeant Rivas glanced at one of them; they placed cuffs on Sergio, read him his rights in Spanish and led him away.

Lacasa watched it all happen with a look of bewilderment and then turned to Rivas.

"How could you tell it was him? He was the only one who didn't know Victor Bueno."

Rivas rose from the table and adjusted his Panama hat.

"Exactly. If the people who knew Victor Bueno didn't kill him, then it had to be someone who didn't know him." He shrugged. "But in the end, none of you really knew Victor Bueno. Did you?"

He bid Lacasa good afternoon, told the guests they could go. On his way out, he picked one plantain off a plate and popped it into his mouth. Then he headed home to his wife.

Made in China

She picked up the large serving platter from the draining board and started to dry it, then stopped. One of the small pink tea roses that rimmed the platter was chipped, destroying the symmetry of the design.

Twenty-five tea roses bordered the platter. The service had been given to her as a wedding present by her sister. Once, during her first year of marriage, she had placed the entire service for twelve on the table, wishing to see if each piece had the same number of roses. That was thirty-three years ago.

The platter in her hand was the only remaining piece from that set. One by one, a piece had been broken, forgotten at some church or club function, "stolen" by one of the children, or borrowed and never returned. Tonight, looking at the chipped rose on the platter, she couldn't help but think that her life, too, was chipped—ending, lost somewhere between the bedroom and the kitchen.

Turning the platter in her hand, she read "Made in China" several times. At least the platter had an identity. She felt as though she had lost hers.

"You still drying?"

Her husband Paul entered the kitchen from the living room. She looked at him, and knowing how much he liked to brag that he never forgot a thing, decided to ask him, with a touch of subtle malice, "Remember this?" She showed him the platter.

"What?"

"This platter?"

"Sure. You served the roast on it tonight."

"No, no, anything else about it?"

"What else is there to know about a damn platter? It's a plate. Nothing more, nothing less."

Warming up to the issue, she asked, "Can you tell me what the design on the platter is?"

"The design? What kind of game are you playing, woman?"

"No game, dear. I just want to know if you can remember the design."

"What do I know about designs on a plate? Ask me who the members of NATO are, that I can tell you. Or who hit the longest home run during a night game on a Tuesday, that I can answer. Or . . . "

She interrupted, "How many years have we been married?"

"Thirty-one. What's that got to do with the design?"

"Thirty-three. And it's a good bet we've had over thirty thousand meals when one or several plates from this set have been on the table, right?"

"You want me to agree? I agree, give or take. Now what are you driving at?"

"The design on this platter. What is it?"

"Again? Who the hell pays attention to a plate's design?"

"These plates are special."

It wasn't often his wife challenged his memory. "A trap," he delighted in thinking. He had to admit to himself that she had him, but why the question? Was it another of those off-the-wall questions she had thrown at him when he least expected it?

Just two days ago, she had asked him whether it was raining. At the time, she had been standing by the picture window that faced the street. All she had to do was look. He had been reading, and the question had so infuriated him that he couldn't continue. Thinking that she had done it on purpose did not escape him. And now he wondered what was behind her plate question.

He glanced at his watch: two minutes before the news. "Give me a clue."

"We've had this set for thirty-three years. It was one of our wedding gifts."

"Okay, and . . . ?"

"You still can't recall the design?"

"What are you getting at?"

"The platter's design, that's all. Do you remember it?"

"What's so important about a plate's design?"

Every night for years now, after supper, their routine had been the same. He would leave the table for the living room, where he would read the city's two newspapers prior to catching the news on TV, and then a couple of hours with the sports channel before going to bed. Meanwhile, she washed, dried and put away the dishes. Not that she didn't care to know what was going on in the world. One of the daily newspapers came early in the afternoon. She read it and didn't think it was necessary to reread the same thing. And she always watched the early edition of the news on the tube. The evening edition was a repeat.

Lately, alone in the kitchen, drying the large platter with the twenty-five tea roses, she had been feeling one with the platter, for she, too, had become a piece of ware. Ensconced at 2222 Robin Avenue. There was one big difference, though, between her and the platter—it had the roses. She had none. And tonight, staring at the "Made in China," she said, "It was made in China."

"So?"

"It has flowers on it. Do you know what kind?"

"I'm supposed to know that?"

"*Yes!*"

Never one to raise her voice, the strong *yes* took him by surprise. It rang with a seldom-displayed anger. He again looked at his watch. One minute before the news. Time to think. It was obviously important to her for him to remember the type of flowers on the platter she held in her hand.

Suddenly, he remembered: They had been married in Texas, at her sister's house, and Texas was known for its bluebonnets. That was it!

"Bluebonnets!" he shouted.

"What about them?"

"The flowers on the plate are bluebonnets. Satisfied?"

"Wrong!"

Her answer angered him, and he threw out a string of names: "Tulips. Pansies. Petunias. Crocuses. Irises. Cactus, yeah, cacti!"

A cloud of wrath followed his exit from the kitchen. In a few seconds, she heard the TV come on, a few decibels louder than usual.

Standing by the sink, she looked at the empty spot where her husband had been standing, then at the platter in her hand. Thirty-three years of washing and drying the odd number of roses. Twenty-five small red tea roses.

It did not occur to her to assuage the anger she was feeling by smashing the platter on the kitchen floor—a predictable possibility, but not for her. She put the platter away—rather, she hid it, knowing that he would look at it, and when she least expected it, he would triumphantly yell out, "Roses!"

Then she went for a walk.

Dolores had one major diversion—to make as many yard sales as possible on weekends, looking for collectibles. After the platter incident, she was determined to find a similar set. Finding it would, she thought, erase the cloud of finality that had come over her since washing and drying the last plate from the set that had been her wedding present.

She found several that were almost alike, except for the rose count. The sets never had more than ten roses. Slowly, a plan began to form in her mind. Forget the twenty-five roses—just so the set's color was the same as the platter's.

She found a set, same color, but rimmed with only eight small red tea roses. She bought it and regularly served supper using the "new" set. Needless to say, her husband commented on the roses, allowing his forgetfulness. A rare admission.

Halfway through the fourth month of using the "new" set of dishes at every meal, her husband began to complain of stomach cramps. One night, during the fifth month, the cramps became so severe that Dolores had to rush him to the hospital emergency room. While being attended to, he died.

Those in the interment business are used to the many odd wishes requested by the deceased's loved ones, such as coloring the hair darker, making a brunette a blonde because "she always wanted to be a blonde," putting dimples on a face, or "Put this sweater on him. It was his favorite." But when they heard Mrs. Ortiz' request, they knew it had to be the weirdest. She wanted her husband to be buried with "his favorite dishes."

She explained to them that her husband had been a very sentimental sort and always talked about the many small things in their lives that had made their marriage a good one. One of those small things that he would talk about was wanting her to use the plates with the "twenty-five red roses" all the time.

With that thought in mind, she said, there was no way she could ever use the dishes again. Her wish was followed, and the set of dishes placed in her husband's coffin.

After the funeral, Mrs. Ortiz could be seen on her patio, painting. She had taken up oils. The neighbors agreed that her newfound hobby had been good therapy, as she seemed to have adjusted very well to life without her "wonderful" husband.

They did find it a bit odd that, instead of using an artist's palette for her colors, she used a large serving platter—a platter with twenty-five red tea roses.

In the Kitchen with Johnny Albino

It was dark when Iris woke up. She rubbed her belly where it hurt, then got up, put on her slippers and waddled to the kitchen. She was a brunette, petite, pretty and six months pregnant—with a big baby she knew was a boy because of the way her belly came to a point, and because she just knew. She went straight for the kitchen and to the dream book.

She got the book out and put it on the table, face down. She tried to remember the dream but couldn't. She lit a cigarette and went to the kitchen window. She looked outside at the clotheslines radiating from the big elm in the backyard to each building. The windows of the apartment buildings on the other side of the yard were dark, like eyes on faces before they wake up. She stared at nothing in particular. She felt that if she kept staring she could somehow reach back to the dream.

The cigarette smoke twirled around her fingers. Tree. Outside. *Río*—river. And there it was—the dream she had been having before the baby inside her kicked her awake. First it came in pieces, then it played like a movie. A woman. Standing with her feet in a river. Drowning. Iris did not recognize the woman, but she knew the river. It was back in Puerto Rico, near her hometown, Guayama, and the water was shallow. The woman could walk across to save herself. Iris told her so, but then a wave came, dark and red as blood, decapitating the woman, just as Iris found a knife in her hand, and . . .

Then a pigeon flew into her field of vision, and Iris was back in Brooklyn.

She went back to the table quickly. The dream book was mimeographed on cheap blue paper. The listings were crooked, on some pages, clear, on others, blurry. Iris had bought the book when she first came to New York City in the sixties, ten years ago. She folded the cover back—it showed a crazy gypsy lady with a crazy smile that always spooked Iris.

In the books, dreams were listed alphabetically, with a three-digit number next to each:

ANIMAL, 369

AUNT, 261

AUTOMOBILE, 522

AUTOMOBILE CRASH, 673

If you dreamed about an animal one night, you were supposed to play 369 the next day and the next few days, because that number was going to hit. Iris searched the Ds and found "DROWNING, 419." She wrote the number down in a little red notebook. She got up and turned on the radio, finding her favorite Spanish station. A song by Trio Los Panchos came on, one of Iris' favorites. She began to sway to its tinny rhythm.

"Mami." Her four-year old daughter, Nancy, stood in the doorway of the kitchen in her pajamas. The girl had the same jet-black hair and sad eyes of her father. Every time Iris looked at her, she was reminded of him.

"Go back to bed."

"I'm awake."

"It's too early. Go back to bed."

"I'm hungry."

She put out her cigarette. "You want some eggs?"

Later, after she dropped Nancy at the pre-K school at St. Peter and Paul, Iris went to the bodega at the corner. The old man, Negrón, was behind the counter, talking to his parrot.

"¿Te pegate? ¿Te pegate?" the parrot said. "¡Negrón!"

"Ratoncito," Negrón said. He called it a little rat because if the cops ever came into the store, they'd know from its limited vocabulary that numbers were being run there. But the cops never came. The parrot was bright green. Negrón was a dark caramel and missing an earlobe—which was why he'd started keeping the parrot in a cage.

Iris told Negrón to play her regular numbers, and then told him to play 419—for a dollar, straight.

"A dollar, straight?" Negrón said. "Did you have a dream?"

"A lady drowning," she said.

"Dios te bendiga," he said, "419, dollar, straight. You got it."

Later in the day, she went back to the bodega to pick up milk and to see which number hit. "¿Quién pegó, Negrón?"

"¡419— te pegues!"

The odds for *bolita*—the numbers game—were six hundred to one. Negrón was from Guayama, too, and had known Iris since she'd moved to the Southside, so he didn't take his normal bookie fee of fifteen percent. Iris had six hundred dollars, more money than she had ever had at one time in her life.

Iris had been laid off that summer. She considered going back to Puerto Rico—again. She'd already been back and forth fifteen times. She got food stamps, and sometimes she cleaned houses for cash. Her friend Maribel was in the same situation and hadn't worked in a year. They spent a lot of the day in Iris' kitchen, drinking coffee and listening to the radio until it was time to pick up Nancy.

"That's pretty nice money," Maribel said.

"You telling me. That's half a year's rent."

"That's pretty nice money."

"I have to go shopping first. Then pay the rent and the electricity. And I gotta put money away for the baby. Then I start saving to buy my own restaurant. Iris'."

"For that, you don't got enough money. You have to dream a thousand dreams. That's a lot of drowned ladies." Maribel laughed.

Iris took a drag on her cigarette and rubbed her belly.

"You know what?" Maribel said.

"What?"

"You know what—you could start your own *bolita*. You make enough money, you never have to work again."

"Run the numbers? Like a crook?"

"Everybody's a crook. Look at the fricking president. It's easy. Look at Negrón. He makes easy money."

Iris nodded her head to the side.

"You have to watch out, though," Maribel said.

"Why?"

"If someone doesn't pay you, you gotta be tough. Business is business."

"I'm tough," Iris said. She looked at the window, remembering her dream.

Maribel laughed. "Little Iris the crook."

"Maribel!" Iris said. Then she got up and took pork chops out of the freezer for dinner.

When Iris got back from the school with Nancy, the girl's father was sitting on the couch in the living room, having a beer. The light was off, but his sad, handsome face was lit by the television.

"¡Papi!" Nancy jumped on the couch and hugged her father around the neck. He kept his eyes on the TV. Iris turned on the light.

"What's new?" he said to Iris.

"I hit the number."

"*Vaya.* Let's go celebrate! We could go to the Copa."

"*¿Así?*" she said, pointing to her belly. "No, thank you. That money is for me and *la niña* and the baby. I'm going to start my own *bolita,* I decided."

"What you gonna do that for?"

The little girl tried to sit in his lap. The father sipped his beer.

"So I can make a lot of money. I could make enough to buy a restaurant."

"That's crazy. Pregnant women are crazy. They get crazy ideas."

"Don't call me crazy, Juan," Iris said.

"What if somebody hits big? They'll take your whole bank."

Iris had met Juan years ago at a club. He got her pregnant but he wouldn't marry her. He hung around, giving her some money for a while. He got her pregnant again, but then hadn't given her any money in months. Iris would tell him she needed to buy groceries and pay rent, but she got tired of asking and knew she would get the money on her own anyway, somehow. She fought with him, but not so much to push him away.

"That's not gonna happen," she said. "No one's gonna hit that much."

"Papi, I want to go to Coney Island."

Juan moved his daughter off of him and got up. "Let me have another beer," he said to Iris.

"Get it yourself."

He got up and went to the kitchen, where Iris was smothering the defrosted pork chops with *adobo.*

"You're a rich woman. Now you can support me," he said, turning on the radio. A slow, melancholy love song was starting. Iris heard it and cursed under her breath.

"You never supported me," she said.

"I don't want to argue, baby."

Just as she thought he would, Juan took Iris in his arms and began to dance slowly with her, humming to the old Johnny Albino song. Iris was stiff at first, then she melted and molded herself to his body, her round belly up against his taut stomach.

"You're my baby, and you got my baby in there."

They danced slowly in place, shuffling on the kitchen linoleum. Nancy watched from the doorway and giggled, covering her mouth.

Iris picked up Nancy at school, then decided to go to Negrón's to get milk. As soon as she opened the door, the parrot said, "*¿Te pegate? ¿Te pegate? ¡Negrón!*"

"Hello, parrot," Nancy said.

"She's getting big," Negrón said, looking at Nancy. He sat on his stool behind the counter. He had once been a big man but now was bent over with age. He rarely moved from the stool, but the store was always well-stocked and neat. The parrot was silent behind him, munching on one sunflower seed after another. Newspapers were spread out under its cage.

"Tell me about it."

Iris told Negrón about her plan and assured him that she would still play numbers with him.

"Don't worry about it. There's plenty of business for everybody," he said. "Every *jíbaro* in the neighborhood plays numbers. And every other *jíbaro* runs a *bolita.*"

Negrón told her not to write a lot down, if anything. He told her not to spend all her money. And then he reached under the counter, balancing himself with one hand, and took out a cracker tin. Inside it was a greasy rag, and inside the rag was an old, dented .38 revolver. "You need any help, you let me know."

"*¡Ay!*" Iris looked at her daughter, who was staring at the parrot. "*Gracias,* Negrón," she said.

Iris knew some ladies back at the elementary school where she used to work liked to play the numbers.

"So you got your own numbers game," said Mrs. Killian in a thick South Carolina accent. Killian was a large black woman who taught second grade. "You're an enterprising woman, Iris. I like that. I always play 731, because the first time I hit the numbers it was July 31. So I'll play that straight and combination."

"Ay, Iris, God bless you," said Olga, one of her old coworkers. "The woman I used to play with moved to Queens. I hope you bring me luck!"

Maribel also played with her, quarters here and there. But Juan wouldn't.

"You don't want to prove that I'm crazy," she said.

"I don't have any money," he said.

"Then how do you eat? How do you live?"

"I work. But I don't got any money to spare on gambling. I need to make more money."

"It takes money to make money," she said.

Iris got into the routine of buying the morning and evening *Daily News*. Two three-digit hit numbers came out every day. The daily number came from the track handle—the amount of money bet at the races—at whatever track was featured in the *News* that morning. The nightly number came from the handle at Yonkers.

While Nancy was at school, Iris would sit by the phone, and her customers would call in. Maribel would play only a quarter every day on 561. Mrs. Killian would play up to ten dollars in numbers, and always 731.

In the first week, Iris made a hundred dollars.

She went to the kitchen cabinet and took down the ceramic pitcher she'd received as a bonus when she worked for the Prince Spaghetti factory in the neighborhood. It had closed a long time ago. She kept her money inside the pitcher in a tight roll wrapped by a rubber band. She sat down and laid out her original six hundred dollars and her newest earnings on the table. She lit a cigarette and looked at the neat piles.

"My God," she said.

If this kept up, she would have no problem paying rent for the first time in months. It meant, she hoped, that she wouldn't have to go running back to Guayama ever again. She had worked for this. So what if it was illegal? Everybody was a crook. Everything was okay as long as she didn't get caught.

"Wow, Mami."

It was Nancy, standing in the dark doorway.

"You should be sleeping."

"That's a lot of dollars, Mami."

"That's right. This is our money. This is for us."

"I'm hungry."

Iris got up and poured a glass of milk for her daughter. As Nancy drank it, Iris said, "You want to go shopping tomorrow? We can go downtown to McCrory's and the toy store and get you a new dress."

"Really, really?"

"Really. Now go to bed."

"How about Papi?"

The girl's father hadn't called or come around all week.

"*Ay*, Nancy. We'll see."

Iris had never even known her own father. All she had was an old picture that someone had crumpled up. After she put Nancy to bed, Iris picked up the phone, then put it down. She wanted a beer but instead poured herself a glass of milk. She shut off the radio, then picked up the phone again.

Juan sounded tired, half asleep. "*¿Qué?*"

"Juan. It's me."

"Why you calling me?"

"What happened? Where have you been?"

"Don't call me here. Don't ever call me."

"You got a daughter here who loves you and misses you. And you got a son on the way."

"Don't call me."

And then he hung up.

"Juan!" Iris took a big drag on her cigarette. "*Come mierda,*" she said, but she collapsed, crying, onto the chair.

It had been snowing. Iris had not heard from Juan in more than a month. Every day Nancy asked her where her father was, and Iris had to lie, had to say he would be coming soon. She knew that no matter what she said, her daughter's heart was breaking every day. Christmas was coming soon, at least, and Iris was happy—after two months with her *bolita*, with some people hitting now and then, she was doing pretty well.

She dropped her daughter off at school in the morning, then picked up the *Daily News* at Negrón's and came home. Because of the snow, Yonkers was closed. The track handle that day came from Tampa Bay. The number was 731.

"Oh, shit," Iris said.

Yesterday Mrs. Killian had said she was feeling lucky and had played two dollars on her favorite number.

"*Coño,*" Iris said.

Iris got up slowly—the baby was due any day. She went into the cabinet and got down the pitcher from the high shelf. She put it on the table and removed the roll of money. Something looked wrong.

She didn't want to think about it. She took off the rubber band, and it snapped on her hand. "*¡Coño!*" It left a red mark. She counted the money. Then she counted it again.

"*Coño,*" Iris said. Mrs. Killian's hit meant she won twelve hundred dollars. The last time Iris had looked at her money, there was more than thirteen hundred dollars. Now there was less than seven hundred. Had she bought something? Did she put it somewhere else? She couldn't seem to remember right.

The phone rang.

"Iris! Good morning," said Mrs. Killian. "It's a really good morning."

"*Hola. ¿Cómo estás?*"

"I am *está muy* boo-eno, Iris. 731 hit! I hit!"

"Yes, yes, you did," Iris said. She could think of nothing else to say.

"So when you coming 'round with the *premio*? I could use it this month, with the holidays and all. You coming at lunch? After work? You want me to come get it?"

"No, no, I'll bring it to you," Iris said. "But I may not get a chance today. The baby . . . "

"Don't tell me that, Miss Iris. I need that money. Don't make me come get it, now," Mrs. Killian said, and she laughed. But it was not a funny laugh.

"I'll bring it to you. Don't worry."

Iris hung up and went to the window and looked out at the big elm and the backyard. Before she came to New York, she had never seen snow. During her first snowfall, she thought it was pretty, the way it covered the dark, low, brown buildings of Brooklyn, the way it seemed to turn the neighborhood into something from a fairy tale. Now, in the silent kitchen, she tried to see beyond the snow-covered backyard, beyond the fairy tale.

She turned, put on her coat and went to Negrón's store. She just needed to talk to him, to understand what to do next.

The snow blew in her face, and it was hard to see more than a few feet. But as she crossed the street, it looked like Negrón's door was open. Snow was mounding in the entrance. For the second time that day, Iris felt something was wrong.

Iris went to cross the street. A car sped directly toward her and swerved to the right, spraying gray slush, to avoid hitting her. She did not hear the driver screaming at her.

Inside the store, Iris was shocked. Negrón was on the floor in front of the counter, face down. She was shocked, first, to see him out of place, to see his whole body laid out on the wooden floor. Then there was the blood. It was dark red and leaked from under him.

"Negrón!" she called.

"¡Negrón!" the parrot called from behind the counter. For a crazy moment, Iris thought the parrot sounded worried.

She got on her knees and touched his shoulder. Then she bent and moved him. He groaned. She turned him over.

"¡Negrón!" the parrot called.

"Buenos días," Negrón said.

"¿Qué pasó?"

"And it's so close to Christmas," he said.

Blood poured from a big gash in his head all over his shirt and face, but he was conscious. Slowly, he told Iris that a kid had come in while he was cleaning. The kid pulled a gun. Negrón was going to smack him. "Sin vergüenza," Negrón called him. Shameless. But the kid had stepped back and shot him.

She called an ambulance and then Negrón's nephew, who worked in the neighborhood.

When the ambulance came, she asked them if Negrón would live. They didn't know. His nephew told her to go, that he would wait for the cops, if they ever arrived. While the nephew was busy, Iris made a decision. She moved to the back of the counter and got the .38. She put it under her coat. "Dios te bendiga," she said to no one in particular, and then left.

She went to the corner and called a car service.

The car service took her to an address in East New York. Iris told the driver, a Dominican, to wait.

She was not surprised when a woman answered the door, keeping it barely open. From what Iris could see, the woman was pretty, a little on the heavy side, and very young. She looked familiar.

"May I help you?" the lady said.

Iris considered pulling the gun in the lady's face to make her open the door. But then she looked down—and saw that the woman was pregnant, too.

"I'm here to see Juan," Iris said.

The woman said nothing. She stepped back and opened the door. The house was cold—Iris couldn't hear the radiators working. She stepped in, and for a second the two women faced each other, big bellies pointing forward. Then Iris followed the woman's turning gaze to an inner door.

As she moved past the woman, Iris realized what was familiar about the lady's face. She looked like the crazy gypsy lady from the cover of the dream book. Iris did not want to turn her back on her. But the door was in front of her, so she opened it. It was dark inside.

"Juan," she said softly, and then louder. Something rustled in sheets in the darkness.

She reached over and turned on the light.

Juan was in bed, lying face down. He looked up at her, his jet-black hair a mess.

"What the fuck are you doing here?"

"I've never seen where you live, Juan. You never brought me. I wanted to see it."

"You're crazy. If this is about her . . . "

"It's not about that. It's about business."

"You're crazy."

"Well, you told me pregnant women are crazy. Your little friend must be crazy then," Iris said, then moved closer to the bed. "I want my six hundred dollars."

"What six hundred dollars?"

He remained on his stomach, not bothering to fully look at her. Iris figured he was naked under the sheets. She remembered he liked to sleep that way. She took a step closer to the bed, took out the old .38 and touched it to his left foot, then moved it up his leg slowly 'til she got to his butt cheeks.

"This could do a lot of damage, Juan. I can't imagine how long it would take to clean the sheets."

"You're crazy."

"You have my money."

He moved and she backed away.

"Careful. I may be slow, but a bullet is very fast."

He opened a drawer and took out his wallet. He threw a messy wad of bills on the floor. Slowly, keeping the gun pointed at Juan, she bent down and picked the money up. There was a sudden sharp pain in her belly—she almost screamed. But she kept it in. She had learned long ago how to keep in pain.

She took them and counted, "There's only three hundred here."

"That's all I got."

"It's my money. And you owe me a lot more."

"Get the fuck out of here."

She put the money in her purse. "Fine. But you're gonna visit your daughter. She loves you. I can't stop that. But a girl shouldn't be without her father, good or bad."

"You're crazy, Iris."

She put the gun right behind where his testicles would be.

"See you for Christmas then."

"Fuck. Okay, okay."

As she left, the young girl stood against the sink. She had a large knife in her hand. She said nothing, but her eyes were full of fear and hate. Iris thought about making the young girl's head disappear but figured the poor thing was headed for enough trouble already. And something was happening to her. She knew she had to get moving. Iris looked straight ahead and walked out the door. The girl never moved.

There was blood everywhere. It flowed like a river and covered the back seat of the car service sedan.

"*¡Avanza!*" Iris screamed.

The driver talked too fast for her to understand. Her water broke in the car, and the liquid pooled dark and red and viscous at the bottom of her feet. She would make it, she told herself. She was a survivor. The car made slow progress through the snow-covered streets. Iris saw whiteness covering the windows, smothering the car. And then all she saw was black.

Later, in the hospital, she opened her eyes and saw Nancy.

"*Hija,*" Iris said.

"Titi Maribel brought me."

Maribel's voice came from somewhere to her left. "Your son is fine. I saw him. He's beautiful. A full head of hair!"

Iris stroked her daughter's face. The girl put something in her hand. Iris looked—it was a roll of money.

The girl giggled. "It's ours, you said."

A Not So Clear Case of Murder

An excerpt from Out with a Bang, *a novel by L. M. Quinn*

I'd never considered myself special or particularly religious (more of a *católica cuando me conviene*, if I was honest), but God definitely had a plan in mind for me. The thing was that I might not live long enough to see it through.

I'd just survived a shitty five-year marriage to the king of *mujeriegos*, only to be hit with a stage-three breast cancer diagnosis and no guarantee of survival. And now I had to solve a murder.

Why me? What did I know about murder? I was a research analyst. Sure, I lived in a big city: LA. And yeah, murders were a daily occurrence here, guaranteed to be sensationalized ad nauseam in the media. But I'd never personally known anyone who'd been murdered, until now.

And who did I have to thank for this latest development? I looked at the photo in the sterling silver frame sitting on my desk, a gift from my late Tía Isabella. She smiled out at me, her love for me shining in her dark eyes. At the bottom of her photo she'd proudly included one of my research firm's first business cards that read: *Norah Sterling, Executive Vice President, Research4You*. In her eyes, I could do anything I put my mind to.

"*¿Estás loca*, Norah? You're ill. You can't take on anything else," my business partner Gladys Fuentes had said when I told her I'd agreed to do a favor for a family friend.

I could see the concern mixed with fear in her eyes as she assessed my gaunt face and cropped hair, results of surviving my first round of chemo. I had two more rounds to look forward to, and God only knew what I'd look like afterward.

"Olivia Atkins needs my help, and she was Tía Isabella's best friend. I can't say no to her."

Just like I couldn't sit around and feel sorry for myself. *Me moriría* as sure as my name was Norah. So when it came out that Olivia was being harassed by none other than infamous and treacherous LA entrepreneur Victor Lohmand, I jumped at the chance to put the king of cover-ups behind bars, something no one had yet been able to do. "Teflon Victor" had connections to dangerous, shady politicians and organized crime figures. People who went up against Lohmand were known to get feet-in-cement-in-the-LA-River dead.

The way I saw it, I had nothing to lose. Being bumped off by Lohmand was a lot more exciting than death by breast cancer. *Por supuesto*, I couldn't tell Gladys that. She'd finish me off before the other two options had the chance.

Now two weeks into my research, I had turned up illegal brothel activities involving Olivia's West Hollywood house and the renters she had in there while she was doing a teaching gig at Harvard for a year. And there was a missing person in this scenario as well. Retired Beverly Hills jeweler Barry Larsen had last been seen at Olivia's house.

An LAPD detective friend told me that Barry's case was on hold pending new information. This translated to sixty something, known-womanizer Barry having run off to Cancún with a twenty-year-old. Case closed. I wanted my own spin on the guy, and when I questioned Barry's wife about his disappearance, I got more than I'd bargained for.

"Empire Properties pressured me to sell my house to them. I had no choice anyway after Barry disappeared and left me nearly bankrupt," Louise Larsen told me in a weak, little-girl voice, tears welling up in her blue eyes.

As if the poor woman didn't have enough on her plate, she was also elderly and suffered from dementia.

Empire Properties was the same real estate company that had pressured Olivia to sell her house to them before she'd moved back to Los Angeles. Empire Properties was owned by Victor Lohmand.

"I've been receiving threatening phone calls to stop looking for Barry, or something bad would happen to me. And my nephew sent me a box of chocolates this week," Louise added, eyes now filled with fear as she clutched my arm. "I don't have a nephew."

¡Ay caray! If that scary scenario didn't send up a red flag—not to mention producing *un montón de escalofríos* down my spine—Louise's fatal heart attack one week later did. Her nephew had just paid her a visit the day before she died, according to the nurse I talked to at Louise's assisted living facility. So who had really been behind those threatening calls?

Sideswiped by chemo and recovery for two weeks, I was watched over by well-meaning but overprotective Gladys. Steven Bender, my on-again, off-again *novio*, was "on" again, as far as he was concerned, to make certain that I followed the doctor's and Gladys' orders, and to carry on his crusade to convince me to marry him.

I'd stopped counting the number of times I'd told Steven it wasn't going to work out between us. But he was clueless about the fact that he needed time to heal from his failed romantic disasters, while I was past that and ready to move on. We were in two separate time zones. Gladys didn't want to hear what I had to say, either.

"No, Norah. You're wrong about him," Gladys had said during my last Steven-dumping lament. "You need someone in your life who loves you more than you love him, not another fiasco like your ex-husband. Steven is your *príncipe azul*, trust me on this."

Although Steven and she both watched me like a hawk as I recovered, I still managed to stay on top of Olivia's case via phone and laptop while plotting my next move.

A techie buddy, Jimmy Galindo (a.k.a. Jimmy G.), confirmed that someone had hacked into Olivia's credit record and fiddled it so she couldn't get a loan when her ailing mother's medical bills escalated her into bankruptcy. Jimmy was still working on who was responsible.

It looked like Olivia would be forced to go into foreclosure if she didn't sell her house in time. And time was something neither of us had much of to halt this march of sudden disasters.

With disappearing husbands and nonexistent nephews starting to pile up, I knew I was out of my league and needed professional help with the case. I sure as hell couldn't go to Gladys or Steven. They'd lock me up somewhere until I saw reason—their reason, of course. I also couldn't go to the cops. I had no solid proof against anyone, only speculation.

On a former client's glowing recommendation, I contacted P.I. Nicolas Martell, who had a reputation for successfully solving quirky high-profile cases, and who wouldn't be bothered by a minor glitch like no proof.

From what I'd heard and read about him, he was a consummate pro and a well-known womanizer. His cases and clients tended to be the ones most agencies wouldn't touch. He'd been successful with most of them, but, as I already knew from my research, not the ones against Lohmand. I figured he must be itching for another chance to nail the guy.

The fourteenth-floor, Santa Monica offices of Martell & Reed, Private Investigators, reeked of luxury. It was a chic, designer-outfitted place of business, with high-end Italian furnishings in teal-colored leather, burnished stainless steel and glass, Magritte art prints on soft gray walls and gleaming parquet floors. The icing on the cake was a spectacular eastern view of LA's skyline through one glass wall. Quirky cases obviously brought in big bucks.

Sitting across from Martell in his office, he listened to me without interruption as I told him what I needed from him and why I thought he was the man for the job.

The guy had a great face up close. The TV interviews I'd seen him in didn't do justice to his looks. He was in his early forties, with dark hair and eyes set in a rugged face that had been recently tanned by sun, either somewhere tropical or on the ski slopes, given LA's current stretch of wet weather.

Not a pretty boy, but a man. His expression, one of polite observation, revealed nothing, a technique he'd no doubt cultivated to keep the bad guys at bay.

"I want to take down that bastard Lohmand just as much as you do, but I don't think this sex house surveillance you're asking me to do is going to tell us much or get us what we want. The cops will just shut the place down and fine him. A few months later, the place will be open for business again."

He gave me a once-over that had the potential to set my clothes on fire. But his rugged good looks, hypnotic cologne and womanizing reputation so reminded me of my ex-husband Tim that I let the seductive insinuation die in a moment of silence.

Sexy good looks and boatloads of charm had been Tim's upside. The downside had included five years of grief and denial on my part that those two things alone could keep a marriage alive.

"You're not giving me the whole story here, are you?" Nicolas' professional demeanor replaced his seductive one.

"No, I'm not. But that's the way it's got to be for now. I'm looking into some other options that could nail Lohmand, and I don't want to involve my client in this until it's absolutely necessary."

LA was crawling with people who'd like to get a piece of Lohmand and see that he got what he deserved. I was just about to hand over to Martell a good chance at nailing the guy. He couldn't say no—not if he was the P.I. everyone said he was.

"Here's the deal. If you agree to help me out, I'll hand over to you all proof I eventually find on Lohmand. I want to keep as low a profile as possible to protect my client and myself."

I was a research analyst who did my best work sitting in front of a laptop, not dodging bullets and running for cover from a hit man.

Nicolas agreed. He handed me a standard contract, which I signed. It allowed him to then turn over all of our proof to the police and handle Lohmand's reaction and the publicity frenzy. Neither Olivia nor I wanted part of that potentially dangerous sideshow.

While Nicolas was looking at the outside, I wanted to know what went on inside of the sex houses. And who would know better about that than service staff?

I contacted and met with two of the cleaning staff who worked inside, *cubanas* Angela León and Zulma Beltrán. Both were transsexuals and former prostitutes. Originally from La Havana, Cuba, they'd left the street life behind and now cleaned houses for a living.

Angela was in the last stages of AIDS. With her gaunt face and skeletal body, she looked like a starving refugee in a famine- or war-stricken country, eyes dull from illness and strong medication and with multiple IV scars in both arms.

In contrast, Zulma was a dark-haired, dark-eyed Latina beauty, curvy in her tight spandex bike pants and long red T. Rhinestones formed the word "Sexy" across her ample chest in three-inch letters.

Both women were afraid to talk to me about the sex parties, so I didn't insist. *Me sentí cucaracha* questioning them in the AIDS ward of Los Angeles County Hospital-USC Medical Center. I tried to make up for it by calling a former client of mine on the spot to arrange for Angela to get a private room in a very good AIDS hospice in West Hollywood that the ex-client ran.

As I was leaving, Zulma stopped me near the hospital exit. Her eyes filled with tears, and she pulled me into a strong hug that took my breath away.

"Thank you, Señora Norah. You good person. I know Angela die soon. I want her to be comfortable and have no pain. This place is crazy. Too many people. Too much noise."

Zulma had then insisted upon providing me with free house-cleaning for helping out Angela. During those weekly cleanings, she did not once mention Lohmand's sex houses or the sex parties that took place there. She did, however, get a look at both Steven and Nicolas, who'd stopped by my place—Steven, for personal reasons, and Nicolas, for business. I could tell from her comments that she was very taken with Nicolas' sexy looks, but Steven's sweetness had stolen her heart. She couldn't understand why I didn't jump at the chance to have both men in my life.

My apartment was spotless, but I was running out of witnesses and options. Was Victor Lohmand about to walk away free and clear once again? Over my dead body. And if the second—and now third—rounds of chemo had their way, that just might be my fate.

Nearly bald, a walking skeleton and intermittently assaulted by chemo-brain memory lapses, I was hanging on by a thread. True, I might be making my last stand, but I swore that I was taking that bastard Lohmand down with me for what he did to Olivia.

One week later, I sent up a silent prayer of thanks when Zulma contacted me to say that Angela and she had decided to tell me what they knew about the sex parties.

"Why did you change your mind about talking to me?"

"Because all my savings gone for my cleaning business. Four years I save. Big Boss steal it from me in one night. I know he did," Zulma said.

Her anger filled Angela's room at the AIDS hospice, as she went on to explain that she didn't trust banks and kept all of her savings in her apartment. The money had been taken from there.

"Who's the big boss, and why would he steal your money?"

"Big Boss is Señor Victor."

"Victor Lohmand?"

"Sí, that right. I do Angela's job at Beverly Hills house two week ago. When I finish cleaning, Big Boss want me to stay and work sex party when one of his regular girls no show up. I tell him no. I no do that kind work no more. On Monday, I come home from cleaning job in Long Beach, my house is trash. Everything broken. All my money gone."

After ID'ing Lohmand and Barry Larsen from photos I showed them, Angela and Zulma confirmed a multitude of illegal activities going on at the sex parties. Angela had also seen Barry Larsen confront Victor Lohmand and his associate Joey Vitanelli the night Barry disappeared. The two men had forced Barry into his office, where they continued to fight. Barry Larsen didn't come out of the office while Angela was there.

There was also another cleaning woman present at the time, a Russian girl called Lana (no last name), here illegally and forced to work sex parties by Lohmand. Lana had disappeared during the sex party that same night.

Without a last name, the girl would be impossible to track down. My last hope of getting and keeping a witness long enough to show up in court bit the dust along with Angela. Both she and Olivia's mother died the following week.

If I couldn't get the living to work with me, I figured maybe I could work with the dead—Barry Larsen, to be precise. Given Angela's last bit of information about the guy, there was a good chance he was dead. And if he hadn't left Olivia's house after his altercation with Lohmand, Barry was still there. It was a hunch that felt more than right.

So I arranged to meet Zulma at Olivia's house, where she was cleaning up following the wake for Olivia's mother. I planned to give the house one last go-through to see if something caught my attention.

I nearly had a stroke when Zulma met me at the door wearing a tennis pin on her sweater that was identical to one that Louise Larsen had worn when I met with her. Zulma had found the pin that morning on Olivia's back property when she was taking out the trash.

Barry and Louise had been avid tennis players, and the pins had been awarded to them for a first-place win in a tournament. Louise had told me that Barry's pin was identical to hers and he always wore it. The initials engraved on the back of the pin confirmed that it was Barry's.

"I'm going to have to keep this pin, Zulma. It's evidence in a murder investigation, and I'll have to give it to the police."

"Murder? Police? I no like police. They no like Zulma, too."

Her past run-ins with the LAPD during her streetwalking days no doubt had left her wary of anything that might bring her to their attention.

"Don't worry. This is not about you. Do you remember the photo of the man Angela said was fighting with the big boss?"

"I remember."

"He disappeared after that fight. His wife never saw him again. This was his pin. His name is on it." I pointed to the back of the pin. "Something happened to this man here in this house."

"He dead?"

"I think so."

Zulma's eyes widened.

"You can't tell anyone about this pin, or about giving it to me. It's very important."

"Zulma like tomb."

That clinched it for me. Barry and Lohmand must have had some deal together that had gone sour. Barry confronted Lohmand, who murdered him. Lohmand then buried Barry's body in a temporary grave on Olivia's property. Lohmand wanted Olivia's house because when Olivia suddenly returned to LA and wanted to move back into her house he hadn't had time to remove the body. Now I just had to find what was left of Barry. But what did I know about bodies, and even more important, finding one without alerting Lohmand?

Scary as it was to admit, that last bit might not be avoidable any longer. A phone call from Gladys this morning had hinted as much.

"What's with Mary Conti, our new researcher? She left me a voice-mail, with no details, about two strange guys stopping by the office yesterday," Gladys said.

"So, what happened?"

"Mary said she was finishing up for the day, when these two 'Mafioso types'—Mary's words—dropped in to ask about our services and who worked the cases. She said they were fishing for information, which she didn't provide, and one of them was casing the office. They told her they'd get back to her. Mary walked out with them to make sure they left the building. She said they took off in a black Beamer with tinted windows. Do you know anything about these guys, *chiquita*?"

A black Beamer with tinted windows? Hadn't I seen a car like that at Olivia's mother's funeral? But so what? There were a ton of cars out there that fit that description.

"No, I don't know anything about them. But it is very strange, since we never get walk-in clients."

"Mary's been reading too many mysteries and watching way too much *CSI*, if you ask me. *Ay, se me olvidó*, Mary got a look at the guys' license plate too, a vanity one that says PAULO."

"Wow, she should work for the FBI, not us."

I gave another thought to Mary's information, watching goose-bumps rise on my arms. I knew from my research and Nicolas Martell's feedback that PAULO was a limo service owned by known organized crime figure—and Lohmand's buddy—Joey Vitanelli.

Finding Barry was now my number-one priority. A recent Ground Penetration Radar (GPR) patent research case I'd worked on had been tickling my memory the last few days as a possible method for locating body remains.

I pulled my laptop out of its case and sat down on Olivia's sofa. I clicked the GPR Web site link referenced in the report and scrolled down to the "What is GPR?" section. Bingo.

GPR traces buried remains, human and otherwise, in the fields of police forensics and archeology.

Since I hadn't a clue how to get my hands on, let alone operate, GPR, I would call my former client, Chuck Grant, today and ask him to refer me to a local GPR expert. I'd tell him that I needed a second opinion to confirm two important points for the final report of another GPR patent case I was working on.

It didn't take an IQ of two hundred to figure out that the police were not about to go digging up Olivia's property based solely on my hunch, which is all I had to offer for now. But with GPR proof on the table, they'd be more inclined to listen and take action.

Later that evening, thanks to Chuck, I made an appointment to meet with GPR expert Dr. Martin Williams the day after tomorrow.

The following day I had to attend a breast cancer fair I'd helped organize. I had a professional makeover by a Disney makeup artist to see what could be done to help my appearance. I wasn't expecting a miracle, but I did walk away looking like one of those gorgeous but gaunt and hollow-cheeked fashion-magazine models. My own mother wouldn't have recognized me.

I almost lost it when I spotted Victor Lohmand at the fair. He was being presented an award for donating a cancer wing to the hospital after his wife Lydia was treated for breast cancer there and survived. This award had been a last-minute addition to the fair's agenda.

I kept my eye on the Lohmands as I watched them being escorted around the fair by Dr. Jeremy Brent, Lydia's oncologist. Brent worked in the same office as my oncologist, Dr. Luis Díaz.

I knew that I had to get out of there ASAP and was making my way through the crowd to the exit when I came face-to-face with

Lohmand and Brent. A one-minute, still-action film unfolded in which no one moved because of the crowd surging around us and the close proximity of the characters in the scene. My eyes locked with Brent's. There was an unsure flicker of recognition in his eyes as he granted me a brief smile and nod. I didn't return his acknowledgment, pretending not to know him. I turned in the opposite direction, only to find my path blocked by Lohmand. His eyes were focused on my chest, which sent a shot of anger through me at his sexist gesture. I backed away from him, my eyes automatically lowering to where his gaze rested. He was staring at the tennis pin that I'd fastened to my pullover pocket during my makeover to avoid damaging or losing it in the bottomless pit of my handbag. Shit, I'd forgotten about the pin.

His gaze rose to meet mine, gray eyes narrowed to threatening slits of steel. His mouth was as rigid as his posture as he opened it to say something.

"Oh, please do excuse me. My husband's waving to me," my voice said in an unrecognizable squeaky-girl timbre, stopping Lohmand before he could say a word.

I held up my hand and waved, causing the two men to avert their gazes.

"I'll be there in a minute, sweetie!" I chirped to my nonexistent hubby.

Quickly sidestepping around the two men, I moved into the crowd and disappeared into the women's restroom. I plunged into the nearest open stall, sitting down on the toilet seat and putting my head between my legs to recover.

Frigging hell!

Lohmand had recognized the tennis pin for sure, but with all the makeup plastered on my face, he might not have recognized me. Like-wise, Brent. I managed a quick escape from the restroom and left the fair still shaking from the encounter.

The following morning, rested and ready for action, I was parked in the Hollywood Hills above Franklin Avenue in front of Dr. Martin Williams' bungalow-style house.

The man himself was at the back of his house standing near a vintage-model Chevy pickup. Clad in a dark-blue and white-striped flannel shirt, cowboy boots and jeans, his short, wiry body was barely visible among the overgrown bushes dotting the property. He stepped forward to shake hands while we exchanged polite introductions.

Returning to his truck, he fought off dipping pine tree branches with one hand and loaded suitcases and boxes into the back as we talked.

Williams confirmed my two questions about the nonexistent new patent case, handing me an envelope containing written input and references to back up his confirmation.

"Thanks so much for this, and for agreeing to some GPR support for the other case I'm working on," I said.

"Yeah, about that. I've had a last-minute change in plans. I might have to leave y'all in the lurch if you need me after today," Williams said in his Southern drawl. "I just got the green light on a consulting gig in China, and I'll be gone the better part of two months. I'm catching a flight out of here late this afternoon."

"You're going to China today?"

A dusty-looking striped orange cat slinked out of the bushes and wound itself around one of his legs. He reached down to scratch its head, and I could hear its purr of contentment.

"Yep, but I still might be able to help you before I leave, depending on what you need. Chuck Grant said something about a dog buried on your friend's property that you need to find?"

He let the cat continue to rub against his legs and resumed loading his truck.

"Yes. My friend thinks her former renters poisoned their dog and buried it somewhere on the property so they wouldn't have to take it with them. She wants to take them to court for animal cruelty, if that's the case." My excuse sounded lame even to me, so I couldn't imagine what Williams thought. "Maybe you have a colleague who could help me, if you're going to be traveling."

Williams kept his back to me as he continued loading.

"Well, now, that might be a problem either way," he said, closing the tailgate and leaning against it as he wiped his hands on a towel. "You see, my colleagues and I don't have the actual GPR equipment. We usually have the dig we're working on rent it for us to use if it's necessary. It involves a lot of paperwork, expense and questions as to why we really need to use it."

He looked at me, his expression telling me clearly that he hadn't bought my story.

"Look, Dr. Williams. Using GPR on my friend's property may be a matter of life or death. I've got to prove that something is buried there, and I've got to do it right away."

"Something—or someone?"

"I can't tell you any more than I have in order to protect my friend and anyone else involved, including you."

He continued looking at me. I could almost hear his mind analyzing the situation.

"Well now, seeing as how my ass is on the line should someone trace what you're doing back to me, I need to know exactly what you need it for, or it's no deal."

So I told him, leaving out actual names.

The guy was unreadable, but my intuition told me to trust him. And as I heard myself pitch my case, it flowed logically and felt right. I finished, watching Williams' next move in silence, with fingers and toes crossed.

"Come with me," he said, walking toward a small, fenced yard next to the garage.

He whistled shrilly, and an old black-and-white border collie came bounding over to the fence where we stood. The dog sat and looked up at us, kicking up a cloud of dust with its tail.

"Hey, Poppy girl. Say hello to Norah. You're gonna work with her today," Williams said, reaching his right arm over the fence to scratch the dog's head, causing her to tremble with delight.

Giving me no time to react or even thank him, Williams filled me in on Poppy, a retired LAPD cadaver dog trained to nose out residual scents like dried blood.

Cadaver dogs were taught not to disturb the crime scene by digging or retrieving evidence. They would only alert to the presence of buried remains. They were also taught how to search a home or vehicle without causing harm to property, discriminating between live-human and cadaver scents, and between animal and human bones.

Poppy caught me staring at her and stuck her nose through a link in the fence, resting her snout on my right foot. I leaned down and scratched her head, and she licked my hand in appreciation.

"You've got until noon today to use Poppy for what you need."

He pulled a pack of Marlboros from his shirt pocket, shook out a cigarette and lit up.

Shrugging off my thanks, he handed me a sheet of instructions for how to handle Poppy and gave me a brief overview about the best way to get the results I needed.

"Remember now, you've only got Poppy for a couple of hours. Make it count," he said. "Oh, and we never met or had this conversation."

On the way to Olivia's house, with Poppy in the back seat of my Honda, I finished off two small bottles of Evian to settle my stomach and soothe my parched throat. I was heading toward a nervous breakdown thinking about all the things that could go wrong if my dog-handling session with Dr. Williams hadn't sunk in.

When under stress and in doubt, eat. So I pulled into a drive-through lane at a McDonald's, ordering large fries for Poppy and me.

We sat in the parking lot and ate in silence. My stomach felt like a churning pit of acid, although it had somehow told me that these greasy fries would calm it down. Surprisingly it worked. Poppy ate her share in a couple of gulps, licking her mouth and giving me a happy face. At least it looked happy to me. She was my responsibility, and neither Williams nor Chuck Grant, my former client, would ever forgive me if anything happened to her.

According to Poppy's bio, she had LAPD forensic evidence expertise that included locating cadavers, decomposing human scents and body fluids from deceased persons. These scents could be on an article of clothing, the actual body, in the ground, or residual.

She'd been a superstar in police detection circles before retiring. So, given all of that expertise, Poppy should have no problem locating Barry's body, provided it was there.

Poppy had settled on the back seat of my car, looking up at me with excitement whenever I glanced over my shoulder. I reached behind me and scratched her head, and she gave me a tiny woof. She seemed to hold her playful nature in check, as if she anticipated an upcoming search and was prepping for it. Or maybe she was bonding with my emotions, picking up on how nervous I felt and trying to calm both of us in case finding Barry Larsen's body turned out to be an on-target hunch.

"Show time," I said out loud, turning onto Olivia's street. I had to circle the block three times before finding the last parking spot in West Hollywood two blocks from Olivia's house.

Poppy strained on the leash as we made our way down the street, no doubt anticipating the important task ahead of us. Three or four other dog walkers passed us along the way. We exchanged the customary polite greetings and commented on the beauty of each other's dogs.

As I hit the end of the second block, a strange-looking guy who had glazed eyes and was wearing a cell-phone earpiece in one ear and an iPod bud in the other boogied past us down the street, singing to himself, before disappearing into the crowd on Sunset Boulevard.

Ducking into the alley that ran behind the houses along Olivia's street, Poppy and I came up to the side entrance to Olivia's property.

I opened the gate. The houses on either side were quiet and shuttered, and there were no gardeners, housecleaners or nannies in sight. Also, no black Beamer to alert Lohmand where I was and what I was doing.

Olivia had told me that she'd be at an appointment with her attorney at this time today. I checked my watch. She'd be away from home for at least two hours. That should give me plenty of time to search every inch of the house and surrounding property.

I'd borrowed Olivia's house key from Zulma, who was now doing a weekly cleaning gig for her. Pulling Poppy after me, we entered the back door of the house. I turned off the security alarm.

Poppy sniffed her way through every room and closet, her body tense with the hunt, her nose to all walls and floor boards. Nothing. No doubt, before Olivia had moved back into her house, Lohmand's cleaners and contractors had erased any traces of Larsen that Poppy might have picked up.

I led Poppy to the rear of the property and walked her around the perimeter. I started circling toward the middle edging, closer to where a patio and fountain were located. In front of the patio, Poppy stopped dead. Then she started making a continuous circle in front of the patio, and then on top of the cement slab. She made a digging motion on the slab, and then sat in "alert" position where she'd been sniffing and digging. Looking up at me, she gave two sharp barks. According to William's instruction sheet, Poppy had told me that she'd located buried human remains. I double-checked the results by having her twice verify that find, as well as those for dried blood and human bones.

"Way to go, Poppy," I said, scratching the top of her head and rewarding her with well-earned doggie treats from the supply Williams had stuffed into my jacket pocket. "It's got to be Barry Larsen, right, girl? This is where Zulma found his tennis pin."

Poppy continued to sit tight, beating her tail on the ground. Her expression was one of alertness and satisfaction at a job well done.

After making notes on Poppy's behavior, I took photos of the patio with a disposable camera I'd picked up at a CVS on my way to Williams' house.

This information had to get into the hands of someone who could do Lohmand damage before Lohmand could get to me. I called Nicolas Martell and my LAPD detective friend to alert them of my find. Neither one picked up the calls, so I left them urgent messages to contact me.

I stopped off at the public library on San Vicente and wrote up a detailed report, including input from Nicolas, Louise Larsen, testimony from Angela and Zulma, the GPR findings and Jimmy G.'s confirmation that someone at one of Lohmand's companies had hacked into Olivia's credit report.

Back in my car, I headed for the post office down the street, bought a large brown envelope into which I stuck the completed report and couriered the report, along with the tennis pin, to Nicolas' office. The ball was now in their court. I had to lie low until I got word that the final inning of the game was about to be played and Lohmand was behind bars.

Williams was waiting for me by his pickup when I dropped Poppy off.

"Find what y'all were looking for?" Williams asked when I'd handed him Poppy's leash and thanked him once again for his help.

"Yes. It was exactly where I thought, and Poppy did an amazing job of locating and describing what was there."

He grunted and gave a sharp whistle, to which Poppy responded by jumping into the back of the pickup.

"Just so you know," I said, as he headed for the front of the pickup, "this story is going to break big-time in the news within the next week or so when the police get the details of my report. Per our agreement, I've left Poppy and you out of it, but you could be tracked down just the same."

"Not likely to happen where I'm going in China. No electricity, no running water and no cell phones." He chuckled as he climbed into the driver's seat, then stuck his head out the window. "But you best be right careful, Norah. Whoever put that body there is not going to take kindly to you finding it."

That afternoon Steven and Zulma took me to my scheduled chemo treatment. Just after the nurse set me up with the IV and made me comfortable, Steven got up to use the men's room, leaving Zulma to watch over me. She started telling me about her latest romance, and then turned the focus on me.

"You know, Señora Norah, that Señor Nicolas is *un papi rico*. And he want you, but he no love you," Zulma astutely diagnosed my love life.

She was still determined to put a little romance in my life, with either Nicolas or Steven as the likely candidate. "Señor Steven is better for you. He love you and no hurt you never, I think."

"Maybe," I replied, wondering whether Gladys had gotten to Zulma without my knowing about it.

Zulma chattered on, instructing me as to why the "maybe" approach might not be enough of a commitment to keep someone like Steven in my life, until she noted that I was nodding off.

When both Steven and she stepped out of my room to get coffee, I dropped off to sleep.

Waking with a start at the sound of an angry male voice, I saw the blurred image of a man in a white coat pulling a syringe out of my IV bag.

His back was to me, and the IV bag was still half full. What was he doing?

"Doctor Díaz?" I mumbled, struggling to wake up.

I tried to see what he was doing by leaning to one side, nearly falling out of the chair. Dizziness forced me to sit back.

Gasping for air, I closed my eyes to bring the nausea under control.

"Dr. Díaz?"

"Son of a bitch!" he spat.

Ultra-polite Dr. Díaz would never say anything like that.

As I slowly leaned closer, the fuzzy profile cleared. It was Dr. Brent.

Sweat beaded his forehead as he struggled to poke the thin needle through the thick plastic of the IV tubing. He got it partially in and then pressed down on the plunger.

What was he doing? He wasn't my doctor.

Recollections flashed. Victor and Lydia Lohmand at the Breast Cancer fair. Lohmand and Brent knew one another. Lohmand asked

Brent who I was. Brent recognized me from the medical office. Lohmand then threatened Brent or paid him to . . . .

¡La puta! The guy was trying to kill me.

I reached out and grabbed hold of the back of his white coat.

Using what little strength I had, I threw my body back into my chair, pulling him away from the IV.

He stumbled, pulling out the syringe and dropping it, then cursing as it rolled under my chair.

"Help!" I screamed. "Someone help me!"

"Shut up!"

He spun, his face flushed with anger, and hit me full-force in the face.

I tasted blood as agonizing pain shot through my body.

Unable to move, I watched him fish the syringe out from under the chair, insert it into the IV tubing again and try to inject the remaining liquid from the syringe.

"Help!"

I couldn't reach him, nor did I have the strength to fight.

His attention was on the syringe. I edged my right hand over to pull out the IV needle.

Brent caught the motion and lunged for my hand. He pulled me toward him, ripping the IV needle from my arm.

I howled in pain, nearly losing consciousness.

Steven and Zulma burst through the door, their eyes wide, taking in the scene.

Blood ran down my chin and left arm onto my shirt and pants as I struggled against Brent's powerful grip on my wrists.

"*¡Maldito! ¡Asesino!*" Zulma screamed.

She threw her hot coffee at Brent and lunged at his face, baring her half-inch red-enameled nails.

Brent brought his hands to his face, screaming in pain from the hot coffee and scratches.

Six-foot, two-hundred-pound Steven decked the shorter, thinner Brent, while Zulma pounced on the doctor's legs to keep him from moving.

The syringe still dangled from the IV.

"Help! *¡Ay, qué horror!* Help!" Zulma yelled. "*¡Ay! Pobre Señora Norah.*"

"Norah, are you okay?" Steven said, looking up at me from the floor. "Talk to me, Norah."

Overwhelmed by pain and the effects of whatever had been in the syringe, I opened my mouth, but no words came out. I wanted to tell Steven that it was too late for me, and for us, as darkness sucked me under, leaving me with a final sense of pride and consolation that I'd had a hand in making it too late for Victor Lohmand as well.

The Skull of Pancho Villa

You've heard the story, maybe read something about it in the newspaper or a magazine. How Pancho Villa's grave was robbed in 1926 and his head taken. Emil Homdahl, a mercenary and pre-CIA spy, what they used to call a soldier of fortune, is usually "credited" with the theft. He was arrested in Mexico but quickly released because of lack of evidence—some say because of political pressure from north of the border. Eventually, the story goes, he sold his trophy to Prescott Bush, grandfather of you-know-who. And now the skull is stashed at a fancy college back east. The story has legs, as they say. There are Web sites about Pancho and his missing skull, and I heard about a recent book that runs with the legend, featuring Homdahl, a mystery writer, and a bag full of skulls, all the way to a bloody shoot-out ending. Haven't read it, so don't know for sure.

That's all bull, of course. Oh yeah, Villa's corpse is minus a skull, but Homdahl never had it, the poor sap. The thing is that everyone overlooks one detail. There was another guy arrested with Homdahl, a Chicano from Los Angeles by the name of Alberto Corral. I'm serious —you can look it up. He was quickly released, too, and then he disappeared off the historical page, unlike Homdahl, who apparently liked the attention and actually enjoyed his grave-robbing notoriety. Corral's role in the tale is given short shrift, something we Chicanos understand all too well. If he's remembered at all, it's as Homdahl's flunky, the muscle who dug up the grave or broke into the tomb, depending on the version of the story, and who was paid with a few pesos and a bottle of tequila while the gringo made twenty-five grand off old man Bush.

I know what you're thinking. Gus Corral is off on another wild hair, this time about his great-grandfather. And I could do that, easy. But that's not it. Whatever happened eighty years ago, happened. I don't know why Grandpa Alberto ended up with the skull and I don't care. No one ever told me how he was connected to Homdahl or

125

whatever possessed him to want to steal Pancho's head, and I don't expect to find out. All I know is that the skull has been taken care of by the Corral family for as long as I can remember. Wrapped in old rags and then plastic bags and stored in various containers like hatboxes, cardboard chests and even a see-through case designed for a basketball. Whispered about by the kids who caught glimpses of the creepy yellowish thing whenever the adults dragged it out, usually on the nights when the tequila and beer and whiskey flowed long and strong.

My grandmother Otilia sang to it, the "Corrido de Pancho Villa," of course. The tiny, dark old woman, hunched under a shawl and often with a red bandanna wrapped around her gray, fine hair, drank slowly from a glass of whiskey while she stared at the box that held Panchito—that's what she called it—for several minutes, and meanwhile all the kids waited for what we knew was coming. And then, without warning, Otilia would rip off the box, grab the skull, expose it to the light and simultaneously burst into weepy lyrics about the Robin Hood of Mexico. One of my uncles, also into his cups, would join in by strumming loudly on an old guitar. Shouts and whoops and *ay-ay-ays* erupted from whoever else was in the house and the little kids would scatter from the room, shrieking and crying, while us older ones were hypnotized by the dark eye sockets and crooked teeth of the skull of Pancho Villa.

You can imagine what a jolt it was when the skull was stolen from my sister's house.

Corrine—she's the oldest, and the flakiest—called me one night, around midnight. Not all that unusual, if you know Corrine. One crisis after another, I swear. One of her boys (they all got brats of their own, but Corrine still calls them her boys) needs to get bailed out and do I have about five hundred dollars? Or she slipped and banged up her knee and can't walk or drive and can I pick her up for bingo? Or the latest love of her sad life went out for a six-pack and hasn't come back, about a week ago, and could I go look for him?

I knew she shouldn't have the skull, but she is the oldest and when only the three of us remained—my younger sister, Maxine, is cute and naïve (I didn't say stupid), but that's another story—Corrine claimed rights to the skull and took it out of our parents' house before Max or I knew what was happening. Which was ironic. Corrine always said she hated that "disgusting *cosa*." But there she was, all over Panchito like he was gold. I kind of understood. Panchito was one of the few things our parents left us and just about the only connection we had to the old-timers of the family.

Anyway, Corrine is totally unreliable; maybe you picked up on that? I'm not perfect, no way, but at least I got a job, managing my ex-wife's *segunda* over on Thirty-Second. Six days a week, from opening at nine in the morning until Sylvia, the ex, shows up around two in the afternoon. I'm also the night watchman, which means I sleep in the place, so I don't have to worry about rent as long as I don't go back to the store until Sylvia leaves. Sylvia provides a cot, but she won't say more than two words to me even when she digs into the cash register and calculates my weekly pay. We both like it like that.

I argued with Corrine about Panchito. I pointed out that the parade of losers that camped out at her house were a major security risk. I added that I could keep the skull at Sylvia's shop. It would fit in with the musty junk Sylvia thinks are antiques, but she clutched that skull like it was a baby. It was clear that the only way I would get my hands on it was to rip it from hers, which I wasn't going to even attempt. Corrine has fifty pounds on me.

She had Panchito for about a year and I hadn't thought about it. The call woke me from a mixed-up dream. I crawled off my cot and answered the shop's phone.

"You got your nerve, Gus," she shouted over the line. "I can't believe you took it. What'd you do, pawn it for beer money?"

"What the hell are you screaming about? It's midnight, in case you didn't know."

I'm not quick with the comebacks with Corrine. She's always intimidated me that way, since we were kids.

"Panchito! Panchito!"

As if that explained everything.

A half hour later I had the story and she started to believe that I hadn't broken into her house and stolen the skull. She had come home from an evening with the girls—right—and found the back door wide open and a pair of her panties on the lawn. She freaked immediately and called the cops. She waited outside, not chancing that the intruder might still be inside. When the cops gave her the all-clear, she entered a house torn upside down and inside out. Her clothes were scattered everywhere, drawers were ripped from dressers, bowls of food dripped on the kitchen floor and a trail of CD cases snaked from her CD player to the useless back door. The final straw made her hysterical. A large wet stain of piss sat in the middle of her carpet.

Did she think I was really capable of that? I could see how she might be suspicious of me concerning the skull, but to trash her place and pee on her rug? Please.

The cops said that they couldn't find any evidence of a forced entry so they concluded that Corrine had left the back door open and one of the neighborhood kids probably saw it from the alley. A crime of opportunity, they told her. I can see her face when she heard that. She must have screamed that she was absolutely sure she had locked the door and then most likely she turned into a blubbery mess, but she was just covering. Corrine often forgot to lock up. Attention to detail never was one of her strong points. One time she came home and found a pot of beans completely black, the beans nothing more than a congealed mass, and smoke as thick as her chubby arms filling every room. A fire truck pulled up a few minutes later. It was months before the drapes and walls didn't smell like burnt beans. She told me she couldn't remember doing anything with beans, much less leaving the stove on. A classic bit of Corrine.

I had to agree with the cops. The way Corrine's house was wrecked and the stuff that was taken—CDs, video tapes, a jar full of pennies and a bag of potato chips—sounded like a kid's thing. But what the hell would he do with a skull?

Corrine never mentioned Panchito to the cops. She told me that she had him in a Styrofoam cooler at the back of her coat closet near the front door. The cooler was still in the closet, empty. The coats had been tossed on the front room couch and she guessed that the thief had taken the skull in one of the pillowcases missing from her bed. The cops said it was a tried-and-true method for burglars to haul away their booty in the vic's own pillowcases or trash bags.

I knew that the cops would never arrest anyone. We got so many unsolved break-ins on the North Side that the police will give you a number to use when you call in to ask about your case—they don't need your name or address, just your number. It's been that way for years, but the new mayor has promised to do something about the North Side crime rate, which means that City Hall is finally noticing all the young white couples with two big dogs and one little blond rug rat that have been moving into the neighborhood. Sylvia calls them yuppies, but I don't think anyone uses that term anymore, except Sylvia, I guess.

The next day after work I started asking around but I couldn't say too much. The Corral family hadn't exactly been up front about Panchito. We had assumed that possession of Pancho's skull was illegal, and that the desecration of the grave of a Mexican hero certainly wouldn't do anything for the family's reputation. Mexico could demand Panchito's return and the U.S. government could back away from us and might declare that we were as illegal as the skull and deport us, although Corrine, Max and I hadn't set foot in Mexico since we were infants, a trip we couldn't even remember. For two days I asked about any kids who had been trying to get rid of CDs that didn't seem right for them—Tony Bennett, Frank Sinatra, Miguel Aceves Mejía—and a jar of pennies. It was ridiculous, but what else is new in my life?

I asked old friends who still called me bro; I quizzed waitresses at a couple of Mexican restaurants. My questions made more than one pool player nervous; and the ballers that crowded the court at Chaffee Park swore they didn't know *nada*. (Those NBA wannabes wouldn't tell me anything, anyway.)

On the second day my search took me to the beer joints. It had to happen.

I got nothing from the barflies, naturally. They scowled like I had asked for money, never a popular question in any bar I'd ever been in, and a couple of the souses didn't even look at me when I spoke to them. I decided to take a break. Detective work had made me thirsty and the Holiday Bar and Grill always had very cold beer.

Accordion music blared in the background and a pair of muscular women wearing their boyfriends' colors played eight ball along a side wall. There were a couple of other guys at the bar, and the three of us were entertained by Jackie, the bartender who worked the afternoon—early evening shift at the Holiday.

Jackie methodically wiped a glass with a bright yellow bar rag and blinked her inch-long eyelashes at me. I worried for a hot sec that the weight of what looked like caterpillars sitting on her eyelids might permanently shut Jackie O's eyes, but it didn't seem to be a problem. Jackie O—that's what she wanted to be called, but I remembered when she was just plain old Javier Ortega, which, as you might guess, is another story entirely. I hardly ever used the O in her name; I just couldn't bring myself to say it. I had to comment about her outfit and headdress.

"Trying for the Carmen Miranda look today, Jackie?"

"Don't be foolish. These are just a few old things I had around the house. A summer adventure. You like?" She twirled and clapped her hands, kind of in flamenco style. The two guys down the bar gagged on their beer. I kept a straight face.

"Nice. That shade is good on you."

"What you been up to, Gus? I don't see you in here too much anymore."

"Same old, you know how it is." She nodded. "But Corrine got ripped off the other night, maybe you heard about it? They broke in her house and took a couple thousand dollars worth of stuff. At least that's what she told the insurance. Too much, huh? I'm trying to find out who would do such a thing, maybe get some of Corrine's stuff back. Maybe kick some ass." I threw that last part in, but I knew she knew it was just talk.

She almost dropped the glass. She turned away quickly and helped the two guys who couldn't seem to get enough of her show. I picked up a bad vibe off Jackie and it bothered me. We went back a long ways and I recognized her signals. I sipped on my beer and out of the corner of my eye I could see her looking at me through her heavily accessorized lashes. Again, I felt foolish. This was not like Jackie.

She reached under the bar and pulled out a bottle of what I was drinking. She opened it and brought it to me, although I hadn't ordered another.

"Let's have a smoke, Gus. I need one bad."

Now we had moved into strange. For one thing, Jackie knew I didn't smoke. For another, although the recent anti-smoking ordinance meant that all smoking had to be done outside the premises, I couldn't remember when that particular law had ever been enforced in the Holiday, especially during the afternoon–early evening shift when there wasn't anyone in the bar to speak of.

But I went with it. She snapped her fingers at the women playing pool. "I'll be right back, Lori," she shouted. "Come get me if anyone comes in."

One of the women shouted back, "Whatever."

I followed Jackie's sashaying hips into the alley.

She lit a smoke and dragged on it nervously. I waited. Like most of the women in my life, Sylvia being the prime example, Jackie loved drama. Jackie could emote, that's for sure.

When she finished sucking the life out of half the smoke, she whispered, "I shouldn't say anything. But we been friends forever, Gus. You backed me up when I needed it. You can't ever let on that you got this from me. I'll call you a damn liar. I mean it, Gus. You swear, on your mother's grave, Gus? On your mother's grave."

See what I mean.

Her face was lost in the twilight and the glowing tip of her cigarette didn't give off enough light for me to see how serious she was, so I took her at her word.

"Okay, Jackie. I swear. I never heard nothing from you. Which so far is the truth."

"Jessie Salazar was in last night."

I heard that name and I wanted a cigarette.

"I thought he was in the pen," I said. "Limon or Cañon City. Supermax."

"He was. Did five years, but he was here last night. I had to fill in for Artie—he got sick or something, or I wouldn't even know Salazar was around. He showed up with his old crew. All dressed up in a suit, smelling like Macy's perfume counter. Talking loud and stupid. Same old crazy Jessie. He said things about your family, and you. That chicken-shit stuff between the Corrals and the Salazars. He said the great payback had begun—that's what he called it—but that there was more hell to pay. He talks like that, remember?"

I felt like someone had punched my gut. I couldn't say anything.

"He never got over that Corrine testified against him," Jackie continued. "I didn't think anything about it last night. That happens in here all the time. Guys blow off steam then the next day forget all about it. More so if the guy just got out of the joint. But when you said someone had broken into Corrine's house, I got to thinking. Salazar's that kind of punk. He could have trashed Corrine's house, easy, but if he did, that's just the beginning. You got to tell her, and you got to watch your back, Gus. He always thought you should have stopped her, controlled Corrine. He blames you for him doing time."

Jackie stomped on her cigarette. I smiled weakly and walked away through the alley. I stopped and turned and waved at Jackie. "Thanks," I said.

"*Cuídate*, Gus," Jackie said. "Be careful."

Crazy Jessie had been my number-one life problem for most of my life. He was the school bully, then the neighborhood gangster and eventually he passed through reform school and the state penitentiary. I tangled with him several times when we were younger. My mother and his mother had been rivals when they were low-riding North Side women, and I had heard many stories about parties gone bad, fights in school yards and nightclubs. That nonsense just kept on when they had their own kids. Corrine and I often brushed up against Jessie and his brothers and sisters, not always coming out on top. But we held our own.

Corrine was having dinner one night about six years ago with the latest love of her life when Jessie stormed into La Cocina restaurant waving a handgun. He terrorized the customers, pistol-whipped the owner and took cash, wallets, purses and jewelry. That happened when Jessie was strung out bad on his drug of choice at the time. Corrine talked to the cops and fingered Jessie without hesitation, but her date denied recognizing the gunman. Hell, he wasn't sure that there had even been a disturbance, if you know what I mean. Didn't matter to Corrine. She gave Jessie to the cops and testified in court. I was proud of her but also a little bit nervous. We all relaxed when they turned Jessie over to the Department of Corrections. We thought he would be gone for a very long time. Five years didn't seem long enough, but then I never understood the so-called justice system.

I knew where to find Jessie. I just didn't know if I wanted to find him. I had to warn Corrine, and I gave serious consideration to forgetting about Panchito. I thought that the thug might leave us alone now that he had vented on Corrine's property and he had the skull. I could see him shaking his head about his discovery in Corrine's closet, thinking that the Corrals were way weirder than he had always assumed.

I tried to call Corrine on my cheap cell phone but the service was weak on the North Side, which meant it didn't do much for me. I got a busy signal, but that wasn't right. It should have gone to her voicemail.

Jessie's crib was in the opposite direction from Corrine. He had a small house on a hill that overlooked the interstate, right on the edge of the North Side where all the new condos were going up. Yuppie hell, Sylvia called it. The house had been the Salazar home forever and it had always been a dump. But with the wave of newcomers and the frenzy of construction, the shack must have doubled or tripled in value since Jessie had been sent away, although Jessie would never know what to do with that piece of information. One of his deadbeat sisters technically owned the place, but as sure as I knew that Jessie's urine had stained my sister's carpet, I also knew that he was living in that house.

Okay, right about now you're thinking, call the cops, Gus. Don't be a *pendejo*. Let the law handle it. But see, you don't live in my world, man. Where I come from, the cops aren't your first line of defense. You didn't grow up constantly squaring off against *cabrones* like Jessie. You never had to accept that every lousy week another clown would challenge your manhood and you would have to beat or be beaten. You never had to explain to your old man why your sister came home in tears and you didn't do a damn thing about the bastard who slapped her around. You never sat in a cell in the city jail staring down the ugly face of what your life could become if you didn't do the right thing.

I had to stop for gas and I used the restroom at the 7-Eleven. Stalling, for sure. It took me a while to make it to Jessie's, but eventually I was there.

I parked about a block away and did my best to be inconspicuous. Construction equipment was everywhere, and a few of the projects had crews working late, overtime. Steel beams stretched to the sky and white concrete slabs waited. I had played ball in these lots, had made out with girls and drank beer with my pals. No one who ever lived in the new buildings would know that or care about those things.

I made my way up the alley behind Jessie's house. I picked up a piece of rebar, two feet long, not thinking about how inadequate it was for the job I had to do. The night had a gray tint from the construction lights. Rap music blared from his backyard. I crawled behind a dumpster and peeked through the chain-link fence.

Jessie was sprawled on the dirt. An ugly hole in his head leaked blood and a messy soup of other stuff.

The guy standing over the body, holding a gun, looked like a junior version of Jessie, except he was alive. Another worthless gangbanger extracting his own revenge for whatever Jessie might have inflicted, maybe in that backyard that evening, maybe in a jail cell that was too small for the both of them, maybe years ago for something that Jessie wouldn't even remember.

I guess no one had heard the shot. The construction could have drowned it or the rap music might have covered up the crime. And sometimes gunshots have no sound on the North Side.

The guy spit on Jessie. He tucked the gun in the back of his pants and jumped over the fence. I inched closer to the dumpster, and my luck held. He walked the other way, whistling, if I remember right.

I swung open the gate and tried to sneak into the backyard. No one else was in the house. Whoever had capped Jessie would have made sure of that. I looked all over that yard, except at the oozing body at my feet.

Panchito perched on a concrete block. A lime-green sombrero with red dingle balls balanced on his slick, shiny head, and an unlit, droopy cigar dangled from his mouth hole. I was embarrassed for him. I removed the hat and cigar and picked him up. There was a dirty pillowcase on the ground. I wrapped Panchito in it.

It was a long walk back to my car and a long drive to Corrine's. I never heard any sirens, and no one stopped me. I drove in silence thinking about what had happened, trying to piece together coincidence and luck. I never thought so hard in my life.

My luck had been amazing and I toyed with the idea of going back to the 7-Eleven for a lottery ticket. But I wasn't the lucky type. Had never won anything in my life. I thought even harder about what had happened.

Corrine opened the door slowly. She let me in but didn't say anything. I set the bundle on her kitchen table.

She smiled.

"How'd you find out about Jessie? Who was that guy?" I blurted my questions as quickly as I could. I didn't want to give her time to make up something.

"You're the smart one. Figure it out yourself."

"Jackie. She called you, told you what she had told me. Said I was probably going over to Jessie's."

"Close. She said you were on your way to get killed by that son-of-a-bitch."

"And the guy? What's that all about?"

"You remember him. Charley Maestas. He lived here about six months, a while back. Too young for me, turned out. He owed Jessie for a lot of grief, something awful about his sister, but he had to wait for Jessie to do his time. I let Charley know that Jessie was out and where he could find him, and the rest was up to him. I said Jessie was getting ready to book so he had to deal with him tonight. I thought the least he could do was give you some help if you got over your head. I guess Charley took care of the whole thing?" She asked but she didn't really want an answer.

I shrugged. It turned out to be simple. Corrine and one of the loves of her sad life. North Side justice often is simple. Direct, bloody and simple.

My older sister picked up Panchito and gave him a quick wipe with the pillowcase. She carried him to the closet, dug out the cooler, placed the skull in it and shut the door.

As I walked out the back I hollered, "I like the new rug!"

Death, Taxes . . . and Worms

After smoothing out the imaginary wrinkles in her flower-print dress, Nellie Gallegos, the victim's elderly neighbor, peered through Coke-bottle glasses at the microphone in front her. She clutched a large black purse tightly to her chest as if it were a life raft. This was her first deposition, and she was ready. A young lawyer, the assistant district attorney, rummaged through papers in his briefcase. A paralegal made notes on a yellow legal pad. The attorney pressed the button to the recording device located on a shelf beneath the table. He cleared his throat and began the questioning.

"How long had you known the deceased, Mrs. Gallegos?"

She leaned forward, practically resting her lips on the microphone, her voice bouncing sibilant s's off the glass walls of the conference room. "*Miss* Gallegos," she said. "Don't get me wrong. I like men, especially if they're handy. You can never go wrong with a man who knows how to fix things, but usually they want you to fix them first . . ." She paused and thought for a moment. "I never found the time to get married." Nellie sat back in her chair, her chin raised to a defiant angle.

The lawyer rose, tightening his already thin lips, and moved the microphone further away from her. The paralegal tapped her pen on the notepad.

The assistant D.A. took a seat again and spoke slowly, enunciating carefully. "Yes, well, *Miss* Gallegos, but how long—"

"My hearing is good, young man, in both English and Spanish. I know my neighbors. Dick made it big in the office products biz. Before the Web, there was Dick—"

"You're referring to the deceased, Richard Metcalf, when you say Dick?"

"That's who's dead, isn't it? Poisoned, cut up like *chorizo* and stuffed in a trunk, then dumped in Lake Wasaka?" Her magnified eyes swept from the microphone to the lawyer.

"Yes, ma'am. Just making it clear for the record that you're referring to Richard Metcalf—Dick—who lived next door to you, for how many years?"

Nellie glared at him for a moment longer, then focused once again on the microphone, as if it had asked the question. "Like I was trying to tell you, Dick was my friend, and he had big ideas. He was way ahead of the average *pendejo*. He sold paper and ink, direct mail order before the Web got popular. I have a computer," she said, "and I know how to use it."

She stopped and took a sip of water, staring at the lawyer with rheumy eyes over the rims of her glasses. Nellie patted her thin gray hair—she'd made a special trip to the salon for this appointment—in a bored manner and leaned toward the microphone again. "Speaking of the Web, it's not what it used to be."

The prosecutor opened his mouth to speak, but something shifted behind the thick lenses of Nellie's glasses—a minute tightening—and he thought better of it. "Yes, ma'am," he agreed. He turned his head slightly toward the paralegal, who raised her eyebrows. As though an unspoken message had passed between them, they both settled back to listen to her story. "Yes, ma'am," he said again. "Tell me about Dick."

Nellie nodded, struggling to get as close to the microphone as possible. "When Office Depot bought him out, he and all of his top management were in the money—millionaires. He lost some things along the way. Got a divorce, lost custody of his children—but he never forgot his roots. By the time he met Betty, he'd decided to slow down, enjoy the time he had left. He was older than her by a good twenty years. She's a good-looking girl. Quiet, but those are the ones to watch out for. They got thoughts that aren't for sharing. He met her at the library, where she was reading books on old furniture. He set her up in the antique business; made her dreams come true. He wanted to stay home and tend to his garden, cook dinner for Betty and chew the fat over the fence with me." She looked at the lawyer. "I live next door, you know?"

"Yes, ma'am," the prosecutor said. "Betty is Mrs. Metcalf, the victim's wife?"

Nellie nodded, resting her eyes on the microphone again. "Yesiree. Now you're cooking with gas. She was his wife. He married her, all right. Before they moved in, four, no, almost five years ago. And she's the one who killed him. Hope you got her locked up tight!"

The lawyer revealed no emotion but said, "I'm interested in hearing more on that"—he held up his hand when he saw Nellie move toward the microphone—"but first, tell me: what was their relationship like, Mr. and Mrs. Metcalf's?"

"When I got to know him, Dick was easygoing, always available for a cup of coffee. We shared recipes, and I even gave him my secret formula for growing the sweetest tomatoes. I eat at least one tomato a day, and I never get sick. See, you just combine good old compost with coffee grounds, and . . . well, I've said too much already. Dick is the only other person who knows that formula, and he's dead."

She turned her convex glare from the microphone to the attorney. He curled his toes and tightened his rectum to keep from talking. He forced himself to relax, sinking into his chair. Just trading stories with the old girl, he thought. Keeping her talking.

"He was going to market that formula, Dick was. Had the plans all drawn up. Said we'd be millionaires." Nellie shook her head. "Well, one of us would be, anyway." She frowned at the microphone, and slumped a little, lost in her own thoughts.

The attorney cleared his throat. "And you think you know who did it?"

Nellie looked up, startled. "Who stole the formula?"

The attorney blinked hard, confused. "No, ma'am. I thought you gave the formula to him?"

Nellie laughed, a nervous twitter that made the attorney uneasy. "Well, of course I did," she said, "and Betty knew all about it, too. She was real excited about being a millionaire again. They'd lost some of Dick's money with his speculating, you see. He said Betty'd be a big help. That was before he met Joan."

Nellie turned back to the microphone, straining to get close to it, her voice booming, causing the attorney and paralegal to flinch. "I couldn't see how, myself. Betty might have known old furniture and such, but the girl didn't have a lick of common sense. I don't know what Dick saw in her. Well, now, hold on there, Nellie old girl, you may be over the hill, but you can still remember where the oats are kept. It was sex, pure and simple. S-E-X. It'll get 'em every time. Men, I mean. And in that regard, Dick was the same as them all. S-E-X is what got him to Betty, and S-E-X is what got him to Joan."

The lawyer and the paralegal exchanged quick glances. Nellie caught their look, and corrected herself. "Well, that's not everything. I'm leaving out money and taxes. Anyway, I bet I knew more about him than she did."

"By she, you mean Joan Archuleta, the IRS agent?"

Nellie fixed him with an impatient glare. "No, I mean Betty, his wife. An audit doesn't take that much time. Even I know that, and he could have had his accountant take care of it. But Dick took a personal interest in handling the matter himself after he met Joan. Soon, she was traveling to his house, and staying the whole afternoon." Nellie sat back in her chair, and frowned at the microphone. "He wasn't seeing to business."

"The formula?"

"He stopped tending to his garden, even let some tomatoes rot on the vine!" she said. "It just wasn't like him, and it could mean only one thing. S-E-X." Nellie squeezed her hands together, the knuckles pale with her anger and indignation. "Next thing I hear, Joan's handling the business, and I got nothing to do but wait for the contracts. He promised me . . ." She stopped, and she laughed again. "Well, business does take time."

"Where was Betty during . . . this period?" the lawyer asked.

"At her antique store. Busy as a bee, and neglecting the hive at home." A twitch at the corner of Nellie's mouth could have been the beginning of a smile. "Like any wife, she's entitled to a change, do something different and come home early." Nellie sighed. "I wasn't home that day and missed the fireworks."

The lawyer sat up, alert. "She found Dick and Joan together?"

Nellie's head tilted up and down, the light from the windows reflecting off her thick lenses like angled daggers. "That was the day Betty tore all his tomato vines down. He was upset and invited me over for coffee. He told me what I already suspected about Joan, and that Betty had walked in on them. *In fragrante*, Dick said. That means naked." Nellie lowered her eyes, and smoothed her dress down again.

In flagrante delicto, the lawyer jotted down. "Why destroy the tomatoes?"

Nellie shrugged. "Can't answer that one. He was upset, though. He'd asked Betty for a divorce, but she said no. He wasn't sure what she was going to do, but he'd seen a side of her that had scared him."

Nellie nodded her head in rhythm to her words. "Yesiree, the man was spooked."

"Betty threatened him?"

"He wasn't afraid for himself. It was Joan he was worried about. He asked if he could give my telephone number to her, in case she needed to reach him. The next morning, I found a note on my door saying he and Betty had gone off fishing together." Nellie's spectacles flashed toward the lawyer. "That sent a cold chill down my back."

"It was unusual for them to go off together?"

Nellie edged closer to the microphone but kept her eyes on the lawyer. "You might want to take this down." She waited for him to pick up his pen. "I got one word for you. Bait." She leaned back in her chair, satisfied.

"Bait?" the lawyer said, his voice squeaking.

"B-A-I-T," Nellie said. "Worms. I know for a fact the man despised worms." She nodded her head once, as if that was the final word. The lawyer wrote *worms* on his yellow pad.

"I'm sorry, Miss Gallegos, but what—"

"I'm telling you he hated them . . . scared the bejesus out of him." Nellie crossed herself. "I can explain later, if you like. And nothing could pull Betty away from her antique store, much less the idea of cleaning fish. Sure enough, she came back from their trip, but Dick was nowhere in sight. A few days passed, and still no Dick. Joan called me, looking for him. And she wasn't cool and calm the way an IRS agent is supposed to be. They're related to the FBI and CIA. Must get some special training? I asked her about the contracts, and she said I'd be paid for my 'input.' As if I was nobody, as if I hadn't invented the formula, as if I hadn't met Dick first. 'Input this!' I said, and hung up." Nellie sat back in her chair, huffing.

The lawyer wrote *contract* on his legal pad. "You still hadn't received the contract?" he asked.

Nellie straightened her back, and looked right at him. "No, sirree, I had not. And I wasn't a fancy consultant, either. It was *my* formula, made up by me, and only me. Me and Dick were partners till . . ." She pursed her lips in a tight O, hundreds of wrinkles gathering there like a drawstring purse.

"Until?"

"Until he showed up dead, of course," she said.

The lawyer glanced at his notes. "You went to the police because of the worms?" He sounded tired.

"The worms were the giveaway. I know what those policemen thought when I told them my suspicions." Nellie tapped the side of her head. "They thought I had the H-O-T-S for Dick. I may know where the oats are kept, but I changed my diet a long time ago. Betty beat me to the punch and had already been to the police to file a missing person's report. She told them she and Dick had come back early because Dick had an appointment with the IRS. Hmphh! That threw me off some, but I knew what I had to do, and who I was dealing with. I went right out of that police station and directly to this place Dick had told me about: Surveillance and Security. I bought videotape equipment, night-vision goggles and a rod and reel with a voice-activated tape recorder built into it." Both the lawyer and the paralegal appeared frozen, concentrating on the old lady sitting in front of them.

"That night, after I was sure Betty was home, I went over there and asked her to show me how to attach the reel to the rod. She just stood there in the doorway, and laughed right in my face. She said she didn't know anything about fishing, that she'd left the whole thing up to Dick. I asked her what kind of bait they'd used. Well, worms, she said.

"'Hmphh!' I said. Did she know that Dick's father had died because of worms? And a slow, ugly death it was, witnessed by Dick when he was a boy. That kind of thing stays with you for life." Nellie crossed herself again. The lawyer and the paralegal couldn't resist another quick glance at each other. The paralegal covered her mouth with her hand and focused on her yellow legal pad. "Well, that got Miss Prissy, and she slammed the door in my face, but now she knew that I knew. And that meant I was next in line."

The lawyer took a deep breath. "I'm sorry, Miss Gallegos, I'm not quite getting the connection—"

Nellie's magnified eyes, like a Halloween disguise, focused on him.

"Hold on. I'm getting there. I couldn't sleep that night. About 2:00 a.m., I heard rustling in my garden. The possums sometimes root around down there, but I was ready for them . . . and her. I caught her red-handed with my night-vision equipment, using a syringe to inject my prize tomatoes with poison. She knew I'd go out in the morning and pick one for my breakfast. She just didn't know which one." Nellie crossed her arms in front of her, shaking her head with disbelief. "I knew she'd come after me, but to use my tomatoes . . . ."

The paralegal passed a note to the lawyer. "The lab has your tomatoes," he said.

"*All* of them," Nellie practically shouted. "The police took *all* of them after I caught Betty and called them. You found the same poison in the pieces of Dick, I bet." She wasn't asking a question.

He cleared his throat. "We haven't found the syringe, and right now it's your word against Mrs. Metcalf's that she poisoned your tomatoes."

"You're forgetting my video camera. The tape caught her red-handed. She poisoned my tomatoes. Just like she done to Dick."

"The camera malfunctioned. The tape shows something moving around your garden, but it's not clear what or who it is. The lab is working on it."

"Did—" Nellie began a question, but the attorney interrupted her.

"Did Mr. Metcalf borrow money from you?"

"How did you . . . well, I might have lent him a bit."

The paralegal handed the attorney another file. "Our records indicate that you had an annuity in the amount of one hundred thousand dollars?" He looked up at Nellie.

She nodded. "Left to me by my mother."

"Which you cashed in seven months ago. A deposit in a similar amount is shown in Mr. Metcalf's account. This is a separate account from his household one with his wife. Another major deposit followed six months later, eventuated by . . . " He turned to the paralegal who produced yet another folder. "Ah, yes, by the sale of one Millennium Tomato Formula to the Bandini Fertilizer company in the amount of . . . let's see, I just saw this." His finger swept down a row of figures. Nellie sat forward. "Ah, here it is: $1,750,000. The royalties to be paid out of gross sales, etc." He looked up, pleased, his finger still resting on the ultimate figure.

"He got the money, then," she said, dully.

The lawyer thumbed through the folders again. "I don't see any checks made out to you."

"I didn't get mine yet. I'm guessing the estate will settle up once the trial is over and Betty is sent up. How long do you think it'll take?"

"Depends. You never had a contract with Mr. Met–"

"But Betty promised she'd pay what was owed." Nellie loosened her hold on the purse she'd had a death clamp on and pulled out an envelope. "I got a contract with her." Inside the envelope was a hand-written note on lined paper promising to pay Nellie Gallegos one-half of any proceeds from the sale of her Tomato Formula. It was signed by Betty Metcalf. The lawyer checked the date.

"This was signed the day before the Metcalfs left on their fishing trip."

"Was it?" Nellie said.

"Didn't she think her husband would pay?"

"Not once she saw him cheating like he was. She didn't believe me, but when I called her. . ." The laugh, now a nervous cackle, came once again.

"You called her at her place of business when you knew Joan was next door with Dick. That's why Betty showed up unexpectedly and caught them?"

"Well, yes," she said with a cackle, "I did. We girls got to stick together."

The attorney stared at her, but said nothing.

"It just wasn't right what he was doing." Nellie sat forward, this time ignoring the microphone and looking directly at the lawyer. "Betty thought so, too. She said it was probably Joan's idea to sell the formula without telling me about it."

"He'd sold it without telling you, yet you found out about it before he died?"

"Betty told me. She was as surprised as me that Dick hadn't told me. At least, she acted surprised. In the end, I guess you could say all four of us knew about the sale."

"But only you and Betty knew that you knew, and she promised to pay you." The room was silent except for the hum of the tape recorder. "Was that right after she caught them together?"

Nellie nodded vigorously. "Oh, yes. She came right over. Crying and helpless like always." Nellie took a deep breath, and clamped her lips tight again.

"So you were not away from home the afternoon Betty walked in on Dick and Joan? You were at home, and you called Betty?"

Nellie nodded, sheepish. "Yes, it's embarrassing, my part in that. I knew what they were doing."

"Betty had come to your house before, upset?"

"Tears come easy to that girl. She's got no backbone. Well, I guess she had spine enough to cut the man up. That was surprising."

"Did you and Betty draw up a contract that night?"

"Pardon?"

"The contract? Between you and Betty? Was it signed before or after you suspected he might try to cheat you out of your share?"

"Well, I guess you got it there, and you got eyes to read. I wasn't born yesterday, and I sure wasn't going to get cheated out of what was rightfully mine, listening to some pot-bellied, sweet-talking, over-the-hill salesman who'd cheat his grandma out of her last crumb. Listen, I don't mean to speak ill of the dead, but a single girl has got to look out for herself. And I said as much to Betty, tried to put a little spine into the girl, put a little too much by the looks of it, and she done him in. With the poison. Same as she planned on doing me in. So she could keep all the money."

"Your tomatoes weren't poisoned, Miss Gallegos."

"They . . . I told you I caught her red-handed!"

"There was nothing in the syringe."

"You said you hadn't found the syringe."

"Betty still had it. She hadn't buried it like you told her to after the two of you murdered Dick. And she wore gloves the night you were videotaping her. There's only one set of fingerprints on the syringe. Yours."

Nellie stood up, not much taller standing than sitting. "He stole my formula for prize tomatoes and never looked back! A man shouldn't be able to get away with that."

"So you poisoned him and cut him up?"

Nellie sat down again, and smoothed the imaginary wrinkles out of her flower-print dress. "The ax job was Betty's doing. You really have to watch out for those quiet ones, you know?"

Under the Bridge

"Chico, wake up," he said, a voice from somewhere in the dark.

"Huh?" I said. "What?" I opened my eyes.

"Get up," Nicky said, flipping on the light. Nicky was full-grown at fifteen, tall, and built to give or take a punch easily. He wore his blue Catholic-school uniform and red tie. His cotton shirt was unbuttoned. The image of a cross was stitched on the front pockets of both the jacket and shirt, just above his heart.

"Partner," he said. "I need your help."

"What's happening, Nicky?"

"Brother," he said, grabbing the *Black Panther* comic book. "You and me are going on a trip."

"Longwood? The movies? What time is it?"

"Man," said Nicky. "Just get dressed and come on."

I forced my exhausted body out of bed. For a moment, I stared at myself in the full-length mirror that was nailed to the door of my dorm room on the top floor of St. Mary's Home for Boys. The push-ups were working. I looked at least twelve, maybe even thirteen.

"What're you doin'?" asked Nicky.

"Nothin'!"

"Get dressed."

I got out of bed and dressed as if my butt was on fire. I would not miss Nicky's adventures for anything—not for comic books, not for movies, not for Saturday morning cartoons, not even at the cost of being grounded for a week by Father Gregory.

Nicky and me were two of the twelve members of the "Dirty Dozen." The first rule of the Dirty Dozen was adventure, the second rule was adventure and the third rule was not to eat yellow snow.

After that, there weren't many rules. But we did practice helping old ladies across the street and saving cats stuck in trees, along with boxing at the Fort Apache gym on One Hundred Forty-Ninth Street and kung fu at Tiger Chang's studio on Fordham Road. Nicky was almost a black belt. I was almost able to get up the long flight up to the studio without running out of breath.

"C'mon!" yelled Nicky.

We snuck down the hall, across the red carpet, past the giant cross and cuckoo clock, while Brother Andrew slept in his room, tired out from the daily headache of trying to watch over, guide, teach and control over a hundred of us orphaned Catholic boys. The sound of late-night Yankee baseball on the activity room's TV competed with Brother Andrew's hard snores.

We opened the large wooden doors of the Home, and Nicky and I ran down Brook Avenue. I followed him into the heat and dark. Side by side we ran, dodging traffic, past the horns blowing and brakes screeching, past the disapproving stares of grown folks talking and drinking, playing cards or dominoes under street lamps that bled light into the tenements, where salsa and soul music sang out and TVs blared, past the windows of Mimi's Cuchifrito, to the 6 train.

First, Nicky and then I hopped the turnstile and took the subway to Whitlock Avenue. We walked along Bronx River Avenue to the fence that blocked the entrance to the train tracks at the dark dead end of the street.

We jumped the fence, climbed down the far side of a boulder-strewn gully and over a stretch of grass, through a small meadow choked with trees. Down to the tracks that gleamed like gold bars in the moonlight, a gold road leading to our hidden place—a bridge above the face of the Bronx River.

Our feet made the tracks ring. We hiked until we reached the bridge, lit up in the night. Down below it, the water shone black between the chinks in the ties. I kicked loose a spike, and it dropped into the water.

Nicky led the way down to the belly of the bridge, the underside of this iron dragon, which was our clubhouse.

"What's going on, Nicky?" I said. "We gonna fight some kids?"

"No." Nicky smiled.

I looked at the dark night, where crickets chirped and lightning bugs blinked around us. "I'm not afraid," I said.

Nicky squeezed the back of my neck.

"Nobody said you was."

Soon we were creeping down the red ladder at the side of the bridge.

I peered over Nicky's shoulder. Two girls sat on the ground with flashlights: Nicky's girlfriend Doreen and her sister Monica, a younger version of Doreen with a camera around her neck. They sat on a jumble of stolen bed sheets amid a surprise picnic of chocolate cake, Coca-Cola and oranges. A small portable radio.

"It's me, Doreen," she said, waving me in like a welcomed guest of honor.

"Don't be afraid!" I yelled down. "It's just us!"

"I'm not afraid!" Monica yelled back up.

We all sat under the bridge on the sheets, sweating and staring into a little fire that Nicky made, pretending that nothing would happen, none of us doubting that something would and that I was just some kinda babysitter for Monica.

Monica started reading aloud from a book called *Aesop's Fables*. She looked so much like Doreen. I refused to smile and make friends with her. Instead, I thought, I'd insult her, say something clever, break away clean and eat cake and drink Coca-Cola in the moonlight all by myself.

Doreen snapped on the radio, and Marvin Gaye sang "How Sweet It Is." She and Nicky began to dance. Doreen had been Nicky's girl for a year. She was a big, graceful, lipsticked girl shaped like a guitar. She was extremely pretty, with her neat Afro and wet, warm, dark eyes. She had the loose and watery moves of a dancer in her short black skirt. She knows all the right moves, I thought as she twirled.

"That's right, baby," said Nicky, and put his hands on her hips.

Monica stood and looked at me as Doreen and Nicky danced.

"May I help you?" I said. "Did you lose something? Like your manners? It's not polite to stare at people."

"Why are you so mean to me?" asked Monica.

I looked away from Monica's face, at Doreen and the way her shoulders sloped, at her tight black skirt and black stockings. I studied the back of her head and her neck. I liked how white her teeth were when she smiled, her plump dark-brown legs. Her flat belly showed between her blouse and skirt. I liked Doreen, and liking her made me feel strange.

"Why you lookin' at my sister like that?" said Monica.

"They're my eyes," I said. "I look at whoever I want."

I bugged my eyes out at Monica and saw her for the first time. Monica was dark and pretty, with deep browns like her sister's. She wore blue shorts, and she hovered over me like a ghost with that damn camera. I was eleven, and she was thirteen. An older woman.

"I love you, girl," said Nicky.

"Say it again," said Doreen.

"I love you."

A wet wind with the feeling of violence blew through the trees that shaded the bridge. And Nicky and Doreen danced, and Monica said, "Hey, Chico!"

Just then Nicky and Doreen stopped dancing, and Nicky moaned and sighed heavily. He had his arm around Doreen, and he pressed against her and kissed her. One of Nicky's hands went inside her blouse. She didn't seem frightened. Then his hand was on her leg and started to move up. Nicky held Doreen, and Doreen whispered, "Come on, sweetie." And Nicky said to me, "You keep Monica company and watch the fire," and he steered Doreen behind a concrete wall. The river rose higher and higher as Frank Sinatra sang "When a Man Loves a Woman."

"What do you think of this music?" said Monica.

"I hate it," I said. "Except for that, it's great."

Something about the whole scene made me want to raise my voice. I wanted to grab the radio and throw it into the river.

Monica stood up suddenly. She went over by the wall and watched Doreen and Nicky through splayed fingers. I had no idea what she was watching. I heard low moans and cries coming from behind the wall.

I turned my back, pretending an interest in the river. It lay raw at my feet, a crust of hard water. It was alive. The trees were alive, too. They sat in the distance and waited and watched, like patient vultures.

Soon I was creeping behind Monica. Cautiously I peered over her thin shoulder, pressed up close behind her.

"They're in love," Monica said.

Nicky and me went back under the bridge a week later to meet up with Doreen and Monica, so Nicky and Doreen could be in love, and me and Monica could watch the fire. That's when I saw it. No, her, floating in the river. At first I thought she was garbage. Then I thought she was a dead dog. But she wasn't. She was a dead girl. I could see her face, and I could tell that she had not been in the water long. Nicky jumped in and pulled her out.

Her name was Doreen.

Doreen. She was my first.

Years later, a slow, hot Tuesday night at Arthur's Bar and Grill. The customers weren't special people; their dreams were little dreams. The booths were full of men and women who worked just hard enough to afford to shop at a bodega. They ruined their minds with liquids and powders and violence that almost made them forget.

Then there was Tomás, who worked as a doorman in Manhattan. He wore a motorcycle jacket, a white T-shirt, and jeans. A forty-eight-year-old weekend warrior on his motorcycle. Tomás had been coming to Arthur's since forever. Everybody liked Tomás.

Everybody but me. I was just pretending to like Tomás. I had also been pretending to be the new bartender at Arthur's Bar and Grill for nearly a month.

My name is Chico Santana. I'm a private investigator. First off, I'm a nice guy. My wife Ramona says so, and she's part Haitian *and* part Dominican, so it must be true.

If you look closely at my nose, you can tell it's been broken twice. And if you pay attention to word on the street, you'll come to understand that the men who broke my nose are no longer eating anything that won't flow up a straw. I'm not a tough guy. A lot of tough guys are six feet under. I'm just lucky.

And I'm also not one of these PIs that sit at a desk with his feet up, waiting for his bosses at St. James and Company to throw him a bone. Nor am I one of those types who are always bragging how close they can come to your chin without hitting you. I have no .38, but I do have a license to bust your ass, and if I have to, I will bust your ass and maybe even the ass of somebody you love.

"What can I do you for, big man?" I asked.

"Big man?" said Tomás, seated on a tall stool. "Did you just call me big man? Yeah, okay, I've put on some weight."

He slapped his big belly like a drum. "Fucking diets. They don't work. Fucking wife and her greasy lamb chops. I'm weighing two-fifty now. But I'm *almost* six feet, so it's not that bad, right?"

"No comment," I said, wiping the bar.

Tomás laughed and slapped the bar. "You won't believe this, Chico," he said. "You love movies, right? One of my so-called biking buddies invited me over to his apartment on Southern Boulevard to watch a movie with his old lady."

"What an animal," I said.

"Animal is right," said Tomás, massaging his thick face with a massive hand. "I need women and money. I'll even settle for food—a steak and some rum. Fuck movies!"

Tomás put his hand up to his ear, and said, as if speaking into a phone, "A movie? Sure, buddy. How about never? Is never good for you?" Then he made as if he were hanging up the phone and said, "Click!" And he laughed like it was the funniest thing in the world.

"Oh!" I announced, pointing at my face. "Did you notice? I got my glasses back!"

I don't need to wear glasses. My vision is perfect. 20/20. But that comes later.

"Great!" said Tomás.

"I just had the lenses on an old pair replaced and tinted," I said. "I picked them up last week."

"They look good on you, Chico."

"Thanks," I said.

"How did you break them again?"

"Girl," I said. "She stepped on 'em." Pause. "By mistake."

An effeminate dude in yellow shorts walked in, swaying his hips. I shook my head. "Disgusting."

"He probably knits," Tomás agreed.

"Truth?" Tomás said. "I think my oldest kid is a fag."

"Serious?"

"Yeah," said Tomás. "If I catch that kid watching the Bravo channel one more time, I'm gonna kill him."

I gritted my teeth and laughed. I let him talk. Tomás loved to talk: "That's what I like about you, Chico. You're not some cheap seal at the zoo who claps every time someone throws it a fish. You have a mind of your own. I wish you were my kid."

I poured myself and Tomás a couple shots, and we clinked glasses and slammed them back.

"Amen," I said. "Are you my father?"

Tomás laughed. "You joke. But I'm telling you. I got lazy fucking kids. The dog needs a license, right? Ten bucks. You think it would kill 'em to get down to the ASPCA? One's a communications major at Lehman College. I'm paying out of my ass so that she can learn to communicate?"

"What the fuck is that?" I agreed, pouring him another shot.

"Read, write, speak," said Tomás agreeing with my agreement. "That's shit she shoulda learned in high school. Waste of fucking money. The other kid? Let's not even talk about him. He's probably a fag, like I said. When the facts come in, when there's confirmation he is a homo, I will deal with it. In my way. Let his mother even try to stop me. I'll take care of her ass, too. Some people gotta learn the hard way."

"I hear you," I said, pouring him another shot. "Did I tell you? I met two chicks here last week. Tourists. They gave me their numbers and everything, and I hooked up with one."

"Must be the glasses," said Tomás and laughed.

I laughed too. "Get this," I said. "I'm meeting them again tonight."

"Hot?"

"Beautiful," I said. "Two beauties. Straight out of those American Apparel ads. Young."

"How young?"

"Eighteen," I said. "Legal."

"Nice," said Tomás and gave me a high five.

"Dumb as rocks too," I said. "I like me some young, beautiful, dumb girls."

"Who doesn't?" said Tomás, excited, and drummed the bar. "Black or white?"

"One is black and one is white," I said. "From Peru."

"You lucky son of a bitch!" said Tomás as I poured him yet another shot.

I slowly scanned the vaulted brick ceiling and the empty tables and chairs and measured the distance between me and a kitchen knife as Tomás sat there on his wooden stool, lips smacking.

He was doing the math. Me and two girls. He was thinking.

Later that night, after my shift, I stepped out into the street. Outside, on the corner of Bronx River Avenue sprinkled with housing projects and three-story red-bricks, the sun was down, but the night was humid. It felt heavy on my skin.

As I started to walk, I saw Tomás rush out of the bar. He slowed when he saw me. "Hey, kid!"

Tomás lit a Marlboro and offered me one. I took it. Ramona wouldn't be thrilled about me smoking, but you did what you had to do. Couldn't break my rhythm with the suspect. Keep telling yourself that, Santana, and maybe one day you'll believe it.

I scanned Tomás' motorcycle goggles with their giant gold frames, baggy blood-red sweatshirt, drooping jeans, black motorcycle boots and ridiculously oversized gold chain with a gold cross and the letter T dangling from it. Classy.

"Where you goin' to meet those girls?" he asked.

"Under the bridge," I said, and took a deep draw on the cig.

"What bridge?" Tomás asked.

"Over the Bronx River. I got everything set up and waiting. Music. Booze. Blankets. Just like when I was a kid. All the kids used to go there. Ever been?"

Tomás puffed on his cigarette. "No. Why don't you take 'em to a hotel?"

"Nah," I said. "This is exciting. This girl's a freak. She likes it outdoors."

"Wow," said Tomás. "Lucky son of a bitch!"

"Yeah," I said, walking toward the bridge. "Night, Tomás."

"I'll walk witcha," said Tomás, dumping his Marlboro. "Wait up for me. I can use the exercise."

I looked at Tomás, and said as if it had just occurred to me: "You wanna meet these girls?"

Soon we were jumping the fence, climbing down the far side of the gully and over the stretch of grass, through the small meadow choked with trees. Down to the tracks that gleamed like gold bars in the moonlight.

We ran along the tracks in the dark.

Our feet made the tracks ring as we hiked until we saw the bridge.

We climbed down the red ladder.

I had set up bed sheets and two bottles of rum and a large portable radio.

"Welcome to Chez Chico," I said.

"What's on the menu?" asked Tomás.

"Long legs of lambs," I said.

We sat under the bridge. I was pretending that nothing would happen, checking my watch, knowing that something would. We told jokes, and I fed Tomás a whole bottle of rum; he downed glass after glass and made witty remarks about his wife's weight.

Classy, sober *and* drunk.

The radio played some Celia Cruz, some Big Daddy Kane; I started humming when Percy Sledge's "When a Man Loves a Woman" came on.

Finally, I shut off the radio and said, "Where the hell are they?"

"Maybe they got lost."

I stood up and whipped my glasses off and let them slip out of my hand and drop into the river.

"Shoot!" I yelled.

Tomás started laughing. "Oh, shit!"

"Don't laugh!" I said. "Those were new glasses! That's my second pair this year!"

"What happened to the first pair?"

Attention. Captain. We got fish. I took a long pause. "Girl broke 'em. I told you."

"I know." Tomás laughed. "Why did the girl break your glasses?"

I took a longer pause.

"I'll tell you a secret if you promise never to tell anybody."

"What?" asked Tomás.

I looked away dramatically. "I killed a girl."

"Say what?" said Tomás.

Silence.

"I killed a girl," I said, slower this time. "The girl who broke my glasses."

I waited. Nothing. After a month, I had thought this was my night. I thought I had him. Maybe I was wrong.

I felt Tomás slipping from my line.

Then I heard him sigh deeply behind me, and I turned. "Shit, man," he said, and started laughing drunkenly.

"I'm not joking, Tomás. I killed a girl."

"I'm not laughing at that," he said.

"What are you laughing at?" I asked, and I sat back down and twisted the cap off a second bottle of rum.

Tomás passed a thick hand over his face. "This is like a dream, Chico."

"What?"

"Like a fucking dream."

"What're you talking about, Tomás?"

"A friend of my daughter's," said Tomás. "I killed a girl, too. Here. Under this bridge."

"What?" I said.

"No shit," said Tomás, looking at the river where my glasses had fallen. "Years ago. She was a sexy little thing. You shoulda seen her. She was down here gettin' it from some kid. My daughter told me. I saw her one night climbing the fence. I followed her. Figured, why not me? She wouldn't give. She got hysterical."

"I hit mine," I said.

"Yeah," said Tomás. "I knew it was a bad match. But she got my head and my heart spinning. Other parts, too."

I forced a laugh. "I feel you."

I didn't.

"She would come sleep over with my daughter," Tomás said. "I was nice to her. She said I was like a father she never had. She looked good in her tight blouse that night; it was knotted at the waist, and she had on tight shorts, like in one of those music videos or something."

"What happened?" I asked.

"I went for the kiss," said Tomás. He was drinking straight from the bottle now. "She pushed me away, looking all horrified and disgusted. I got so mad."

"What did you do?"

Tomás just shrugged. "I remember going home and changing my clothes and dumping them in the trash. I don't know why. There was no blood. And I don't remember how I got to work the next day. I just looked up, and there I was in my uniform, boss at the door complaining about a delivery, like it had all been a dream."

"Wow," I said.

"Why did she make me do it?" asked Tomás.

"Mine was a tease," I said.

"Yeah," he said. "Mine would sleep over with my daughter and walk to the bathroom at night in panties. Why did she make me do it? I don't usually like them that young. But I liked her. I saw her once; she was wearing all gold—shirt, pants, shoes—but not tacky. Well, almost tacky, but she made it look good."

"What did you do later that night?"

"I went home. I ate dinner. Watched the tube. Got to sleep."

"Wild," I said. "You left her there in the river?"

"Fuck was I supposed to do?"

"Damn," I said.

"I'm really sorry about it. I regret it. You? You regret yours?"

I watched the river.

"You okay, kid?"

"Yeah, I'm okay. I understand," I said, pouring him his last drink. "Been there."

"Jesus," said Tomás. "I never told anybody that story, Chico. Never."

"Why'd you tell me?"

"You told me yours."

"Yeah," I said.

"We're like blood brothers now, kid," he said, slamming back his drink.

"Yeah," I said. "Blood brothers. Guess that would make Doreen my blood sister?"

Tomás looked at me like his heart had stopped. He had wanted to forget, to bury Doreen in his mind like her body had been buried so many years ago, at the funeral.

The cemetery was gray like death, I thought, and everybody was dressed in black, like night would last forever. The long car, the red curtains, the glass chandelier, the crying and the wooden box with Doreen inside. I wanted to forget, too. Her smooth brown skin had turned pale. Her hair was combed to the side, and they put a childish smile on her, as if she were happy. Then they shoveled her under the dirt, covering her up like dogs bury bones.

"How'd you know her fucking name?" asked Tomás.

"You told me," I said. "You said the girl's name. The girl you killed. You said her name was Doreen."

"No," he said. "I didn't. And I didn't tell you she fell in the river. What's going on here, Chico?"

I stood up. "I think you know."

"Who are you?"

"I'm a private investigator."

"How did you know?" he asked. "About Doreen?"

"Doreen's sister came to see me," I said. "Said she had a dream, and saw you in her dream killing Doreen. She saw you push her down, and she saw Doreen fall into the river. At first, she said, she didn't know how she knew. Then she remembered she was there, hiding behind that wall. She saw you."

I pointed. "She put her hand over her mouth, and when you were gone, she fainted. When the police questioned her, she said she had been asleep. She couldn't remember, until she dreamed about it years later. Last month. But cops are funny. They won't arrest a man based on a dream. So she called my buddy Nicky Brown, and you got lucky 'cause Nicky called me instead of paying you a special visit. He's not as hospitable as I am."

"You can't prove anything," said Tomás.

I picked up the rum bottle and took a small swig, then I popped the tape out of the radio. I had switched it to record when I stopped the music. Then I saw the knife in his hand. But before he could get to me, I slammed the side of his skull with the rum bottle.

His head fell into his chest, and his large arms went limp. As he stumbled forward, his motorcycle goggles fell off. He stepped on them and broke them, and he fell to the ledge with a heavy thud.

Tomás lay there, blood pooling around his head, not complaining or anything. Something inside me was satisfied. Not happy, but satisfied. I looked down at the gash in my hand.

I shoved the tape into my coat pocket, took out my cell phone and dialed 911.

I looked down at Tomás one final time and said, "Monica says hello."

Caring for José

"Who would care if they killed José Matos?" Gonzalo thought.

José Matos had been a bully since grade school, and that was thirty years ago. He was well over six feet tall, and well over three hundred pounds. Luis Gonzalo, the sheriff of the small town of Angustias, Puerto Rico, had arrested José Matos nearly two dozen times for fighting, for intimidation and for assault, and once for removing the pool tables at Colmado Ruiz and pushing them off a cliff.

Gonzalo had always known someone was going to kill José. He expected the phone call in the middle of the night; he expected to have to gather his two deputies to "lug the guts." He just never expected the avenger of Angustias to be the petite, still-teenaged bride of José Matos.

He nodded several times as though the speaker on the other end of the line could see him. He "uh-huhed" into the receiver several times. Finally he said, "Okay, okay. I'm coming over. Just let me get my pants on." Then he hung up before the person on the other end of the line, Rachel Matos, could say another desperate word.

"Who was it?" Gonzalo's wife asked.

"Rachel Matos."

Mari Gonzalo nearly sprang out of bed.

"Did that monster beat her?"

"No," he said pulling on a pant leg.

"Did he kill her?"

Gonzalo turned to his wife across the bed.

"I just told you that was her on the phone."

"Oh, right. What about the baby?"

"The baby's fine."

"How do you know?" she demanded.

"Look, Mari. Get dressed and come with me. See the baby for yourself."

She shook her head violently.

"I don't want to see José, that monster," she said.

"Not much to see anymore," Gonzalo answered, retrieving his gun from its lock box. "He's dead."

Mari was out of bed and into her clothes in less than a minute. This was a long-awaited event. Gonzalo made a call to the station house, asking to be met at the Matos residence. "Emergency?" he was asked. He thought about it a moment before saying, "No. No emergency."

It was a ten-minute drive through the cool of the night, deeper into The Valley of Angustias, a town sparsely sprawled over several hills and valleys. The valley is where several other valleys of the town meet to flow out south toward Comerío and eventually Ponce. Most of this land was farmland, and the festivities of the weekend were now long over, this being the very earliest part of Monday morning. The night was now as silent as a night could ever get in Angustias—over the slight humming of the car's motor, a thousand crickets could be heard individually, along with the occasional overripe fruit crashing through the leaves of trees to hit the forest floor. Gonzalo and Mari were accompanied on the trip by the constant two-note whistle of the *coquí*, a tiny tree frog that is the national mascot of Puerto Rico. It was in this silence that Gonzalo told Mari everything Rachel Matos had hurriedly explained to him on the phone.

"She said they got into a fight again. His food was cold when he got home. It was midnight, and . . . "

"And he wanted his food to be warm still? That idiot. If he were my husband . . . "

"Can I finish, please? Thank you. They got into a fight. I guess he started to chase her around the house. She said he hit her a few times. Poor girl," Gonzalo said. "She hardly weighs a hundred pounds. Anyway. He chased her into the kitchen; he grabbed a knife, she grabbed a frying pan, frying pan won."

"How? He's so big. A frying pan killed him?"

"No. Frying pans don't kill people. People kill people. I don't know how. She called from her neighbor's house. She has the baby with her. The baby's fine."

"She's in Irma's house?"

Irma Pagán was a nurse who worked in the only clinic in Angustias.

"Yup. Killed her husband, took the baby and ran."

Mari was silent for half a minute, staring at the tall grass rushing by her window.

"But how could that little girl kill that big monster with a frying pan?" she asked.

"My guess is that she didn't. I'll bet she knocked him out and thinks he's dead. That's why I brought the gun—when he wakes up, he's going to be pissed."

They pulled up in front of the Matos family home. Irma Pagán's house was a hundred yards further up the road. Both women were in the street with Rachel's nine-month-old girl. The lights were on in the Matos house.

Gonzalo looked up at the night sky before attending to business. It was 1986, and though Angustias had finally joined the rush of technological development—people were buying Ataris, and his middle daughter now owned a Commodore 64 for her college work—this area was not well-lit. The Milky Way was visible, and Gonzalo spent three seconds picking out constellations before turning to work that might be gruesome.

When he walked over to the women, it was his wife who was dandling the baby. Rachel Matos had fresh bruises around her left eye and on the right side of her chin. She was only nineteen, younger than Gonzalo's Commodore 64 daughter. She had been married to José Matos for two years, and as he stepped closer, Gonzalo could tell that she was pregnant again; she was just beginning to show. Certainly this had been a hard life for the girl, but if what she said over the phone were true, if José Matos were really dead on the floor, her life had just gotten easier.

"¿*Qué pasó*, Rachel?" Gonzalo asked.

Rachel lifted her hands to wipe tears from each eye. Her hands were shaky, and Gonzalo noticed an old bruise on her upper right forearm and a patch of red that was sure to become a new bruise around her elbow. She had probably twisted out of one of José's paws a half hour before.

"What happened?" he asked again.

"I told you already. I killed him. I killed him with the frying pan."

"Okay, but how? You're such a little woman. Are you sure he wasn't just knocked out?"

"He's dead," Irma Pagán broke in. "I checked."

She wrapped an arm around Rachel. Mari drew herself up to her full height. In her mind, these questions were irrelevant and impertinent. Who cares how he died? Why poke around for specifics?

Gonzalo looked at his wife and could hear her thoughts: "Dingdong, the witch is dead." Who could blame her? Who would care if someone killed José Matos? Still, there was an investigation to be made.

"Okay. Just one question."

Rachel looked up at him, sniffling.

"How many times did you hit him?"

"Once," Rachel said.

Gonzalo couldn't help but whistle in amazement as he turned away to enter the Matos home. Irma Pagán followed him.

The Matos home was hardly more than a few plywood boards nailed together into the form of a giant box; the bedroom was curtained off from the rest of the house, and the kitchen was separated from the front room by a plywood partition. While José Matos was the biggest man in town and could have gotten work on any number of farms or gone to a big city to load and unload trucks, he had spent most of his adult life either in bars or behind bars. Earlier in life, José had gone through a series of jobs, sticking around long enough to become eligible for unemployment benefits. Recently, he hadn't had the energy even for that. Puerto Ricans living on the island are not eligible for Welfare money from the government, but they are eligible for food stamps. Rachel Matos had made do with the food stamps for the two years of her marriage.

Inside the house, Gonzalo immediately noticed a wrinkle to his investigation. José Matos was not on the kitchen floor where a good dead man who was killed there ought to be. Instead he was on the living room floor, a trail of blood smears and drips showing that he had dragged himself or crawled there or maybe been dragged there by others.

"Who could have moved the body?" Gonzalo wondered. There were only two other houses in this nook of the valley: those of Irma Pagán and Don Julio who lived further in the woods, in a shack. Don Julio was approaching one hundred years of age. That was a no-go.

Maybe Irma Pagán and Rachel Matos worked together? Yeah, he thought. Together with a couple of horses. Okay, José had dragged himself to the living room.

Gonzalo looked to Irma. As a nurse, she had seen death before and had often assisted Gonzalo on cases where medical knowledge was useful.

"Was he here when you checked on him?"

"Yes."

"Was he dead then?"

"Oh, no. Soon after, though."

Gonzalo stared a little more intently into Irma Pagán's face. His look asked the question for him. "Did you do anything to scoot him on to the next world?"

"José was obese," Irma volunteered in the unhelpful way medical professionals sometimes have, expecting others to be able to figure out the appropriate conclusion from a bit of medical evidence.

Gonzalo was proud of his own intelligence, so he tried to come to that appropriate conclusion on his own for a moment. He looked at José's mass of flesh on the floor; prodded it with his toe. There was a deep gash on the forehead as one might expect. There was a small puddle where the blood came trickling down off his forehead, down to the bridge of his nose and from there onto the floor. His right hand was smeared with blood. Together with the blood smeared and dropped between the kitchen and his final resting place, there were three or four tablespoons worth. Not nearly enough for him to have bled to death. Gonzalo looked at Irma again.

"So he was fat? So what? So was my grandmother, may she rest in peace. What does that have to do with anything?"

Irma rolled her eyes. It was more than just an annoyance eye roll. This eye roll told Gonzalo that Irma would rather not say much more. This was beginning to feel suspicious to him.

"What does that have to do with anything?" he insisted.

"He had several medical problems. Diabetes was one. A bad heart was another. He was on thyroid medication, and he had hepatitis. In a patient, all of this was terrible, but the worst medical problem he had was himself. He rarely took the medicine that was prescribed for him. When he did take it, it was usually late, or half the dose, or double the dose to make up for missing doses. You could check his charts at the clinic if you don't believe me."

"Why would I not believe you?"

"I don't know. You're asking a lot of questions. The man lived like a dog and died like a dog. Who cares? Just bury him before he stinks so this girl can get her life back together."

Gonzalo crouched down next to the body. He searched for a pulse to give his hands something to do, not that he would have been able to find one through all the flesh. He was surprised to find how much of the mass before him was solid. Not quite muscular, but more than just fat. He probably could have done the work of two men, if he had cared to. Gonzalo tried to turn the body over, but he didn't have the strength to do it without entangling himself with the body more than he wanted to at the moment.

Throughout the inspection of the corpse, he kept Irma Pagán in the back of his mind. He wondered what her role was. One of his deputies drove up to the front of the house. Hector Pareda, his young deputy, twenty-seven years old, was heard outside. His other deputy was off-duty but would probably show up soon, too. Emilio Collazo was well over seventy but with a work ethic only the people who had lived through the Depression Era could ever understand. Or so he claimed, at least. Hector poked his head through the doorway as Gonzalo was trying to look at a mark on José's left upper arm.

"Anything you want me to do, chief?" Hector asked.

"Nope. Stay out there with Rachel Matos. Keep her company. Don't say anything awkward, but keep your ears open."

Hector ducked out again.

Gonzalo managed to roll José's sleeve up far enough to see the mark. It was a tattoo heart, maybe three inches wide. A banner across it read "Rachel." Strange.

"What are you thinking about now?" Irma asked. Her tone indicated that she wanted all of this to be over with.

"I was just thinking about this tattoo. It's a heart with Rachel's name on it."

"And you think that's a sign of true love?"

Gonzalo frowned at her.

"No," he said. It was a lie.

"Good. Can we call Santoni now?"

Santoni was the funeral home director. When there was no doubt about the cause of death, he was called in to care for the body. He filled out all the necessary paperwork and got the right signatures without disturbing anyone, silent, like a ghost.

"There's been foul play. The medical examiner has to see this."

"You don't need a doctor. I can tell you the cause of death."

"Well, don't tell me he died from a frying pan to the head. I've hit him with a nightstick harder than that girl could ever hit him."

"He had a heart attack."

"A what?"

"Matos has had trouble with his heart for years. He's had two heart attacks that I know of . . . "

"How can that be? He's not even forty yet."

"He was forty-three and a hundred and fifty pounds overweight. It's not that uncommon."

Gonzalo paused for a moment. In everything Irma said, there was a sense of wanting to get José Matos underground as fast as possible. He understood that no one would care much for José, but that didn't explain Irma's desire for speed here.

"I have a question for you."

"How do I know all this about him?"

"No. That's obvious. You're one of the few nurses in town. I have a personal question for you."

"What?"

"Five years ago, I knocked on your door. Your husband, Antonio, had died in a car accident, remember?"

"Of course I remember. We were married ten years."

"I mean, do you remember the moment you opened the door with me standing there?"

"Yeah." Slowly.

"You were already wearing sunglasses. The same glasses you wore at the funeral."

"So?"

"When did Antonio start hitting you?"

Irma was taken aback by the question.

"What makes you . . . Who told you . . . How did you . . . ?"

"Oh, I had seen bruises on you a few times before that day. Not too often, but I even asked you about them once. A bruise on your arm. You said you hit a doorknob. It was a little high for a doorknob, but I let it go."

Irma set her jaw. "Why'd you let it go?"

"It's not my job to pry into the private lives of the citizens of Angustias. You know better than I do what an angry husband might do if he thinks I'm asking too many questions. They won't take it out on me. They'll take it out on the wife. On you. On Rachel. Sometimes it's better to let the woman decide how to handle the situation."

"But sometimes that backfires."

"Sure. No question. It's a tricky thing trying to decide when to step in. Look at this case. I've come here three times before. Arrested José twice. I bet you think I didn't do enough." He waited for a response. None came.

"Well, whatever you think, I tried hard here. It backfired. Everything I did fell to pieces. Now someone's dead."

"Of natural causes."

"Well, that's for somebody else to decide unless you have more to say."

"I don't have anything else to add. It was a heart attack."

"What makes you so sure?"

"When I came in here, he was in the middle of dragging himself to this spot. He stopped about where you see him now. He got up on his knees and grabbed his arm . . . "

"His left arm?"

"Uh huh. He was starting to have a heart attack."

Gonzalo had his notepad out, and he was writing.

"And what did you do?"

"I . . . I asked him how he felt."

"Anything else?"

"Sure. He said, '*medicina*.' I went to the bathroom and got his heart medicine: nitroglycerin tablets. He suffers from angina. I was trying to open the bottle, standing right here . . . " She moved closer to the body.

"But he snatched the bottle from me. He was desperate. He shoved the bottle into his mouth, but it was too late. You can't take nitroglycerin tablets once a myocardial infarction begins. Also, you can never take as many as he did. He precipitated his own death. A minute or two later, and he collapsed face down as you see him."

"CPR?" Gonzalo asked.

"CPR? How was I supposed to turn him over? He weighs two hundred pounds more than I do. Even you can't turn him over . . . "

"Okay, okay. Sorry. Where's the bottle now?"

"In the bathroom."

Gonzalo walked over to the bathroom. The light was on. The door to the medicine cabinet was swung open wide. Inside there were the usual feminine products and over-the-counter drugs: Pepto-Bismol, Alka-Seltzer, etc. There were also several prescription-type bottles. The top of the cabinet had a dozen or more small bottles for prescription drugs; too high for Rachel or Irma to reach without a chair. Just barely within the reach of his fingertips if he tippy-toed.

"How many medications was he on?" Gonzalo called out to Irma.

From the living room, after a hesitation, "Four or five. He went to different doctors and pharmacies. Nobody has a complete history for him."

"How did you get the bottle?" Gonzalo called out again.

"It was on the bottom shelf," Irma said speaking from right behind Gonzalo now.

The bottom shelf did have several empty spaces where the bottle might have been. Now the bottle was on the edge of the bathroom sink, the lid off, empty and with a smudge of blood on the label. Gonzalo squatted to have the bottle at eye level. He tried to read beneath the smudge.

"Whose blood?" he asked still studying the bottle.

"His, of course. I tried to loosen his shirt collar. I still have blood on my hands," she said and reached to turn on the faucet.

"No, no, no!" Gonzalo said, turning the water off.

"What? Am I a suspect in anything? I didn't stab him."

"No, but don't clean up just yet."

Gonzalo thought for moment. What should have been a simple accidental death or a case of self-defense was turning complicated.

"Did you check the bottle before administering the pill?" he asked.

"What? Nitroglycerin is nitroglycerin. It has a distinctive look to it. I didn't give him the wrong medication. Besides, he swallowed them on his own."

"That's not what I'm talking about."

Irma looked away. Gonzalo knew he was on to something.

"Did you look at the date?"

"No." Still looking away.

"It's right under the smudge. Right there." He pointed to the smudge. "These pills are two years old."

Irma looked back at the sheriff.

"Really?" she asked with not nearly enough interest in her voice.

"Yeah," he said. "What happens to a patient when they take one of these expired pills in the middle of a heart attack?"

"You want to know the truth?" Irma asked. She looked angrily into Gonzalo's eyes.

"Sure," he said calmly. "Why would I want to hear a lie?"

"The truth is, if a patient takes one of these pills, and it's expired, nothing happens. Nature takes its course; God has his way. Ask the doctor; look it up. The pills were dangerous because they were taken when his angina had progressed into a heart attack, not because they were old. Even if I made the *mistake*," she emphasized. "Even if I made the mistake of giving him an expired pill, I think it was a little understandable, no? If those pills were still good, it was the fact that he took them at all, the fact that he took so many of them that is important. If they were no good, then they became harmless, like a placebo, and he died of a simple heart attack. I'm telling you, he killed himself."

"Okay, but one question. If he wasn't supposed to be taking nitroglycerin anyway, why did you get him the bottle?" Gonzalo asked.

Irma looked at him with deathly cold in her eyes.

"Because he grabbed my robe."

She pointed out the large red handprint on her yellow bathrobe.

"Because he could have killed me. Because he told me to. I was afraid, Gonzalo. Nobody in this town has ever done anything to stop him from hurting people. I didn't want to be his next target. I would have gotten him any pill he wanted. Cyanide even. Are you going to arrest me for being afraid of José Matos and not caring whether he lived or died? Or because I was too weak to keep him from taking the bottle from me?"

Gonzalo didn't know what to say. He looked at some of the other bottles in the medicine chest; some were bloody. He imagined himself before a jury making the case against the nurse.

"Ladies and gentlemen of the jury, the defendant rushed to the home of José Matos at midnight after being told that the bully might be dead. She found him in the middle of a heart attack, blood gushing from a wound. She flew to his medicine cabinet, blood on her hands, fumbled about quickly for a bottle of nitroglycerin pills, the pills that might have saved his life. With blood on the bottle, with blood on several bottles (a sign that she was looking for the right medicine, or a sign that she was looking for precisely the wrong medicine? I ask you, ladies and gentlemen; it's for you to decide), she misread the label. (Did she read the label at all? I ask you, ladies and gentlemen. It's for you to decide.) She rushed back to her patient, watched as he popped pills into his mouth, popped the whole bottle into his mouth and watched him croak and unceremoniously plop face down to the ground. No CPR, ladies and gentlemen. No CPR. Remember that. Ladies and . . . "

"Luis."

His wife was beside him now.

"What are you doing in here?" he asked her.

"Collazo and Hector are both outside. They want to know what you're doing; whether they have to do anything," Mari said. "The baby has to get into a bed, Luis. What are you going to do?"

"Well, I'm not going to arrest her. There's no case."

"Arrest her? Who? Rachel? How could you think of such a thing?"

"No, no. I was thinking . . . Oh, forget it. I need to get into a bed myself."

He walked his wife back to the door and surveyed the group outside. Collazo was looking at him, waiting for something to do. Hector was talking to Rachel. She was smiling and even laughed at something he said, and Gonzalo wondered if his young deputy hadn't hit it off with the newly minted widow. They made an attractive couple.

"What would investigating this further do but wreck the poor girl's life more than it already was?" he wondered to himself.

Together with Collazo and Hector Pareda, Gonzalo pushed, pulled, dragged and carried the corpse of José Matos to the pickup truck Emilio Collazo had driven over in. The younger deputy, Hector, would drive the body to the morgue in Ponce. If they asked him any questions, he was to say that Gonzalo would call later, when it was properly morning rather than this dim imitation. Gonzalo wondered what he would tell them. An autopsy would be coming to find the exact cause of death, and he didn't doubt the coroner's findings would match the explanation given by the nurse—she hadn't lied, he just wasn't sure whether the truth made her guilty of anything. Probably nothing criminal; certainly nothing a jury would convict her of. She didn't, after all, force-feed José the pills. She had simply given him what he asked for, not sure if the pills would help him and not caring.

Gonzalo shuddered, thinking Irma Pagán had stood, cold-blooded, and watched José Matos fumble useless pills down his throat. She had watched his heart attack progress. She had watched him die.

The older deputy, Collazo, was sent home again. Mari got back into the car, and Gonzalo walked over to Irma Pagán's house. Irma, Rachel and the baby were all on the front porch, the baby playing on Rachel's lap. The sheriff motioned to Irma, and she walked over to him to a patch of grass some yards from her house. They spoke in low tones.

"I'm going to check on what you said about the pills. If you're right, if those pills just become useless but not harmful, then you have nothing to worry about. Still, even if this was really a mistake . . . "

"If? You think I forced him to eat those pills, a man who could kill me, kill you, barehanded?" Irma asked. She wasn't happy.

"If it was a mistake," Gonzalo ignored her. "I want you to remember one thing."

"What?" Eyes rolling again.

"I want you to remember that if this is a mistake, then it shows a carelessness that is never seen in good nurses. You were responsible for a patient and now that patient is bouncing around in the back of a pickup truck headed for an autopsy. That's not good nursing. It may not be criminal. Under the circumstances, it may not even be punishable by whatever authority nurses work under, but it was not good care on your part. Understood?"

Irma looked at her porch where Rachel and child were playing together, the baby gnawing one of her mother's hands while punching the other hand with her baby fist. The child let out a squeal of delight, and the mother at that moment snatched her baby close to her heart and began to nuzzle the nape of the child's neck. A picture of sheer joy.

"Yeah, whatever, Gonzalo. I didn't kill José Matos. But I'll tell you one thing: José wasn't my only patient. I have other people in my care," Irma said.

Then she went back to her house and, with Rachel and the baby, went inside and turned out the porch lights.

Gonzalo stood outside the house a minute, watching the lights go on in different rooms.

"Sleep easy," he whispered.

But as he walked to his car, he wondered whom his words were for.

A New York Chicano

Ricky Quintana's fingers nervously slipped and skipped over the keys of his black MacBook, his fingernails too long, as he returned an e-mail from his boss at Merrill Lynch who wanted to know when the quarterly report for consumables in the biotech sector would be ready. Ricky's report was already a week late, and he had never been late delivering a report before, but nobody else would or could do it.

"Hey, Rick, come over here!" He heard Marisa's high-pitched, he-still-thought-sexy voice from his living room as his quivery pinky hit the delete button repeatedly to correct his mistakes. In fact, it had been Marisa Yoshimoto's voice, with its squeaky, come-hither quality, that had tickled him in that special place one night less than nine months ago, at the Parlour, an Irish pub on Eighty-Sixth Street and Broadway. Ricky had been attending a birthday party for an analyst buddy also at Merrill Lynch, and he had overheard, above the reverberating cover of Bonnie Raitt's "Something To Talk About," above even the chirps of the Ms. Pac-Man/Galaxaga machine behind him that had momentarily reminded him of his days in El Paso and Ysleta High School, this lilting laugh, this fluttering, mesmerizing song from an otherwise unintelligible conversation. He had turned away from the bartender and the outstretched Corona Light to lock eyes, for two seconds, with a slim, somewhat slight and pretty Asian woman of deep brown eyes, the blackest short hair and that intoxicating voice. It had taken Ricky less than five minutes to introduce himself to Marisa and less than five minutes after that for Marisa's girlfriend to excuse herself to search for the Parlour's restroom with a wide-eyed glance at her, and about half an hour after that for Marisa to hand Ricky her phone number—actually, she had scribbled it on his palm with another laugh that seemed to hit him like a lance to the chest. The next Saturday night, they had dinner at the boisterous Gabriela's on Columbus and Ninety-Third Street, and the rest was, well, their short history. "Hey, come over here. I wanna show you something."

But today, Ricky ignored his girlfriend for a moment, finished typing his e-mail and said loudly to his MacBook, a drop of perspiration just grazing the fleshy nub outside his left ear, "I'll be there in a second! I just gotta finish this for work!" Ricky buried his head in his hands as he waited for the rainbow wheel of the Mac to stop spinning, to power the computer down and he smelled it again. This briefly sharp, musty, unmistakably dead-animal scent that seemed to waft in from his window, which was open only an inch. It wasn't coming from the Astor's courtyard, he suddenly realized, it was coming from the gurgling radiator. Ricky jumped up from his desk, yanked open the beige metal cover that housed the bedroom radiator of his otherwise amazing prewar, rent-stabilized apartment, less than half a block from Fairway Market, the culinary Mecca of Manhattan's Upper West Side, and saw it: a furry gray mouse, dead probably for days, its little shrunken head caved in.

"Come here," Marisa begged him sweetly, as Ricky rushed into the bathroom at one end of the living room, pushed the door half-closed and quickly pulled a wad of toilet paper into his hand.

"Just one second. Just one second," Ricky said as he rushed past her again, hiding the toilet paper in his palm and hoping she wouldn't follow him into the bedroom and freak out. Marisa, still in her work clothes, her black pumps already abandoned like useless relics under his slatted coffee table, seemed like a cat perched on his downy navy blue sofa, her sleek legs tucked under her. She was watching the news on the Sony that sat in an alcove next to the wide, six-foot-high window overlooking Broadway. As Ricky pushed the mouse onto the toilet paper, and the mouse's little body crumpled into a curvy L, finally on its soft white shroud, he remembered first making love to Marisa on his sofa, she rushing to shimmy out of her jeans and happy to be guided, not to the bedroom, but back onto the sofa by his hands, over the sofa's edge, into the most delicious of L's and arching her unbelievably beautiful butt, just for the right angle, just for him. That crazy Friday night—a near two-hour lovefest on the sofa, on the floor, on his bed—one of them had inadvertently smacked the coffee table and propelled the magazines and what was left of their margaritas onto his sky-blue Navajo rug. Palming the now-weighty toilet paper, Ricky marched briskly into the bathroom again, flushed the toilet and stepped into the living room. "Okay, what's up?"

"He's dead."

"Who's dead?"

"That guy on the news. *America's Watch.* Or whatever they call it. Armstrong Ferry. Listen, here it is again. They're running clips from previous shows."

"Oh, yeah," Ricky sat down distractedly and put his arm under her as if suddenly cold while Marisa snuggled closer to him on the sofa. He began to kiss her neck, which smelled deliciously of Shalimar again. "I heard. Are we going out or staying in?"

"Didn't you hate him?"

"He was an ugly prick."

"Heart attack last night. Aren't you thrilled? I thought you'd be absolutely thrilled."

"Don't care anymore. I just care about this sweet delicious thing right next to me, who I can undress and make love to, who keeps my motor hummin' all week. TV's got nothin' on you, *mi preciosa.*" Marisa—her body, her scent, this squeaky-voiced affability—had always taken him out of his obsessions, the outrages in his head and even now, his vague, secret fears.

"Sweetie, I'll take care of you a little later," Marisa purred into his ear, which sent a shiver up his spine. She didn't take her dreamy brown eyes off the television. "You know what you do to me when you start talking Spanish."

"Well, what are we doing tonight?" he said, pushing away, a coldness suddenly rising from deep within him. Ricky Quintana shivered from head to toe as though a lightning bolt had coursed through his lanky body. He glanced out the window, listened intently for any sounds beyond the blathering television, possibly in the dimly lit hallway, but nothing seemed out of place. "Let's celebrate, let's do something fun, *mi reina.* Let's get outta here."

"Celebrate what?" she said, smiling hopefully, but with a quizzical look on her moon-shaped face.

"Life. Happiness. Fridays."

"There he is again. No more rants against illegal aliens. Against 'the foreign invasion of our Anglo-Saxon culture.' You know, he hated the Chinese; he hated the Japanese, too—anyone who was beating Americans at their own game. Not just Mexicans. He hated anyone who wasn't like him."

"Armstrong Ferry was an idiot. I really don't want to talk about him now."

"I just imagined you would be jumping for joy at the news."

On Sunday evening, the temperature had dropped drastically, even for late February in Manhattan. After just the short walk to Fairway, Ricky was panting, his asthma clogging up his lungs, his face, which Marisa claimed appeared more Greek than Chicano, so numb he had to wait a few seconds inside the market before consciousness seeped up from deep inside his skull to his eyes, to stepping away from the well-put-together blonde jostling past him in the chocolate-brown mink, to the items on his grocery list. Julio from Guanajuato was perched on a stepladder arranging the uncannily shiny Honey Crisp apples in a pyramid, and Ricky for a moment thought about saying hello, but Julio was busy and out of reach. El Güero with the mustache, who could be an asshole with his *trabajadores* and turn on a dime and smile pleasantly if you were wearing the latest North Face jacket over a rose Oxford shirt, was also prowling the vegetable aisles to keep them clear for the men with dollies racing into Fairway from the double-parked trucks with boxes of asparagus, carrots, scallions, giant California oranges and arugula. The to and fro, Ricky noticed, left a trail of sawdust that, with each gust of arctic air, disappeared from the dark sidewalk on Broadway. The stocky Julio, an illegal—as were most of the workers who minded the gigantic produce department—had a few months ago declared to Ricky ("You mean, *como el esposo de* Lucy Ricardo?") in Spanish, "At least I'm not at the warehouse anymore! They work you like an animal over there."

As Ricky marched in and out of the aisles to get what he liked to eat—Red Delicious apples, extra-large navel oranges, St. Lucien brie, calamata olives, Fairway's pinon nut pesto sauce, chicken tenders—he glanced at his friend Julio and the other *trabajadores* at Fairway. Those who had seen him occasionally chat with Julio grinned silently at Ricky; others just ignored him, stoic, busy, on the lookout for El Güero. Ricky noticed Julio's ragged, dark-skinned, leathery face was lost in thought, and Ricky wondered what had happened to Julio's sixteen-year-old daughter, whom Julio had recently told him was pregnant by "*un pinche puertorriqueño*," whom he wanted to kill along with his daughter. When the squat Julio had blurted out the news to Ricky, it had been an uncomfortable revelation for Julio, and for their easy, usually safely pleasant conversations at Fairway, from "*¿Como está ahora, señor?*" and "*¡Qué bonito día nos tocó!*" and "*¿Está seguro que usted es mexicano? ¡Es el mexicano más alto de Nueva York!*" and "*¡Debe de tener usted buen trabajo y estudios, porque aquí se me hace la comida* *muy cara!"* to, well, the tears that welled up in Julio's tired gray eyes as he revealed this bitter disappointment, this loss of hope for his child.

Was he—Ricky thought weeks after this exchange—still like these *mexicanos*? Julio's white stubble on his dry cheeks; the soft, nameless, faded baseball cap on his head; the way Julio moved from fruit to fruit in a semi-hunch, determined to do his work above all else routinely deferential to any customer who crossed his path, really, sheepish and excessively kind—all these things reminded Ricky of his *abuelito*. Ricky remembered how he had worked for his grandfather in grade school and high school in Ysleta, cutting grass on Colonel Smith's farm, planting flowers in the spring in Socorro, whitewashing the gigantic cottonwoods next to the irrigation canals, Saturday after Saturday. Ricky remembered the calluses on his grandfather's puffy knuckles and yet how happy Don José always was to be under the sun at lunchtime, reclining against the dry banks of the canal, at times peacefully asleep. Their exchanges: "Why don't you ask Colonel Smith for more money?" and the retort, "*Ay, mi hijo*, I have what I need. It's good to know what you need, or else you end up chasing your own tail, like Lobo." Ricky, the teenager, had made it a point to get out of Ysleta, out of El Paso, to ask for more, to risk failure for success and to apply to colleges across the eastern seaboard. When Merrill Lynch recruited him five years ago from NYU, and he had signed the lease on his Upper West Side apartment, Ricky believed he had taken an irrevocable leap beyond the Chihuahuan desert of the Mexican-American border. He was beyond his father and mother, who begged him to return home whenever he mentioned he was lonely, beyond begging for help from anybody, beyond depending on the good graces of others, especially *gringos*, toward self-achievement, to demanding what he wanted, to expanding, even, his ideas of what he could possibly desire. Ricky Quintana had escaped Ysleta, yet, every Sunday night, after he saw Julio in the fruit aisles at Fairway, Ysleta would invade Ricky's mind like an uneasy spirit that refused to die: He couldn't help Julio, he wanted to help Julio, he was like Julio and he was not like Julio anymore and perhaps never would be.

At the checkout lane, which was so narrow that Ricky had to turn sideways to avoid bumping into the Belgian chocolate squares and the cracker-like pale orange sponges in row upon neat row on impulse-buy racks, the Jamaican or possibly Antiguan checker snarled at him and violently shuffled his groceries from the electronic scanner to a grocery bag and waited with an open hand and a red-eyed, somnolent stare at the space above his head as Ricky signed the credit card slip. Once Ricky had questioned the scanned price on a bag of prewashed spinach, and this checker had dramatically summoned the manager and grumbled something about *"espece d'imbeciles"* slowing down the checkout lines, and threw Ricky this look that seemed to split his head open like a machete. Ricky had been right, but who cared if he had been right? Since then, this checker (who was indeed the fastest) hated his guts, or appeared to loathe his very presence, Ricky now the oppressor in her eyes, the disgusting white yuppie, the one who symbolized her abysmally low pay, her pressure-filled minutes, the simultaneous near and far of what and who she was not.

Finally in his apartment again, Ricky locked his steel door and put away his groceries in the kitchen that was no bigger than his bathroom and slumped into the sofa. He could hear the Broadway traffic echo through his massive window, the whistle of the cold winter wind and he heard creaks that seemed to emanate from his fireplace or beyond it. He walked into his pitch-black bedroom and flipped on the light, and of course no one was there. No one was also in the bathroom; no one lurked behind his shower curtain. Ricky Quintana was alone in this warm, shadowy darkness above the lights of Broadway. He turned on the TV and flipped to the cable news channel's *America's Watch*, which was still running retrospectives on Armstrong Ferry, the causes he had taken up over the years, his unrelenting, three-year attacks against illegal immigrants to the United States, hour-upon-hour of "news" filled with Ferry's red-faced diatribes, his asking a "question" of a guest only to rudely interrupt and answer his own question with more simplistic, incendiary pronouncements, Ferry's smile mocking any view, any group, any person who did not immediately recognize his greatness, his rightness, his "impeccable logic." In fact, when Armstrong Ferry grinned to silently disgrace anybody who dared to counter him or his arguments, Ricky thought, it looked as if Ferry wanted to eat them. The TV light intermittently illuminated the darkness like faraway thunderbolts, and Ricky began to masturbate to images of Marisa Yoshimoto, to making love to her again soon, to watching her head grind into his pillow in ecstasy. But at once Ricky stopped. It was better with the real thing; it was better with her scent and her softness at his fingertips; there was no need to rely on images for ecstasy, or a false ecstasy; he had but to ask Marisa for her to say yes to him, to metamorphose his dream into reality, to turn the suspense of a fictional mystery into the thrill of an actual killing, to escape and fly free. The TV images kept bursting into the darkness of the living room, illuminating the night as well as obscuring it.

"The Mexican culture is fundamentally incompatible with American culture, and we're just importing their poverty and the poverty of their values! Our government refuses to secure our borders, and where has that left us? Higher crime by illegal aliens who have already demonstrated no respect for the law! Higher high school dropout rates as Hispanic students, their parents and entire communities refuse to learn English! An education bureaucracy that shoves bilingual education and multiculturalism down our throats! America is still vulnerable at our borders, this, years after terrorists invaded this country and killed thousands on 9/11!"

"But, Senator. If I may, Senator. I just have to laugh at your arguments. Racism? This is not about racism, Senator. It's simply about what's right. The white middle class in this country has been abandoned by your pro-NAFTA polices, by a government which simply refuses to aid local communities fighting against the deluge of illegal aliens sucking up resources, on welfare, in the hospital emergency rooms, in schools where our own children are receiving a substandard education! Now you're arguing about the rights of illegal aliens? That's preposterous! You should be ashamed!"

"Deport them! Send them all back! Door-to-door if necessary! Get the army to patrol our borders! Give INS the resources to do it! We can't start talking about anything, and certainly never about amnesty for illegals, until our borders are secure! What is wrong with this country? We are losing our way of life! We are losing the achievements, let me add, of the white, Anglo-Saxon, Protestant, European immigrants, who, I admit, may or may not have arrived here illegally, yes, but that's not the point. That's a red herring. Today's massive illegal immigration from Latin America is overwhelming us, and this country needs to get serious about stopping it before it's too late!"

Long ago, Ricky had seethed at these words that emanated every night from his television set, right at about dinnertime when he would flip through the cable channels and stop at *America's Watch* to torture himself by listening to Armstrong Ferry. This warbly, deep-throated voice unleashed, unopposed, even encouraged and lauded by small-town mayors, Minutemen with microphones in the no-man's-land of the Arizona desert, self-selected viewers who also ranted against illegals and waved a metaphorical American flag in honor of *America's Watch*. How could a major news network, these sponsors, allow this moron on a supposed "news" show night after night? Ricky had thought, gritting his teeth. Ferry's not calling us spics, but he might as well be. He reduces us to stereotypes, he picks the worst portrayals, the scandalous examples and applies these images to everybody, to all Latinos, illegal or not. And they let him. And they have been letting him do it for years. Let's not talk about what the English and the Dutch did to the Algonquin in New York. Let's not talk about slavery, what about those "great values"? English immigrants, Irish immigrants, Italian immigrants, they just came and they took, and there was no legal or illegal! It's bullshit! And they simply let him do it night after night.

Tonight, however, Ricky Quintana just smiled at Ferry's words and added an extra dollop of pesto sauce to his pasta, and more grated Pecorino cheese. He turned off the television and listened to the wind, for any noise, and for the first time in a long while, Ricky believed he was safe in New York.

What had changed everything for Ricky Quintana almost three weeks ago was an innocuous decision he had made one morning. Since returning from visiting his father and mother in El Paso for Christmas —tamales, *buñuelos, arroz con leche, champurrado*—Ricky had decided to walk to work in Midtown, to Merrill Lynch's research division on Fiftieth Street, right before Park Avenue. That Monday, a wintry blast from Canada had left the cracked sidewalks on Broadway slippery with muddy snow, and Ricky had woken up early, knowing his walk would take extra time, and trudged south toward Columbus Circle and the fancy Time Warner Center, at which point he would decide whether to turn on Fifty-Ninth Street, toward the Apple cube store next to FAO Schwartz, or to continue south on Broadway to Fiftieth Street, just before Times Square, and then have his cup of coffee at a Starbucks. His blood pressure was borderline high, his triglycerides were twice normal—his doctor had warned him at his annual December checkup—and Ricky needed to avoid alcohol and sugar, and exercise every day, if he could. But he had never reached Columbus Circle on foot.

At Sixty-Third Street and Broadway, right after the Sony IMAX and Gracious Living stores, Ricky's lungs had had enough of the bitter cold, and he couldn't breathe, but he had remembered passing a Starbucks on Amsterdam, behind the Barnes & Noble superstore in front of him. He had hurried into the coffee shop, found the restroom ensconced in one far corner, miraculously vacant, and immediately inhaled two puffs of Primatene Mist, which he always carried with his laptop. In line for his Venti Mild, Ricky could feel his lungs expanding, his heavy wheeze receding, the blood coming back to his head and clearing his mind. That's when he had seen him. At the front of the line and already paying for his coffee. Others at that Starbucks, which Ricky had never been to before, also staring, one woman pointing to another with a subway map—tourists—and barely able to contain her glee at spotting a famous personality on the streets of New York. Ricky had seen Harrison Ford strolling on Broadway; one night he had sat next to Richard Dreyfus for a few stops on a downtown No. 1 train; finally he had even shared a bench-seat with Frances McDormand on the M-104 bus for about twelve blocks. And like most New Yorkers, Ricky had never done anything or said anything, but had simply returned to minding his business. But Ricky Quintana had never seen this famous reporter before. When the reporter, instead of leaving, wiggled onto a stool next to the corner of the bathroom and snapped his newspaper open, Ricky had decided to linger in the warmth of this Starbucks.

Ricky, sitting next to a small table a few feet away, had noticed the sandy-haired, somewhat-heavier-than-expected reporter sip his coffee for a few minutes, pop a pill from an open black portfolio at his feet— "Plavix" Ricky had read as the plastic bottle had been left momentarily on the counter—and altogether ignore everyone else at that Starbucks. Others, except for the tourists who were walking out the door, also ignored each other, and read newspapers, or typed on their BlackBerrys or iPhones. Outside on the street, on Amsterdam, Ricky had focused for the first time on the television studio for the cable news network, the double glass doors constantly swinging open with a shiny flash and many workers rushing across the street, right into the Starbucks. After about fifteen minutes, the reporter, whose hair was also much thinner and stiffer than Ricky had expected, almost Donald-Trump-like, had abruptly left the coffee shop and marched into the television studios and disappeared behind a set of heavy wooden doors with two guards in red blazers. Ricky would have been late had he continued his walk to his office at Merrill Lynch, but he had hailed a cab and arrived just in time.

In Ricky's head, for days after that non-encounter, he had imagined shoving the reporter from behind into the traffic on Amsterdam, he had imagined stabbing the moron in the neck with a pen, he had imagined, he had imagined . . . but had done nothing. Each night, as more words and their images assaulted him from his Sony again, as Ricky sat there and ate his dinner alone, sometimes distracting himself by thinking of Marisa, Ricky had hated himself for having done nothing. This hate had overwhelmed him and only seemed to sharpen his sense of outrage at what he heard, at his missed opportunity, at his own cowardice, at the cowardice of everyone who heard what he heard night after night but did nothing, lifted not one finger, for Julio, for his *abuelitos*, for his mother and father, for anyone who did not deserve these lies in the name of the God of High Ratings, these well-worded distortions, these self-serving provocations masquerading as intelligent arguments. Ricky had hated himself until on his way to work again, he had returned to that Starbucks on Amsterdam. He went back again the next day, and waited anxiously, when the reporter had not appeared the day before. And then there he was! Perhaps the reporter was not there every day, Ricky had reasoned, but only a few times a week.

Ricky had quickly found the news item through a Google search, the reason why *America's Watch* would have had a substitute anchor for a few weeks last summer. One major pharmaceutical company— a giant with seventy-percent gross profit margins—along with a smaller rival, were the two makers of stents for opening up clogged arteries to the heart, an incredibly profitable business Ricky was intimately familiar with at Merrill Lynch. But the pharma giant had taken it a step further: it also manufactured the drug to correct the blood-clot problem that plagued many stents, a delicious paradox not uncommon in this industry, which Ricky admired, of a company making money to correct the shortcomings or mistakes of this selfsame company's products. Heads I win; tails you lose. At a vitamin shop, Ricky had scoured the shelves until he found the small, round, rose-colored pills that matched the bestselling anti-blood-clot drug.

At the Starbucks, early this time, and at the appropriate seat, close to the bathroom but with a stool free next to him, between him and the dark corner into the bathroom, Ricky Quintana had waited, his nose deep inside a *New York Times*, had waited until, until, yes, the opportunity appeared again, a second chance, yes, the perfect chance. The reporter had shoved open the Starbucks glass doors, dropped his black portfolio to save the stool next to Ricky's and, as the reporter had waited in the back of the long line, away from this dark corner and any possibility of getting a clear glance at it, Ricky had stood up, as if searching his jacket pockets and so blocking anybody's view of the portfolio, reached in, grabbed the medicine bottle and sat down again. In a few seconds, his black North Face jacket open and providing more cover, Ricky poured out the Plavix and poured in the vitamin pills. His heart thumping inside his chest like a trapped, enraged *duende*, Ricky had stood up again, dropped the medicine bottle back into the portfolio and picked up his coffee and started for the door. He imagined Armstrong Ferry's huge, soft body lunging at him like an old bull, outraged, that familiar pale face blushing and demanding an explanation; he imagined others pointing him out, asking what he had done, but not one pair of eyes had even bothered to look his way as Ricky pushed open the Starbucks doors and walked hurriedly around the corner, into a cab, away.

As the taxi sped around the statue of Christopher Columbus atop a granite pillar, the explorer depicted more like an Oxford don rather than an adventurer for slaves and gold, suspended seemingly amid the space created by the glass skyscrapers around it, Ricky felt elated, he felt like a New York Chicano and he believed, even in a Halston suit with a Ferragamo tie, that his blood was still a brownish-red.

Mario Acevedo

Mario Acevedo will never be known as a quick study in this writing biz. One day he sat down to write a book, and six manuscripts and seventeen short years later, he finally wrote a story that got the attention of a literary agent. That led to a three-book contract with Harper-Collins, which has been renewed for another two books. Mario started to write serious literature and instead found success writing about Felix Gomez, Iraq war veteran and vampire detective. His first book, *The Nymphos of Rocky Flats*, was published in 2006, followed by *X-Rated Bloodsuckers* in 2007. *The Undead Kama Sutra* was just released. Mario is a former army helicopter pilot, paratrooper, engineer and art teacher to incarcerated felons. He lives and writes in Denver, Colorado.

His Latino heritage, besides the fact that he likes to drink Carta Blanca and eat jalapeños: His dad's side of the family had their property taken by Pancho Villa; his mom's side were the ones who helped take it. He was born in El Paso, Texas, and grew up in Las Cruces, New Mexico.

Lucha Corpi

Poet and writer Lucha Corpi was born in Jáltipan, Veracruz, Mexico, and came to Berkeley, California, as a young wife in 1964. Corpi has a degree in comparative literature from U.C. Berkeley, where she served as a student member of the newly established Chicano Studies' Executive Committee. She is a founding member of Aztlán Cultural, an arts service organization, and of Centro Chicano de Escritores.

She earned her master's degree in world and comparative literature from San Francisco State University. Primarily known as a Spanish-language poet, she is also the author of five English-language novels, four of which are mysteries featuring Brown Angel Investigations and Gloria Damasco, the first Chicana detective in American literature.

Her novels include *Delia's Song*; *Eulogy for a Brown Angel*, which received the 1992 PEN Oakland Josephine Miles Award and the Multicultural Publisher's Exchange award for best fiction; *Cactus Blood*; *Black Widow's Wardrobe*; and *Crimson Moon*.

Her poetry is collected in *Variaciones sobre una tempestad / Variations on a Storm* and *Palabras de mediodía / Noon Words*, with English translations by Catherine Rodríguez Nieto. She has also authored the children's books *Where Fireflies Dance / Ahí, Dónde Bailan Las Luciérnagas* and *The Triple Banana Split Boy / El niño goloso*.

Lucha lives in Oakland, California, where she was a tenured teacher in the Oakland Public Schools Neighborhood Centers Program for thirty years.

Sarah Cortez

The poetry of Sarah Cortez (*How To Undress A Cop*, Arte Público, 2000) brings the world of street policing to the reader in a way that poet-reviewer Ed Hirsch describes as "nervy, quick-hitting, street-smart, sexual." Winner of the 1999 PEN Texas Literary award in poetry and other juried designations, Sarah is much in demand as a creative writing teacher and visiting poet. She was awarded two consecutive one-year appointments as a visiting scholar at the University of Houston's Center for Mexican American Studies. One of her poems was chosen for the nationwide Poetry In Motion program, and many others have been anthologized both in the United States and in Europe. One of her poems was recently awarded Honorable Mention in the Texas Poetry Calendar 2008.

Sarah has been named a fellow at the Virginia Center for the Creative Arts. She has edited *Urban-Speak: Poetry of the City* (University of Houston, Center for Mexican American Studies, 2001) and *Windows into My World: Latino Youth Write Their Lives* (Arte Público, 2007), an anthology of short memoir essays written by young men and women across the United States, reflecting the diversity of growing up Latino. She and Liz Martínez are also coeditors of the forthcoming anthology *Indian Country Noir* from Akashic Books. Sarah has been a police officer in the state of Texas since 1993.

Carolina García-Aguilera

Cuban-born Carolina García-Aguilera is the author of eight books and a contributor to many anthologies (among them: *Mystery in the*

Sunshine State, *Mystery Street*, *Miami Noir*, *Havana Noir*), but she is perhaps best known for the first six, a series featuring Lupe Solano, a Cuban-American private investigator who lives and works in Miami. Her books have been translated into twelve languages and optioned out for film and television. Carolina, a private investigator herself, has been the recipient of many awards, including the Shamus and the Flamingo.

Alicia Gaspar de Alba

Alicia Gaspar de Alba is a writer/scholar/activist who uses prose, poetry and theory for social change. She serves as the chair of the César E. Chávez Department of Chicana and Chicano Studies at UCLA and is also a professor in that department. She has published eight books, including the novels *Sor Juana's Second Dream* (University of New Mexico Press, 1999), which was awarded Best Historical Fiction by the Latino Literary Hall of Fame; *Desert Blood: The Juárez Murders* (Arte Público Press, 2005), which was the recipient of both the Lambda Literary Foundation Award for Best Lesbian Mystery Novel and the Latino Book Award for Best English-Language Mystery; and *Calligraphy of the Witch* (St. Martin's Press 2007). Alicia was also the recipient of a Ford-Pellicer Border Literature Award in 1998 and the Massachusetts Artists Foundation Award in Poetry in 1989.

On the academic side, Alicia has published *Chicano Art Inside/Outside the Master's House: Cultural Politics and the CARA Exhibition* (University of Texas Press, 1998), and the edited volume *Velvet Barrios: Popular Culture and Chicana/o Sexualities* (Palgrave, 2003). Her writing has been translated into Spanish, German and Italian.

Alicia was born in El Paso, Texas, and has lived in Iowa City, Boston, Albuquerque and Santa Barbara. She currently resides in West Los Angeles.

Carlos Hernandez

Carlos Hernandez is a writer and educator living in New York. He cowrote the novel *Abecedarium* (with Davis Schneiderman), wrote the novella *The Last Generation to Die* and to date has penned seventeen short stories that have found homes in journals and magazines including *Happy*, *Interzone*, *Fiction International* and *Cosmopsis*.

He was born in the greater Chicago area in 1971 to Osmundo and Emma Hernandez, both recent emigrants to the United States who left Cuba to wait out the Castro regime. In 2000, Carlos earned a Ph.D. in English with an emphasis in creative writing from Binghamton University. He teaches composition, literature and creative writing at the Borough of Manhattan Community College, part of the City University of New York and could not be prouder to serve as a steward of accessible public education.

He wishes to assure readers of this anthology that, while mamey seeds do contain cyanide, there is virtually no risk of being poisoned by accident. Purposeful poisoning is another matter entirely.

Rolando Hinojosa-Smith

Rolando Hinojosa-Smith, a native of Mercedes, Texas, is the Ellen Clayton Garwood professor at the University of Texas. Parts of his Klail City Death Trip series have been translated into Dutch, French, German and Italian. Theses on his works have been written in this country and in Germany, Netherlands, Italy, Sicily, Spain and Sweden. Aside from numerous presentations in the United States and Europe, he has also read in Cuba, Iraq, Mexico and Panama, and has judged manuscripts for the National Endowment for the Arts and the National Endowment for the Humanities. He holds a Doctor of Letters from Texas A&M University.

Bertha Jacobson

Bertha Jacobson is a federally licensed court interpreter who lives in San Antonio, Texas. Born in Chihuahua, Mexico, Bertha moved to the United States after graduating from high school and attended the University of Texas at El Paso, where she received her BSEE and MSE degrees. She then moved to Dallas and spent fifteen years working as a software engineer, while nurturing her interest for the written word both in English and Spanish.

Currently, she is a freelance court interpreter and translator at work on her first novel. She graduated from the Institute of Children's Literature in West Redding, Connecticut, and is an active member of the Society of Latino and Hispanic Writers of San Antonio. Her Spanish-language short story, "Las babuchas de su santidad," was published in the UTSA literary magazine, *Labra Palabra*.

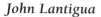

John Lantigua

John Lantigua was born in New York City. His mother was from Ponce, Puerto Rico, and his father from Matanzas, Cuba. He has published six novels, including *Heat Lightning*, which was nominated for the Edgar Award for Best First Novel by the Mystery Writers of America. His last three books, *Player's Vendetta, The Ultimate Havana* and *The Lady from Buenos Aires*, all feature Miami-based Cuban-American private eye Willie Cuesta. Several of his novels have been optioned by film companies. His short story "The Jungle" was a finalist for a Shamus Award from the Private Eye Writers of America.

John has also won various journalism prizes, including the Robert F. Kennedy Journalism Award, the World Hunger Year Harry Chapin Media Award and the National Association of Hispanic Journalists Award for Investigative Reporting. He has lived in Mexico, Honduras, Nicaragua and Thailand, and has reported from numerous other Latin American and Caribbean countries, including Cuba, Colombia, Argentina and Venezuela. He currently lives in Miami Beach, Florida.

Liz Martínez

As a child, Liz Martínez lived with her parents in her father's hometown: Mexico City. Her father was a mobster, and her mother was a secretary. After escaping a later suburban existence in Northern Virginia, she returned to her birthplace, New York City, where she earned her undergraduate degree from John Jay College of Criminal Justice. She went on to get a master's degree in writing popular fiction from Seton Hill University.

Her short stories have appeared in the anthologies *Manhattan Noir, Queens Noir* and *Cop Tales 2000*, and in publications including *COMBAT: The Literary Expression of Battlefield Touchstones* and *Police Officer's Quarterly*. Her short story "Kris Kringle" was Orchard Press Mystery's Christmas 2000 feature. She is also the author of the non-fiction book *The Retail Manager's Guide to Crime and Loss Prevention*, and her articles about security and law enforcement have appeared in publications around the world. She is a member of Mystery Writers of America, Sisters in Crime, Wordcraft Circle of Native Writers and Storytellers and the Public Safety Writers Association.

Liz is at work on a young adult mystery and an adult mystery. She and Sarah Cortez are also coeditors of the forthcoming anthology *Indian Country Noir* from Akashic Books. She is currently employed as a New York state investigator.

Arthur Muñoz

Arthur Muñoz was born in Los Angeles in 1924. As a teen, he lived in Corpus Christi, Texas, and later, in Colorado Springs, Albuquerque and San Diego. Weeks after Pearl Harbor, he joined the Marine Corps and saw action in the South Pacific during World War II. He returned to the Marine Corps during the Korean war as an infantry instructor at Camp Pendleton in San Diego. He was interviewed for Ken Burns's PBS documentary *The War*.

Art attended Texas A&M in Kingsville, where he was given a poetry scholarship by the Nueces County PEN organization. He has had two books of poetry published: *In Loneliness* (Naylor Company, 1975) and *From a Cop's Journal* (Corona Publishing Company, 1984). His articles and poems have also been published in magazines and the San Antonio *Express-News* newspaper. He recently won third place in a poetry contest sponsored by the San Antonio Museum of Art.

Art retired as a homicide detective from the San Antonio Police Department. He has also worked as a fraud investigator for the state of Texas and was chief of the San Antonio City Transportation Department. In addition, he taught poetry for two years in the gifted and talented classes for the San Antonio Independent School District.

R. Narvaez

Nuyorican writer, blogger, podcaster and performer R. Narvaez was born and raised in Williamsburg, Brooklyn. His mother came from Ponce, Puerto Rico; his father from Naranjito. Narvaez received his master's degree from the State University of New York at Stony Brook and later attended the Humber School for Writers on a scholarship. He has taught at the high school and college levels and worked in magazine publishing and advertising. His literary and crime fiction have been published in *Mississippi Review, Murdaland, ñ, Pocho, 11211, Street Magazine* and *Thrilling Detective*, among others. He lives in Brooklyn and is currently working on a novel.

L. M. Quinn

L. M. Quinn lives in Los Angeles and works as a technical writer for the business end of Warner Bros. *Una ensalada mixta (mitad mexicana, mitad rusa)*, she was born in Michigan, but raised in Los Angeles (*¡Gracias a Dios!*). She is also actively engaged in writing mysteries, short stories and book reviews, and has been published in *Travel 50 & Beyond* and *ELLE* Magazines. She has written two unpublished mystery novels, *Out with a Bang* and *Deadly Recollections*.

Manuel Ramos

Manuel Ramos is a lawyer and former professor of Chicano literature and a past winner of the Colorado Book Award and the Chicano/Latino Literary Award. He is the author of six crime fiction novels, five of which feature Chicano lawyer Luis Móntez. The Móntez series debuted in 1993 with *The Ballad of Rocky Ruiz*, which was nominated for an Edgar award by the Mystery Writers of America. His published works include the noir private eye novel, *Moony's Road to Hell*. His other publications consist of several short stories in various genres, poems, nonfiction articles and legal handbooks.

Manuel is a Chicano, born and raised in Florence, Colorado, and is a current resident of Denver, where he is the director of advocacy for Colorado Legal Services, the statewide legal aid program.

S. Ramos O'Briant

S. Ramos O'Briant was born and grew up in Santa Fe, New Mexico. She currently lives in Los Angeles. Her work has appeared in *Whistling Shade, La Herencia, AIM Magazine, Ink Pot, NFG, The Copperfield Review, The Journal of Modern Post* and *Café Irreal*. In addition, her short stories have been anthologized in *Best Lesbian Love Stories of 2004, Latinos in Lotus Land: An Anthology of Contemporary Southern California Literature* (Bilingual Press, 2008) and *What Wildness Is This* (University of Texas Press, 2007). Her book reviews have been published on La Bloga and Moorishgirl.

A. E. Roman

A. E. Roman (Alex Echevarria Roman) is the author of *Chinatown Angel*, the first book in the Chico Santana mystery series, coming soon from Thomas Dunne Books/St. Martin's Press Minotaur. He's also a co-author (with Emily Adler) of *Sweet 15*, to be published by Marshall Cavendish.

He has read his poetry at the Nuyorican Poet's Café, the Cooper Hewitt Museum and the John Coltrane Society, among other venues. His poems have been published in Howard University's *Amistad* (of and about Black art and literature), *The Orange Room* and *A Gathering of the Tribes* magazines.

He was born in New York City and raised in the South Bronx. His parents (both of mixed African and Spanish ancestry) are originally from Isabela, Puerto Rico. He has traveled through much of the United States and Puerto Rico, the Canary Islands, Serbia, Croatia, Germany, Italy, France and Spain, but he still lives and works in his beloved New York.

Steven Torres

Steven Torres was born and raised in the Bronx, but lived in Puerto Rico with his parents for over a year in the 1980s. He is the author of the Precinct Puerto Rico series for St. Martin's Press. *The Concrete Maze*, his latest novel, is set on some of the meaner streets of 1992 New York. His Bronx-set short story, "Early Fall," can be found in the anthology *Bronx Noir*. He now lives and teaches in central Connecticut.

Sergio Troncoso

Sergio Troncoso, the son of Mexican immigrants, was born in El Paso, Texas, and now lives in New York City. After graduating from Harvard College, he was a Fulbright Scholar to Mexico and studied international relations and philosophy at Yale University.

Troncoso's stories have been featured in many anthologies, including *The Norton Anthology of Latino Literature* (W. W. Norton), *Latino Boom: An Anthology of U.S. Latino Literature* (Pearson/Longman Publishing), *Once Upon a Cuento* (Curbstone Press), *Hecho en Tejas: An Anthology of Texas-Mexican Literature* (University of New Mexico Press), *City Wilds: Essays and Stories about Urban Nature* (University of Georgia Press) and *New World: Young Latino Writers* (Dell Publishing). His work has also appeared in *Encyclopedia Latina, Newsday, El*

Paso Times, Pembroke Magazine, Hadassah Magazine, Other Voices and many other publications.

In 1999, his book of short stories, *The Last Tortilla and Other Stories* (University of Arizona Press), won the Premio Aztlán for the best book by a new Chicano writer and the Southwest Book Award from the Border Regional Library Association. His novel, *The Nature of Truth* (Northwestern University Press), was published in 2003 and explores righteousness and evil, Yale and the Holocaust.

Arte Público Press publications by authors in *Hit List*

Lucha Corpi

Black Widow's Wardrobe: A Gloria Damasco Mystery
Cactus Blood: A Gloria Damasco Mystery
Crimson Moon: A Brown Angel Mystery
Death at Solstice: A Gloria Damasco Mystery
Eulogy for a Brown Angel: A Gloria Damasco Mystery
Palabras de mediodía / Noon Words

Sarah Cortez

How to Undress a Cop
Windows into My World: Latino Youth Write Their Lives

Alicia Gaspar de Alba

Desert Blood: The Juárez Murders
Sangre en el desierto: Las muertas de Juárez
La Llorona on the Longfellow Bridge: Poetry y Otras Movidas